FRANK STREEK

The Arctic Connections

iUniverse, Inc.
Bloomington

The Arctic Connections

iUniverse books may be ordered through booksellers or by contacting:

iUniverse
1663 Liberty Drive
Bloomington, IN 47403
www.iuniverse.com
1-800-Authors (1-800-288-4677)

ISBN: 978-1-4759-2893-8 (sc)
ISBN: 978-1-4759-2895-2 (e)
ISBN: 978-1-4759-2894-5 (dj)

Library of Congress Control Number: 2012909273

Printed in the United States of America

iUniverse rev. date: 6/12/2012

A mother is a mother still
The holiest thing alive.

Samuel Taylor Coleridge

1

Emigration

"What is your name?"

Aleksandras Girnius, a poorly clad Lithuanian who had been looking around the Halifax docks and its many ships with amazement, did not understand the immigration official's question.

The person behind him said in Russian, "He wants your name."

"Aleksandras Girnius. I am called Aleks," he replied, his voice faltering.

"Sounds like another Russian. All right. I got Alexander. What was the other name?"

The unofficial translator prompted him to repeat his surname, which Aleks did.

"Oh, Greenus. Strange name. Have you a passport?"

"He wants your passport."

Aleks handed him a Canadian Certificate of Sponsorship, a Canadian Health Certificate, a baptismal certificate, and a sheet of paper with a Montreal address.

"No passport? Sorry. You will have to go over there," said the official, and he pointed to an office at the other end of the room.

Aleks hesitated.

The friendly man behind him pointed out to him where the office was and told him to go to it. Aleks followed his directions and once inside stood there bewildered until a pleasant Russian-speaking lady requested his papers. She examined them carefully and asked why he did not have a passport. Aleks explained that he would have been refused one because he had not served the compulsory time in the Lithuanian army. The official said Canada did not recognise escapees from military service as refugees, but he could use his uncle's sponsorship. If he did, he could be cleared on a temporary basis. He would have to report to the police in Montreal on arrival. He would not qualify for welfare benefits, so if he could not find work, his uncle would have to support him.

Aleks agreed to that arrangement. She endorsed his papers, wrote something on a card, and encouraged him to enjoy some refreshments outside. She told him he should then to go to the nearby train station, buy a ticket to Montreal, and wait on the platform for that train. She wrote it all down on a sheet of paper and told him to show it to the ticket seller at the train station.

She asked if he had any money. Aleks showed her the Canadian dollars he had obtained in Danzig. She whistled, told him it was not enough, and gave him a rail warrant and the money for a Montreal bus fare. As she returned his papers to him, she smiled and wished him luck.

"You must safeguard these; they now include an Immigration Identification Card in the name of Alexander Greenus," she offered a final piece of advice.

He thanked her and went outside, still confused by these most recent events, his surroundings, and the mix-up with his name.

I am now a new person in a strange country. What does the future hold for me?

He stared at a sign on the building that read "Pier 21" and wondered what it meant. Still uncertain, he joined a line of immigrants at a table where coffee and sandwiches were being distributed by a welfare association. He was impressed and thanked one of the helpers in French.

She told him that because he spoke French, he should go to Quebec. He told her that was his destination, and she said he would be happy there. Aleks was pleased that the limited French his priest Father Staugaitis had insisted teaching him was now proving useful.

He enjoyed the refreshments as he made his way to the station platform. Once there, he spoke to some fellow passengers from the ship he'd come over on and then stood at the back of the platform, a forlorn figure in a bedraggled overcoat with a worn backpack.

He looked across the expanse of water to a distant town and reminisced about recent events. It seemed ages since his father had said he would have to go to Canada, because he could no longer support him. He would soon be eighteen, and he did not want him conscripted into the Lithuanian army, a fate suffered by his two older brothers, Jonas and Stasys. Lithuania had become an unhappy country since Antanas Smetona seized the presidency in 1927. In 1928, he had dissolved the parliament and introduced a new constitution, which increased presidential powers.

Aleks and his four sisters, Sofija, Marija, Janina, and Terese, had helped his father and mother eke out a meagre subsistence from their landholding and also assisted with the raising of the three smaller children—a daughter called Julija and twin sons, Algirdas and Kazys. His mother, who had lost two children in infancy, was worn with toil and childbearing.

Aleks was slim and of medium height; he had brown eyes and curly hair. His muscled arms and rough hands were the result of the physical work he'd done on their small farm. He smiled easily and had been diligent at school. At home, he had read whenever work was finished. His family was religious, and Aleks was a member of a small choir the local priest Father Staugaitis enjoyed coaching.

In 1937, Aleks's father said he had received an official letter from his brother Juozas in Canada in which he agreed to sponsor Aleks. It was time for him to leave. The problem was that he could not get a passport unless he had completed his military service, so he needed to find his way to the nearest Canadian emigration office in the Free City of Danzig on the Baltic Sea where he could be cleared into Canada without one. From there, he would have to catch a coastal ship to Copenhagen and then travel by a German boat to Halifax.

Aleks's father told him not to worry, because the escape route was well used. He gave him all the money he could spare and after a tearful farewell to the rest of the family, took him to the train station at Mosedis. There he caught a train to Klaipeda. He had been told to go to the harbour and look for a fishing boat *Skuodas,* whose captain, a relation of his mother's, would get him to Danzig.

He had no trouble finding the boat. Its skipper, a huge, black-haired, barrel-chested man shook his hand. He had been expecting him and welcomed him aboard. He remarked that Lithuania would soon have no men left.

"We have to do some fishing on the way, and I'll sell the catch in Danzig. It is a free port, and you'll have no trouble entering the town. We sail tomorrow morning. You can sleep in my cabin tonight."

After an excellent meal of fresh fish fried in a tasty batter, Aleks slept soundly and woke to the sound of the boat casting off. Once the ship was off, Kranz nets were cast and dragged.

"It's a good catch," said the skipper. "We'll hang around a little longer."

Late that afternoon, they set course and arrived in Danzig a day later. Aleks thanked the skipper, who wished him luck and suggested he join a fishing boat in Canada because there were huge catches made off the Grand Banks. He had served there on a Norwegian boat for several years, earned enough to put a deposit on *Skuodas*, and never looked back. He said cod were caught by the tonne year after year off the Canadian coast. Alex told him he would think about it.

The Free City of Danzig was created in 1918 to give Poland access to the sea. It had proved popular, and its harbour was busy when Aleks arrived. He had no trouble getting into the city. He simply blended in with a group of sailors. They greeted a customs official, who smiled and waved them on. Aleks bade them farewell and sought the Canadian consular office.

The city's inhabitants were mostly German. When he asked where the Canadian consul was, they shrugged their shoulders and responded with, "*Ich weiss nicht.*" He entered a store and tried again, using his limited Polish, the city's official language. He received directions to the consulate. The informant commented that he hoped he would get into Canada.

At the Canadian consular office, he was interrogated by a friendly official, subjected to a medical examination, and given a document certifying that he was healthy and "cleared for vaccination and distemper (disease)" He asked where he could change some money into Canadian currency and was directed to a bank opposite the office. The officials gave him some more papers and told him to get a passport. He knew that was impossible, so he hung around the docks until he could find a sailor to ask where he could find a boat to Copenhagen. The seaman pointed to a rusty ship and told him to try that one. Aleks was not impressed by the vessel's appearance, but he knew his options were limited. He climbed aboard and found his way to the captain's cabin. There, a cheerful, husky, redheaded seaman asked him in Polish what he wanted.

Aleks replied in Russian that he was a Lithuanian and had to get to Copenhagen.

"You're lucky. One of the crew broke his arm, and we need someone to help us load and offload goods. You look strong enough. Farm boy, eh? So was I, but I had to get away. Just like you. Where're you going?"

"Canada," Aleks replied.

The captain told him he would be at home there, because the winters were just like Lithuania's. When he asked for his passport, Aleks handed him all his papers. He told him that officially, he could not take him without a passport, but if he stayed on board at the ports they were due to visit, he would smuggle him ashore at Copenhagen. It was easy for sailors to disembark there. He gave Aleks some clothing and gloves and handed him over to the bosun, a husky, weather-beaten man of medium height with a grip of iron. Aleks winced when the man shook his hand.

The sea was calm as the ship headed down the coast for Stolpmunde, Rugerwolde, and Kolberg and then set course northwest for Copenhagen. Away from the coast, the Baltic Sea was rough. Aleks felt queasy but stayed on his feet. The captain laughed and assured him he would get used to the ship's movements.

At the Danish port, Aleks thanked the sailor. He told the captain that he had enjoyed helping load and offload cargo, but it looked like too tough of a life for him. The skipper smiled and said that maybe he'd land a job that made sailoring seem a picnic. He wished him well.

Aleks was ready for the bosun's grip this time and squeezed back hard.

"You've grown up in a few days!" The sailor laughed. "Stick around; we'll make a man of you."

"And break my hand," Aleks retorted. He asked if the bosun knew where the office of the German shipping line he had been told to use was located.

"All the shipping lines' offices are in the dock area. One of my crew will walk you there. I know he's going that way."

He called a sailor and asked him to guide Aleks to the shipping offices.

The two of them walked along the quays, conversing in Russian. The sailor knew Aleks was going to Canada, and he envied him. He would like to live abroad, but he had a wife and kid to support and they were committed to paying a mortgage on a small house they had bought.

"The skipper is a first-class sailor. He knows where the fish are. We work long hours, but the bonuses we earn are worth it. I know he suggested you become a fisherman. You were comfortable on board despite some rough weather. If I were you, I'd think about it. Canada is a good fishing country."

"Yes, I'll give it some thought when I get there."

The crewman showed him the company he sought, and the two parted with mutual good wishes.

At the shipping office, he booked a passage to Halifax. The clerk advised him that he would be allowed aboard without a passport, but it would be up to him to clear his entrance with the Canadian authorities. He was obliged to sign a disclaimer exonerating the steamship company from any liability he incurred. Aleks smiled. Apart from his meagre clothing, he had no possessions that could be used in settling claims against him.

The ship was a tramp steamer whose owners augmented their revenue with a limited number of passenger fares. Aleks slept in the steerage with the other emigrants. He listened with interest to the reasons his fellow passengers were leaving their home countries. Many were alarmed at the prospect of war in Europe. The Jewish passengers told harrowing stories of Nazi abuses. Aleks wondered if the evil they described would spread to Lithuania and put the many Jewish families in the Mosedis area at risk.

It was not a comfortable voyage. He and his fellow passengers were obliged to help with cooking and serving food. He was not seasick and impressed them with his energy and willingness to tackle all chores.

There were many fond farewells when the ship docked at Halifax, whose huge harbour impressed Aleks.

His reverie ended at midday when someone shouted that the Montreal train was coming.

Aleks found a window seat and stared out at the activity on the platform. He pondered the idea that the others would be scattering across Canada. The train moved towards the city and stopped at the Halifax Railway Station, an imposing limestone building.

Aleks did not relish the thought of the 22-hour journey that lay ahead. He studied pictures of the train's dining saloon and the bedding that could be hired. He knew the use of either was beyond him. His negative mood changed to one of interest when he was joined by a well-dressed middle-aged woman with two children. He jumped up and helped with her luggage.

She smiled at him, greeted him in French, and rattled off something else he couldn't understand.

Aleks responded with a phrase he had memorised: "*Desole. Je ne comprends pas. Si vous parlez lentement je peux comprendre que vous dites.*"

She and the children laughed. She said slowly with appropriate body language that she had thanked him and asked where he came from and where he was going.

He explained.

She said she did not know where Lithuania was. She too was going to Montreal, for a holiday with her parents who were immigrants from Germany. Her father always commented favourably on the treatment of the officials and the kindness of the Quebec people. She had gone to a French school, as her children did now.

About an hour later, she nudged Aleks, who had dozed off and offered him coffee and cake. He thanked her and enjoyed the succulent food.

The train travelled alongside the St. Lawrence River. Although there was snow on the ground, the river was not frozen this time of year, and he saw several large cargo ships. They reminded him of the advice he had received to become a fisherman. He thought about that and wondered what he would end up doing. He was fit and knew a little about farming but was ill equipped for anything else. He had heard the world's economy was in a mess. He could not expect anything but the lowest-paying job.

At six o'clock, a steward announced that it was time for the first sitting of the evening meal. Aleks indicated that he would not attend it.

"Yes, you will," said the mother. "You will be my guest."

Aleks protested, but she laughed. "My husband has a good business and was generous with my holiday money. My father would be cross if I did not look after you, so it is my pleasure to do so."

Aleks was bewildered by the cutlery and the food, so he watched what the others did and copied them. The food was excellent. He thanked his benefactor and told her he had enjoyed the meal.

"You looked hungry and proved it. You set an example for my children, who sometimes leave food on their plates."

Aleks was surprised to see that four beds had been made up. He looked at the mother. She smiled and said the children would occupy the top beds and she and he the lower two. He again thanked her and went to the toilet to give her time to change. When he returned, she was in bed and had turned her light off. He bade her good night and turned off his own light. He took off his boots, socks, jacket, and trousers and got into a comfortable bed. The movement of the train lulled him to sleep. He was awakened by a steward announcing breakfast. The mother ordered milk for the children, coffee for herself and Aleks, and croissants and brioches.

"You must have been tired. We have been up for some time. I'll take the children to the corridor while you dress," said the mother.

Aleks quickly dressed. He enjoyed the croissants and brioches with marmalade and had two cups of coffee. He again thanked his benefactor. He showed her the note given to him in Halifax and asked her to help him in Montreal. She said that she would be pleased to assist him.

On arrival at the city, she bought his bus ticket and showed him where to wait. She wished him happiness in Canada. "In the end, we got along fine in French. Yours is as good as many in Quebec. If you stay in this province, as I suggest you do, you will soon become fluent."

Aleks told her because she spoke clearly and used her hands and eyes, he understood her. That was a lesson to him. He would never forget her kindness to him, a complete stranger.

"Il n'est rien," she said. *"Bonne chance et adieu."*

He waited for an East Montreal bus. He boarded it and gave a Montgomery Street address to its driver, who said, "Another one for the European Quarter, eh?"

Alex nodded his head.

He understood what the driver meant when he saw the mixture of races in the area of Montgomery, Hogan, and Hochelaga Streets.

The bus dropped him off on the hilly Montgomery Street, and he soon found 123 A, which was on the ground floor of a three-storey building similar to others in the vicinity. He knocked on the door, and a cheerful lady wearing an apron opened it and greeted him.

"I am Aleksandras Girnius. Does Juozas Girnius live here?"

She hugged him and said, "You are Aleks, and I am Juozas's wife, Nelle, and therefore your aunt. We wondered when you would arrive. Juozas is working, but come in and I'll show you where to sleep."

There was not much space. She showed him a drop-down bed that he would use. The main room had a sofa, two easy chairs, and a dining room table with four chairs. There was a picture of a snow scene on the wall. The other rooms included a small kitchen with wooden shelves and a bedroom and toilet. Everything was spotless. Aleks was impressed by the humble home. He felt comfortable and enjoyed answering the barrage of questions his aunt fired at him. She said she came from Marijampole in Lithuania. She and Juozas had been married three weeks and had met at a church function.

"I was a seamstress but gave that up. I shall probably take in piecework because Juozas does not earn much despite the long hours he works. Life is tough around here, but it is a close community and we all help each other. Where will you get work?"

"I hope Uncle Juozas will help me find something."

"I am sure he will, but don't be surprised. It is bound to be rough work. That's all immigrants can get."

Juozas, a strongly built man with long white hair and a worried face, arrived at 6:30 looking tired. He greeted Aleks warmly and asked after his family. Nelle had a meal ready and served it. The pork dish was familiar to Aleks, who expressed his pleasure with it.

Conversation was animated. Aleks had many questions about Montreal and Canada. He thanked Juozas for sponsoring him. He said he was impressed with the courtesy of the officials and the generosity of the social workers at the docks and in particular with a mother on the train. He explained his language difficulties and how they had been overcome. The lady was generous and converted what would have been an uncomfortable trip into a pleasant one. He sensed he would be welcomed in Quebec.

"Don't be surprised by your experience. You will find friendliness everywhere. Like in Lithuania, the Catholic religion predominates in this province. As you know, it is part of our creed to help our Biblical neighbours and they include strangers."

Aleks nodded his head. His priest told him that if he maintained his faith, God would look after him and that had happened so far.

"I have to report to the police. I hope they are helpful, not like those in Lithuania."

Juozas told him where to go and which bus to catch to get there. He said there was no work in the city, but there were opportunities in the logging camps to the north. Life there was tough, but the work provided a start. There was higher-paying logging work in the United States, but he suggested Alex learn that trade in Quebec and advised him to call on the Mauricie Development Company on St. Joseph's Street. He knew they were looking for workers.

Aleks agreed to see the company. The following day, he reported to the police. He was asked where he lived and what he intended to do. He explained, and the police officer endorsed and stamped his Immigration Identification Card. He was told that until he obtained Canadian citizenship, he would have to report annually.

He then found the logging company's office, where he was interviewed by a husky, rugged-faced man, who laughed at his French. Aleks explained that he was fit and strong and used to rough work and frigid weather. They offered him a job in the cookhouse of a logging camp with wages of ten dollars a month all found. He accepted and was given a bus ticket to St. Georges. When he arrived there, he was to stay at the bus terminal and watch for a company vehicle. It would take him to the camp via St. Tite. He thanked the official, returned to Montgomery Street, and wandered in the area. He could not believe the different languages he heard the children using. They played in the lanes at the back of the buildings and were noisy but happy.

Nelle was delighted that he had found work. She said he needed winter clothing and took him to the Lithuanian St. Casimir Catholic Church in Rue Parthenais, where there was a room full of clothing. She helped him choose suitable garments, including steel-toed boots and tough mittens.

"Aleks, you are now fully equipped for the winter. You can throw your old clothes away."

He was quite pleased with his new possessions but worried about payment. The church worker smiled and said that in his case, there would be no charge. One day, when he had some money, they would appreciate a donation. Alex thought of Father Staugaitis, his family's priest, and realised his advice to keep his faith in God had again proved sound.

That evening, he discussed his plans with Juozas. His uncle told him to avoid bad company, to work hard, and to keep in touch with them. He embarrassed Aleks by insisting he accept some money.

"You will be short of cash to start with. You can repay me later."

The next day, he set off for the central bus station.

He wondered what lay ahead.

The ride to St. Tite was long. He thought of his family and wondered how they were doing. He was lonely, but that changed in St. Georges when he boarded the company's truck, which contained a motley collection of men. They greeted him, and one asked what he would do in the camp. Aleks told him he would be in the cookhouse.

"You speak funny," said one of the men.

"You will spend hours peeling potatoes and washing pots," forecast another.

Aleks told them he was desperate and would do any work offered to him.

"The cook likes pretty boys, so look out. He'll add some crude words to your vocabulary too. He has a vile temper and doesn't hesitate to express his feelings."

Aleks had heard that unpleasant things happened in groups of men when they were isolated from women and smiled knowingly at the warning. He would take care with the cook.

The logging camp had a cookhouse, eating hut, stables, bunkhouses, a forge, and an office, all of which were timbered buildings. Beyond it lay trees in a white landscape. At first glance, it was depressing, but later, Aleks would come to find the buildings comfortable and the hinterland manageable.

He reported to the manager, Jean Pettit, who sat in a log cabin office. He was thickset with intelligent blue eyes. Like his workers, he was dressed in practical clothing.

Aleks said, "Sir, I am Alexander Greenus, known as Aleks. I am a Lithuanian immigrant and speak some French. I was told I had a job in the cookhouse."

Pettit shook his hand and said, "Welcome. Yes. You will be well received in the cookhouse. You have an unusual name, Alexander Greenus. We all go by first names here. We'll call you Alex. You'll receive instructions from the cook, Elov Stravinsky. He's a Pole. He has a quick temper and uses a lot of strong language. One can hardly blame him, slaving as he does in the hot kitchen preparing food for hungry workers. Just be careful. Beneath his noisy appearance, he has heart of gold. Alex, we are still in the middle of the Great Depression. I do not know what it was like in Lithuania, but things are difficult here. There is not much money around, but you will be fed and have protection from our frigid winters. I hope you will settle down to our way of life and enjoy the weekends when we put our feet up."

"Sir, life was not easy in Lithuania. My large family had a small farm, and we all had to get stuck in and work the fields and care for the animals. You will not have to worry about me."

"Excellent. Your companions will be rough but ready. Elov will show you the ropes. The kitchen is the second building in the row, and you will find him there. Good luck, and again, welcome to the camp."

Alex walked to the cookhouse where he met Elov. He was a swarthy, potbellied man with piercing black eyes, a straggly beard, and long grey hair partly covered with a cook's hat. He wore an old-fashioned butcher's apron with broad, blue, horizontal stripes. He greeted Alex with a fierce hand grip.

"What's your name?"

"I am Alexander Greenus. Mr. Pettit said I would be known as Alex."

"Alex? Well, Alex, I have been waiting for you. I have to feed 50 hungry men three times a day, and I could do with some help. Life in the cookhouse is prepare, serve, and clean up. Keep your hands clean at all times. The men work in tough jobs in cold weather. They have good appetites and need warm food. My problem is that I am on a tight budget, so I have to use my brains to keep the peace. I use lots of potatoes, squashes, and rice to fill their bellies and cook stews and broil meat and fish. We have good ovens, and I make tons of bread. I'll show you how to do everything. You'll have to get up early to make the fires.

"On the wall, you can see the menus I have planned for the next four weeks. We will follow them unless we run out of things. That happens when the delivery system fails. You'll hear lots of grumbles. I think the men moan because of the hard life they lead. I am an easy target for their anger. I laugh it off. They know only too well that there are thousands of men out of work, sleeping in the streets, and hitching rides on trains. Here, they have shelter and food, and most of them earn a reasonable wage.

"You'll sleep in the cabin opposite the cookhouse, alone. We store food in there. There's nothing for you to do today, but be here at five in the morning. I will start training you on making porridge."

Alex went to the wooden hut. It had a table and a chair, a bed with rough blankets, and a kerosene lamp. The walls were stacked with food in sacks, bottles, and tins. The room was surprisingly comfortable. He dumped his few possessions there and strolled around the camp. He then went to the kitchen and watched Elov putting the finishing touches on the evening meal. He asked Alex to help him. In the dining cabin, men sat around waiting.

One said, "Oh ho, Cookie! You have a young boy to help you. Be good to him," and leered.

"He will have lots to do. If you upset him, I'll get even with you," said Elov.

"Really? Your punishment is usually another helping of your lousy stew."

Alex smiled at the good-hearted repartee, but the lumberjack's innuendo did not escape him.

Elov reminded Alex that in the morning they would make porridge.

"These guys would eat a dozen eggs each if we gave them the chance, so it is usually porridge, scrambled eggs, and grits for breakfast. As I said, I bake bread. The men stuff themselves with that. Once they're working in the forests, it's easier in the kitchen. We have to take hot food to the cutting sites, and that means using the ponies. You'll get a lot of abuse slung at you because of the food. Ignore it. There is a depression on, and these guys would be starving if they weren't here. We get meat from the village and produce from local farmers, who deliver it, so we manage. The lake near here is full of fish. We often get some, even in winter. On the whole, the bleeding loggers do well.

"I have a bread-mixing machine, so it is easy to make lots of loaves. I bake pumpernickel, rye, whole wheat, and white breads and get them to rise near the ovens. What else? Oh yes, we keep kitchen slops for the pigs. Your job is to feed them. You see these large bowls? We fill them with food; put them on the tables, and the men help themselves. We have to refill them quickly, or there are complaints. You may be surprised to know that I look after the first aid, so I'll show you what to do for that too."

Alex soon fitted into the cook's routine. He was tired by the time of the evening meal. One day, he stumbled when serving at a meal and said, *"Perkunas!"* (Damn it). Afterwards, a tall, languid, black-haired man approached him. He had noticed Alex had used a Lithuanian word. He wanted to know if he was a Lithuanian. Alex said that he was, and the other man introduced himself as Arturas Naujokas, known at the camp as Arthur. He had taught in Panevezys in Lithuania but had fallen afoul of the government. He opposed the dictatorship of Antanas Smetona. The political police hounded him until he immigrated to the United States. There was no work there, so he moved to the Canadian logging camps where he spent the winters. In the summers, he moved around the eastern United States doing odd jobs for farmers.

He asked if Alex was interested in reading. Alex said he was but had no books. Arthur had a few Russian books and could obtain some in other languages through a rural library. Alex told him how he had been persuaded by a priest to study Russian and was familiar with the Cyrillic script. Arthur said he would lend him books, provided he gave him a written appreciation of the contents of the books when he finished reading them. It was agreed that he would use the Roman script in his answers.

He has remained a teacher, thought Alex, who before long was absorbed in Tolstoy, Pushkin, and Dostoevsky. In the discussions that followed, Arthur said Alex understood the books, but his writing needed improvement. Alex wanted to read books in languages other than Russian. He was told he would have to improve his French based as it now was on the camp language, which differed from classical French.

Arthur gave Alex about 300 words to learn and said they would enable him to handle most conversations. He then started on conjugations. Alex was fascinated and was soon at home in the language. He read every French newspaper and magazine he could find. The cook often shouted at him to put the damned papers down and watch the pots, which were boiling over.

"Why the hell are you reading all the time? You should be practising with an axe and become a man like the rest of us. What is the use of reading and writing? That tall jackass who teaches you should forget logging and work in a school. Mind you, he is good with first aid and in settling disputes with the managers. He talks their language and sticks up for the men. It takes all sorts to make a world. You should finish your work before any more reading."

"I usually read when I have finished my work. You don't mind when I write your letters. You should learn to read and write. Then you will be able to do your own letters, and that will give me more reading time."

"You bloody Russkis are all the same—bluff and bargain."

"I am Lithuanian, not Russian."

"It's all the same to me. I'm a Pole. We should still have all the Baltic lands, but you seem to prefer the Russians. I would still like some letters written by you, so you can read as long as we get the work done. I was kicked out of school when I was a kid, so I don't write well."

"You should ask Arthur to teach you to read and write properly. It will make all the difference to your life."

"Do you think he would?"

"Yes, I'll ask him."

Arthur agreed, and he and the cook were thereafter seen at night working together. Others were curious, and before long, Arthur had a small class. Jean Pettit encouraged his work and provided a blackboard, exercise books, and writing paper. He told the proprietor that he preferred the men to be busy learning to drinking home-brewed alcohol and fighting.

The cook decided to slaughter one of the pigs that had been fattened by the kitchen slops. He was delighted when Alex asked for a knife and said he could handle things. All he needed was a beam from which to hang the pig and buckets for its blood and head. He selected one of the bigger animals and quickly cut its throat, collected the blood in one bucket, and the severed head in another. Alex skinned the carcass and split it down the middle, after which, he and the cook dismembered the rest. Alex told the cook that he had learned the technique from his father, who always gave him a piece of the tenderloin in recognition of his help.

"I get the message, and you'll get your meat. You have no idea how much work you have saved me."

As a reward for the slaughter, the cook gave Alex one of his precious knives and told him to keep it handy. "Make a sleeve in your trouser leg and practice pulling the knife out quickly. Also, practise throwing it. You never know when you'll need it."

He shook Alex's hand and then stroked his arm and said that Alex should move out of the small cabin and join him in the warm room off the kitchen. Alex thanked him, and mindful of the remarks of the logger on the truck on his first day in the camp and subsequent ones by others, he declined the invitation.

The loggers looked at Alex in a new light when they heard he was responsible for the tasty pork.

"Hey, Cookie, when are you going to kill another pig? That meat was delicious!" asked one.

"There will be one in three weeks, and I have got a sack of beans to go with it," the cook responded.

Alex kept his knife sharp. It was beautifully balanced, and he practised throwing it. One evening, he slipped while serving and spilt some hot soup over a logger's arm. The man swore and said the book-loving, Bible-thumping kitchen mutt was a stupid bastard who needed a lesson. He stood up and moved towards

Alex, who calmly took out his knife and moved it from one hand to the other.

"If you stay where you are," he said, "you're safe. If you move, I'll either pin this knife to your shoulder or slice a bit off your face. Whether I read the Bible or Quran has nothing to do with you. Leave me alone. Are you still going to teach me a lesson?"

By now, other loggers had moved towards the assailant. They persuaded him to sit down. Alex stood back and threw the knife at the wooden wall where it entered point first.

"I was not bluffing," he told the crestfallen logger. "That wall could have been you."

Alex often went to St. Tite to collect provisions and to shop for the workers. Arthur had an arrangement with the postmaster to send requests to the rural library, and Alex would return with a load of books, which were soon read.

One day, Arthur said he would lend him a long book, *Das Kapital*, written by one of the cleverest intellectuals of the past 50 years. He was Karl Marx, a Prussian of Jewish descent, who worked on political philosophy and developed communist theory with another revolutionist Friedrich Engels. Marx's revolutionary and communistic views resulted in his expulsion from Cologne. He settled in London and used the British Museum for his work.

"You may not agree with his views, but he and Engels, who completed Marx's work after his death, provided the Bolsheviks with the philosophy they needed to overthrow the Romanovs. You know what Russia is like today. They have their eyes on our home country for one thing. Marx believed that a diminishing number of Capitalists get rich while the labouring classes end in increasing dependency and misery. Sounds familiar, eh? Here we are slogging away in the woods for a pittance for the benefit of an absent owner. Think about it, but don't start a revolution."

"Of course not. I am grateful for the food and accommodation and some money. Hell, it's a thick book. Written in London, did you say? I don't read English."

"No, it is in the original text, German. You have some German, and here is a dictionary. You'll soon pick up the meanings of German words. In any event, I shall grill you on the book, so you'll know all about it by the time we leave here."

This proved to be the case, and they had many animated discussions on Marx's views and the Bolsheviks' misinterpretation of his work.

"For example, they took Marx at his word when he said *'Die Religion ist das Opium des Volkes,'* religion is the opium of the people, and they wrecked churches, synagogues, and mosques," said Arthur. "I notice that you have a rosary, so someone kept the faith in your village."

"Yes, it was Father Staugaitis, who not only practised the Gospel but ran classes on the history of Lithuania that showed Communists in a bad light. I miss his talks on our customs and beliefs. He gave me this rosary when he heard I was leaving and told me to keep my faith in God as I have done. It has helped particularly here where there are some rough, uncouth people."

"You are right. I keep my distance. I learnt to look after myself and keep fit. After a fight I had with a drunken lout who tried to hit me with a chair because I refused to drink with him, I have been left alone. I ducked the chair and kicked him where it hurts and to make sure he was finished, kneed him in the face as he bent over in pain. It was quite amusing, because at the time, I was doing all the first-aid work so I was the one who patched his nose. We have been good friends ever since. I see you help the cook with first aid. I'll train and test you, because you never know when you will be needed."

Alex thought about Marx, the equality of men, and communal living. His present life illustrated Marx's point about Capitalism, because he was a virtual slave to the logging camp owner, who lived well off the sweat of the loggers. But was it any different in Communist Russia? Its leaders lived well and had their dachas for relaxation, but the masses were as miserable as ever, and there were also pogroms and massacres. He did not think Marx intended that.

I'll avoid trouble, he thought. *I'll work hard, save what I can, study under Arthur's guidance, and hope for better days.*

Before long, he was writing to Arthur's satisfaction, could speak French well, and knew a lot about broken legs, arms, and ribs; bruises; cuts; sprains; and stomach disorders.

He showed an interest in the horses used for hauling logs and communications. He often spoke to a blacksmith, whom he helped shoe the animals with studded shoes to prevent slippage on the ice. The blacksmith was a powerful Pole, who laughed when Alex found one of the hammers too heavy to wield.

"Use that smaller one," he told him, "but continue trying with the big brute. It is effective when one has a large piece of iron to shape."

Jean Pettit noted his interest in the horses and smithy and put him in charge of the animals. He replaced him in the kitchen with a logger whose leg had been damaged in an accident.

Cut logs were loaded onto sleds and dragged to the banks of a frozen river, and the horses were always busy. At the end of the day, Alex had to feed, water, groom, and stable them. Some of the men complained that the horses were better accommodated than they were. They were told this was true because the success of the logging depended on the animals. When they suggested that the company buy the machines that modern logging companies used, they were told the owners were satisfied with proven methods. It was pointed out that when machines broke down, as they often did, work came to a standstill. One worker observed that the bosses did not hesitate to use motorcars, so why not use tractors and mechanical loaders in the forests? Alex was interested in the discussions but did not participate in them.

A doctor made regular rounds of the logging camps, and Alex accompanied him when he visited sick workers. He observed his diagnostic techniques and noted which medicines he prescribed. He questioned the physician, who explained his methods. He suggested Alex add more medicines to the first-aid cupboards. He told him he was impressed with his treatment of fractures and said he should not hesitate to use tourniquets when there was excessive bleeding.

"So many people die unnecessarily from loss of blood and shock," he said. "I'll show you the pressure points, so you'll know where to tie tourniquets. They have to be loosened every few hours. I congratulate you on the camp hygiene standards you introduced. The toilets are clean, and I see you have made an incinerator for burning rubbish. I am a great believer in preventing illnesses in preference to curing them, and you are saving the men from sicknesses. You should see how filthy some of the camps are. I also like your idea of having first-aid boxes in the remote parts of the camp for emergency use."

Alex was impressed with the lean, middle-aged, bespectacled doctor's concern for the loggers. His lessons came in handy two weeks later when an anxious lumberjack rushed to the stables and said his mate had gashed himself with an axe and there was blood everywhere. Alex grabbed his first-aid kit and ran to the victim. He wrapped a wet pad around the wounded leg and applied a tourniquet.

"You'll be okay now. I'll get a horse and sled and take you to St. Tite where we'll get our doctor to attend to you," he said to the distressed worker.

He collected a pony and hitched it to a sled, made the logger comfortable on it, covered him with furs and a blanket, strapped him down, and set off. It was bitterly cold, and the logging road was slippery. He drove through the darkness, stopping frequently to check the tourniquet and to rest the horse. Finally, he could see lights in a building on the outskirts of the town, so he stopped and obtained directions to the logging doctor's house. The doctor helped Alex carry the injured man inside, and after examining him, he told the man, "You're lucky. Someone who knew what he was doing looked after you. The bleeding has stopped, but you need stitches. I'm going to inject you against tetanus, and then freeze the area of the cut and stitch it." Afterwards, he suggested that the injured man and Alex spend the rest of the night at his house. If there were no complications, in the morning, they would return to the logging camp. He would examine the injury on his next visit in ten days' time.

"Until then, it will be light duty for you. Give this note to the manager; he'll understand. And you, young man, have made good use of the lessons I gave you. Have you thought of being a doctor?"

"It had crossed my mind," said Alex, "but I know nothing of science and my English is weak."

"Those are just hurdles to cross. I think you are a natural healer. All that stuff we learn in college is important but valueless if not used properly. You can train at a French university. Do you have Latin?"

"No," said Alex.

"Well, think about it."

"Thank you, sir. I'll do that."

The two men spent the night in the warm building and the next morning returned to the camp where the injured man told the manager how good Alex had been. "The doctor said he saved my life, and that means he saved the company a lot of compensation money."

"Oh, nonsense. It would take more than a small cut to wipe you out. You can take things easy until the doctor's visit. I am sure you will be 100 percent by then."

He read the doctor's note, which stated that the man probably would have died but for Alex's timely intervention. He called Alex, thanked him for his initiative, and increased his monthly pay by two dollars, for which Alex was grateful.

Arthur wanted to know all about the incident, and when he heard that his young friend was interested in becoming a doctor and would need mathematics and Latin, he assured him it would not be a problem. Mathematics was really logical thinking, he said. Latin was a discipline, and Alex would have to repeat words and phrases over and over until he got their meaning. The old language would open up a new world, because it was the basis of many languages. He said he would start the next day with it and basic mathematics. Alex could get some textbooks and push ahead on his own during the summer months.

"By the way, Alex, what will you do over the summer?"

"Well, I could go to my uncle, but that would be unfair because he is struggling. I'll look for farm work. I was told there are lots of dairy farms south of here. I am sure help will be needed in haymaking and in harvesting corn. I can handle horses, and there are still farmers using them. I wonder what will happen to the horses here. I have grown fond of them."

"The owner has a farm where they graze in the summers. They are good stock and are used for breeding."

In the spring, as the lumberjacks prepared to leave, Jean Pettit told Alex he would have a job for him in the fall. If he put on some weight, he could join a cutting team and make some real money. He gave Alex his address and hoped he would have a good summer.

Arthur said he would head for the eastern United States. There was much history, which he found interesting, and lots of seafood, which he enjoyed, there. He would get jobs on the farms. There should be no difficulty in getting work, because the regular workers liked to take holidays in the summer when the schools were closed.

"If they will have me, I'll return for one more year with this outfit. They plan to move to a new camp five kilometres from here, and it will be years before they finish logging in this area. Keep at your books. By the time we meet, I expect you to know all of Euclid and Pythagoras and Caesar's *Gallic Wars*. You have the translations, so you can teach yourself. *Au revoir.*"

Alex thanked Arthur for his help and presented him with a book, *English Romantic Poets*. Arthur had mentioned Byron, Keats, and Shelley. Alex hoped he enjoyed this latest anthology. Arthur was delighted and told Alex he could not have given him a better present.

"You are a dark horse. If you conquer Latin, you will find English easier to learn. It is an interesting language, and you'll be able to read socialist Charles Dickens's books, which were so much admired by our friend Karl Marx. There is also the work of that incomparable genius, Shakespeare, waiting to be enjoyed. Pushkin was fond of him, as you may have noticed. You will hear plenty of English south of here, so keep your ears open and do not hesitate to try speaking it. You will be corrected, but you have a flair for languages and should welcome that. You know the Russians forced Lithuanians to speak their language. Although they did not intend to help us, they did so, because most of us picked up their language as kids and other languages followed easily. I even speak some Polish. Once again, adieu—sorry, *good-bye*." They shook hands and parted.

Alex made his way to his uncle's home in Montreal and told him that as indicated in his letters, he had enjoyed the rough life in the logging camp and had learned a lot. He repaid the money Juozas had lent him and left a donation for the church. Juozas thanked him. He commented that Alex had grown and put on weight.

"Yes. I am fit, and I had the good fortune to meet a former Lithuanian schoolteacher, who improved my reading and writing and coached me in Latin and mathematics."

"Well, young man, if you are interested, I suppose learning is important. I have always been so busy trying to feed my family that I have had no time for anything else."

"Uncle Juozas, you are a good man, and I am eternally grateful that you sheltered me when I arrived in Canada. From the letters my parents sent me, it is obvious that things are uncomfortable under the dictatorship at home. I wish more of my family could emigrate, but the authorities have clamped down. What can I do to help you?"

Juozas said that he would be grateful if Alex would collect and chop some wood in preparation for the winter. Alex readily agreed. He scouted around and found a firm that delivered logs. He ordered a sufficient supply for the winter, split and cut them into practical pieces, and stored them neatly under cover. From time to time, he stopped to listen to children playing in the street and again was amazed at the number of languages he heard. *They sound happy, and there are no racial hang-ups. Canada must be a melting pot for immigrants and their offspring.*

Juozas told him the best chance for a job was in the Eastern Townships area and suggested he contact the government agriculture department. Alex called at the department's office at Rue St. Jacques and was shown a notice board on which vacancies were advertised. He made a note of three in the Eastern Townships area and phoned them to fix interviews. One vacancy had been filled, but two farmers said they would see him and gave directions to their farms. He took a bus to Sherbrooke and hitched his way to the first farm, the appearance of which upset him. The buildings were dilapidated, the fences were broken, and there was rubbish everywhere. He did not bother to present himself and made his way to the second farm near East Angus. It had a neat appearance, and there was an attractive garden around the house. He saw a young man in overalls tending to a tractor and enquired about M. Bourassa, the name on the vacancy notice.

"That's my father. You'll find him in the small barn," was his response.

He found the farmer, a tall bronzed man with smiling eyes. Alex told him he wanted to apply for the job advertised in Montreal.

"You are the third applicant today. What do you know about farming?" he asked.

Alex explained that he was a farmer's son and was familiar with animals and crops. He could plough with horses and could handle a tractor. He had spent a season in a logging camp, was fit, and would like to work through the summer.

"Well," said the farmer, "times are changing, and horses are fading out. Fortunately, my son Emile works with me and is up-to-date, thanks to his studies in agriculture at Macdonald College. Join us for lunch, and I'll think about the other two applicants. They were students, not farm boys. I would have to train them and am scared they would hurt themselves. As you know, accidents are common on farms."

"And in logging camps," said Alex. "I was looking after the first aid, and there were some nasty cuts and bruises."

He was introduced to the farmer's wife, daughter, and son. His wife was a strikingly beautiful, middle-aged lady. She said she was glad to meet him and wished him well at the farm. The daughter was an attractive young lady with sparkling blue eyes, who also said she was pleased to meet him. Alex noticed that she spoke classical French, not the local *joual* of the Montreal streets and logging camp. The son, Emile, whom he had met earlier, immediately launched into a lecture on the necessity of buying new machinery. His father said he was sure he was right, but his debts did not permit him to buy more equipment. If they had a good season, the bank might help.

The farmer said grace and noticed that Alex crossed himself.

Alex said he assumed the farm was a mixed enterprise, because he had seen cattle, hogs, free-range Rhode Island Red chickens, and even some bantams. Bourassa said that they were self-sufficient and had survived the depression. Although things were still tough, both his children had gone to high school. Emile was at a college, and Giselle would leave soon for training as a nurse. He said that Alex's accent was not local and asked where he came from.

"I am from Lithuania. There is a lot of poverty there, and, as you probably know, there are many Baltic immigrants in Quebec. I learnt most of my French in the logging camp, but a friend taught me the classical language, so I am inclined to mix the two."

"You'll find *joual*, local French, used around here. We tend to query people with fancy accents, but don't let that bother you. Look, I'll give you a job. There is a convenient room in an outbuilding where you can sleep. We will feed you, give you farming clothes, and pay you twenty dollars a month. You will have to perform all chores, including milking the cows, looking after the horses, helping with haymaking, filling the silos, and any other work that might be needed. After chores, you would have Saturday afternoon and Sunday free. You are a Catholic, are you not?"

"Yes," said Alex.

"Then you could come to Mass with us. You will like our priest, Father Levesque. He is well educated and lively. He plays on the local hockey team, and woe betide anyone on the ice who gets in his way."

"Thank you. I would like to work here. I can assure you that you will not be sorry you hired me."

"Where are your things?"

"I have a bag and my books, so I can settle down straightaway."

"Those books seem heavy."

"Yes. I missed some years of schooling and a friend is helping me catch up. I have French, English, and German dictionaries, a copy of Karl Marx's work, and some Latin and mathematics books."

"I doubt if you'll have much time for reading here, but if you chat with Father Levesque, he might help you with Latin. He curses that it was removed from the schools and encourages youngsters to study it. There is a movement in the Church to change the Latin graces and responses, and he is opposed to that. Emile will show you your room, and you can spend the rest of the day with him learning the routine. We plan the next day's work at supper each night."

Alex's room was airy and furnished with a bed, a table, a chair, and a reading lamp. There was a washbasin with a jug, some pictures of rural scenes, and a small cross on a chain.

It will be a change to be with religious people and to enjoy home cooking, he thought.

Emile said that Giselle was responsible for milking the cows. Alex would have to learn quickly because she would leave soon for Montreal. It would mean getting up early. Alex said that would not bother him. The next morning, someone knocked on his door and told him to get up. He dressed quickly and made his way to the milking parlour where Giselle was already busy. She told him to watch carefully, because there was a routine to follow. She then instructed him to do some milking. He surprised her by performing the task correctly. He told her that he had learnt from his mother, but they only had two cows, not ten like the Bourassas. She laughed and said they had plenty of buckets. They could each milk half the herd and that would give her more leisure. Their hands had touched when she instructed him, and he sensed hers had lingered.

The rest of the day was spent in cutting, bundling, and stacking hay. Emile said they would have to work until dark, because once the hay was cut, it had to be covered in case of rain. There were ominous clouds in the sky, so they worked nonstop and finished the first field as planned. Alex slept soundly and was again awakened in the early morning by a knock on the door. They finished milking the cows quickly. Giselle, who had proved most friendly, thanked him for his help.

On Sunday, he joined the family for church, and they drove to East Angus in the farmer's Chevrolet. Alex felt at home with the service and the familiar Latin used in it. The priest, Father Levesque, who had heard that he wanted to pursue his Latin studies, greeted him warmly and said he could help.

Alex thanked him. The priest told him to be at the vestry on Tuesday evening.

"My day of rest is Monday, and after my hospital visits, I put my feet up. See you then, on Tuesday," said the priest.

On Tuesday, the farmer told Alex he could use the pony. He enjoyed the late-afternoon ride. The priest was affable and wanted to know why Alex was running against the tide in learning Latin. Alex gave two reasons. First, he hoped to become a doctor, and he understood Latin was a prerequisite. Second, he wanted to improve his knowledge of languages, and his mentor had said familiarity with Latin would help in that pursuit.

"Quite right, my boy. You'll need to know a tibia from a deltoid for medical reasons, and the Romance languages are based on Latin. What do you know? Ah, the *Gallic Wars*. I suggest we work through them. We'll concentrate on passages you do not understand. Then we'll move on to more interesting things, like the classical poets and logicians. There is a wealth of knowledge to be tapped while you are conquering the conjugations."

The first evening was the forerunner of many pleasant meetings. When he heard that Alex had been a choirboy, he persuaded him to join his small choir. Giselle was also a member, and they attended practices together. He said he would miss her and her lively humour when she went to Montreal. She smiled and told him how pleased her parents were with his work. Her father needed to have an operation but had put it off because of farm work. He had now made an appointment because he was confident that Emile and Alex could manage in his absence.

One Saturday night a few weeks later, he was almost asleep when heard his door opening. Giselle slid into bed next to him. When he realised she was only wearing a flimsy nightdress, he was shocked and asked, "What on earth are you doing?"

"I have been waiting for this opportunity. Emile is with his baseball team, and Mum is visiting Dad in hospital. I know you like me, and I was lonely, so I came for a chat," she said and snuggled against him.

"Giselle, I am fond of you, but I am a man and you are exposing yourself to trouble moving your lovely body against me like this, as much as I enjoy it."

"Alex, from the first moment our fingers touched when I showed you how to milk a cow, I have wanted this moment. Your fingers fascinated me. Although your hands are rough, you have the tapered fingers of a pianist. You must have noticed that I shake hands with you often. Of late, you have lingered before releasing your hand."

"You are a crafty person. I am very fond of you but did not dream that you were more than casually interested in me. You have excited me, but it must end there, or you may regret my taking advantage of you."

"Don't worry. Just hug and kiss me and relax."

She kissed him warmly and removed her garment. He was aroused. He kissed her eagerly and moved his hands across her body. She said she could feel that he was interested and pulled off his pyjama pants.

"Whew, you certainly are. Put this on," she said and produced a prophylactic.

"Wait a minute," he said, "here you are, a good Catholic girl with one of these? What would the Pope think? You are ahead of me. I do not know how to use them."

"Alex, I went to a convent school, and there is nothing we did not know. I had a boyfriend here. He had a good supply, and I kept some of them. I'll help you." She did, and he became more excited. When she guided him, Alex was astonished but delighted. Giselle told him to rest, and they would try again. They did so, to their mutual satisfaction.

He could not believe his good fortune, but their opportunities to make love were limited. They tried in the early mornings before milking, but it was too hasty and unsatisfactory. They welcomed choir practices, but the car was not ideal for lovemaking, and, all too soon, it was time for Giselle to leave. They had hidden their romance as best they could and were formal in the presence of others. On her departure, they simply shook hands and wished each other well.

They arranged that she should write to him poste restante at East Angus, because they did not want her family to know about their relationship. Letters sent direct would have exposed them. He missed her badly and took refuge in his books. At the end of three weeks, he told Emile that he was going to Montreal the following Saturday to see his uncle and asked him to do the Sunday chores. Emile agreed.

He would see his uncle, but the weekend visit coincided with some free time for Giselle and they had agreed to meet. She met him at the bus station, and they hugged and kissed. She said she had a surprise for him. One of the trainee nurses who lived away from the hospital had left for the weekend, and she told Giselle to use her apartment. They made their way to it, and as soon as they were inside, Giselle urged him to hurry up while she undressed.

"You are a wanton hussy," he said, "but I love you."

"I don't know what *wanton* means, but I'm wantin' you. I see that you have got the message."

They made love all afternoon. Giselle said that if he planned to be a doctor, he should know all parts of the body and their functions. She was busy learning them, and she gave him some practical lessons, concentrating on the areas of pleasure. He told her that he would soon return to the logging camp. It would be difficult to see her in the winter, but he would try. She responded that her course would keep her busy, but she knew he would be faithful to her because there were no females in the camps.

The two days passed quickly. She had to be on duty at Sunday midday. After parting from her, Alex visited his uncle. He repeated that he was very grateful for his help. They discussed family affairs. Alex said he heard from his parents regularly and planned to send them money, because times were still bad in Lithuania. He had hoped his sisters would emigrate, but the authorities had clamped down and that was now impossible. His father told him Lithuanians were concerned with the aggressiveness of the Nazis and that of a pro-Fascist group in the country that supported Germany's claim to Memel. Alex said it was a relief to be in Canada and in a logging camp where one was so busy that sad external affairs were forgotten.

He helped Emile and his father complete the season's work and thanked them for employing him.

"On the contrary," said the farmer, "you worked well, and I am pleased to give you a small bonus. Keep in touch; we could use you next year."

"Thank you. I would like to do that. We'll have some new equipment by then, eh, Emile?"

"Now, now Alex, don't encourage him."

Mrs. Bourassa gave him a hamper of food. He said he would never forget her wonderful meals. Despite the rigours of farming, they had added to his weight, which was something he needed. He asked her to give his best wishes to Giselle, which she promised to do.

"You two got on well, did you not?" she asked with a wink.

She knows, thought Alex. *I wonder how much?*

He agreed they did get on well. He liked her sense of humour. He hoped she succeeded in her nursing training. He thought of her as he travelled to the logging camp and contrasted the journey with his first one.

No more cookhouse for me. I can swing an axe and pull a saw. I am strong now and can communicate with everybody. I can earn good money and send some home. It will be difficult to pursue my studies, but if Arthur is there, he'll help me, and there are the weekends when we relax.

Mr. Pettit greeted him. He put him with an experienced team and wished him well. He hoped he would continue to look after first-aid matters.

"Did you know that the government health officials now inspect the camps and that they gave us full marks thanks to your hygiene improvements? They agreed that it makes sense to keep workers healthy and on the job. We will probably have visitors from other camps to study what you have done. The owners have their eyes on you."

"Yes, I'll look after first aid. I hope to be a doctor one day, so the practice will be helpful."

Arthur arrived and told Alex about his experiences in Maine and Massachusetts. "Maine is just like Canada, but don't mention potatoes, because they compete with New Brunswick and you'd think it was the 1812 war all over again. I told them there were starving people everywhere, who would welcome their surplus potatoes. In fact, we could do with a lot more in this camp. I spent some time in Boston. Do you know American history?"

Alex said he knew there had been a revolt against the English, that the revolution had inspired the French masses to rise, and that the Russian Marxists used the American example to justify their actions.

"It is far more interesting than that. The colonists were fed up with unjust taxes. They were not represented in the British Parliament, and 'Taxation without representation is tyranny' became the catchphrase of the American Revolution. It all started in the Boston area. In 1773, there was the so-called Boston Tea Party, when colonists climbed onto British ships and threw cases of highly taxed tea into the sea. The first skirmish took place at Concord nearby. I walked all over the area during my breaks from farm work. It is not often that one can visit the scene of such momentous events. I am sure this does not interest you. How did you get on?"

"You are wrong. I am interested in those events. I came across people called Empire Loyalists, Canadians who left the United States or were kicked out and came to Canada. They are proud of their background. They told me that in 1812, the British with local help, including some Indians, beat the Americans. If I am to live here, I should know the history of the country. It is obviously linked to that of the United States. However, that will have to wait. I had a great summer. I worked my hide off on a mixed farm enterprise. It was self-sufficient with a pleasant family. As you can see, I have put on weight. I also fell in love."

"You did what?"

"I fell in love with the farmer's daughter, and we had some great times. I shall miss her, stuck as I am in the wilderness."

"So I suppose the studies you contemplated fell by the wayside?"

"No. The local priest is a Latin scholar and coached me. In return, I sang in his choir. The family was French-speaking, and I managed comfortably. I am on a cutting team here, so I will not have as much time as before to read, but I'll keep at it. I battled with Euclid on the farm and must tackle calculus if you will help me."

"Of course, but you are lucky. There is some new equipment here, and the engineer in charge has a university degree and studied maths and physics. When I mentioned your studies, he said he would help you. He heard from the manager that you were a keen student."

"Thank you once again. I am glad you returned to this outfit."

Alex almost regretted changing jobs because the work was heavy, and at the end of the day, he was exhausted. Logs were cut and skidded to log piles and then carted by sleigh on frozen tracks to a riverbank ready for the spring river drive. He realised that his companions were testing him by loading him with the heavy jobs. When they were satisfied that he would not be a drag on their performance, they lightened his load. He found time to study instead of going to bed early exhausted. The weekends were blissful, and he loafed and read. He and Giselle exchanged letters and planned to meet in the summer.

He was unhappy with the turn of events in Lithuania. The dictatorship was leaning towards Communism and a closer alliance with the Soviets. There was talk of collectivisation of farms. Taxes had been increased, even for the poor, and life was uncomfortable and unsettled for his parents. They appreciated the help he gave them and asked him to check if immigration were possible. He asked Arthur what he thought. He said Canada needed immigrants, but the present government did not encourage refugees. The main problem was getting his relatives out of Lithuania. Alex said he would visit Lithuania in the summer and try. He was advised to become a Canadian citizen first so he would be protected against the Lithuanian authorities, who otherwise would force him into their army. Unfortunately, five years' residence was required before one could become a citizen and get a Canadian passport. Alex said he would go and use his immigration papers to prove his identity.

At the end of several hard months of cutting, sawing, and lifting, he went to Montreal and enquired at a shipping office about a trip to Lithuania. When he said that he did not have a passport, he was told that he had no hope of travelling to his homeland, because shipping companies faced the expense of returning people who were refused entry into Lithuania back to the port of departure. He called on the immigration authorities and asked if he could get an emergency passport. He was told that he did not qualify as a Canadian citizen and therefore could not be issued with a passport. He explained that his family was suffering, and he wanted to get them to Canada. He was told that the authorities were not sympathetic to refugees, but if people were sponsored, they could be admitted.

Alex explained his dilemma to Giselle, whom he met at the hospital where she worked. She wondered if he could find someone with a Canadian passport to go to Lithuania on his behalf, but they realised there would be language problems. Alex shook his head and said he would tell his family to send a family member to the Canadian authorities in Danzig to see what could be done. There was nowhere to make love, and Giselle told him he would have to be patient until she arrived at the farm for two weeks' holiday. Her father was pleased that Alex had applied for summer work there again. He and her mother planned to take a holiday when Giselle was at the farm and could do some of the chores.

The Bourassas greeted Alex warmly, and he settled into a routine straight away. On the first Sunday, he spoke to Father Levesque, who enquired about his studies. Alex said he had continued and felt comfortable with Latin. He had also progressed in mathematics. He had started on English and could read reasonably well. The priest said that if Alex wished, they could continue their meetings and discuss biology, which would be helpful if he pursued his intention of becoming a doctor. Alex appreciated the offer, and the evening sessions were resumed.

Giselle was as cheerful as usual and tackled her chores with zest, but she was reserved with Alex and their lovemaking lacked its earlier spontaneity. One fruitless evening, she told him that she had formed an attachment to a doctor, and, much as she loved Alex, she felt their close association should end. He tried to dissuade her without success, and it was a relief to both of them when she returned to Montreal. He again sought solace in his books.

He failed in his attempts to bring his family to Canada. In discussions with his uncle Juozas, whom he visited from time to time, it was decided that Juozas would keep in touch with authorities through the St. Casimir Church and would advise Alex if prospects changed.

For the 1938–39 winter, Arthur and Alex decided to work in a logging camp in the Algonquin Park at Kiosk on Lake Kioshkoqui, where the Stanforth Lumber Company, a progressive organisation, needed experienced workers. Horses had been replaced with trucks and tractors, and trains were used to transport lumber to sawmills. The camp had electricity and telephones. Loggers were paid $30 a month, and Alex and Arthur earned an extra $5 for taking care of the first-aid work at the new camp. They suggested improvements in its hygiene, which were implemented. The management was relieved to have two experienced men, because the Ontario government's health inspectors now visited camps regularly. They were on the same cutting team and were impressed with the innovative equipment that speeded up the dispatch of timber.

Arthur continued to tutor Alex and told him that if he were serious about being a doctor, he would need to pass some examinations in order to be admitted to a university. He thought that the high school diploma or its equivalent could be obtained by writing examinations in September. He would check to see what needed to be done. He found that Alex could write the exams, and he was entered for Latin, mathematics, and biology.

Arthur said he would again visit Massachusetts in the summer and work his way to Washington DC in pursuit of his interest in early American history. Alex said he would return to East Angus where Father Levesque had undertaken to tutor him, and at the end of a strenuous winter, they agreed to meet in the fall and parted.

Alex and Emile worked hard on the seasonal chores, using new equipment, and once again, the farmer and his wife left them to it while they took a holiday.

Father Levesque was pleased to see his pupil, and when he heard of the forthcoming examinations, he framed a course of study that kept Alex busy. One night, the priest asked Alex if he had thought of the priesthood or work as a medical missionary, because the Church was in dire need of men such as he. Alex said he had not considered the matter and, in any event, doubted if he had the strength to honour a priest's vows. He was told God would provide the power to serve the Church.

Alex said he would like to achieve his first objective, namely to qualify for university entrance, and then study medicine. How he would do that, he did not know, because he did not have money for fees. The priest did not press the point, but they frequently discussed religion and its opponents, including Karl Marx. Alex's knowledge of him impressed the priest.

Early in September, Alex went to Montreal and in the examination room felt old, as he was surrounded by youngsters. He blessed Father Levesque for his tuition in Latin and biology. He felt he had a chance of passing those subjects but was doubtful of mathematics.

He lived with Juozas and Nelle during the exam period, and they often discussed the war that had broken out in Europe. They were upset by the German invasion of Lithuania in which local Fascists greeted the Nazis with enthusiasm because they would get rid of the oppressive Communists. Alex and his uncle felt the Germans would plunder their small country and impose their racialism on the many Jews there.

Two weeks later, Alex heard he had passed the three subjects. He called on Father Levesque with the good news; the priest told him not to rest but to plan the next subjects. Alex told him he could not have passed without his help and presented him with a statuette of a beaver carved from wood by a lumberjack. His teacher was delighted and said all students of biology should study the animal's habits. He asked his housekeeper to fry the juiciest steaks she had. They had a splendid meal. The priest was surprised when Alex declined his best wine; he had heard that the logging camps were the scene of much boozing. Alex acknowledged that they were. As a result of his experiences, he had decided to leave the alcohol to others. The priest said he enjoyed wine and an occasional Dom, a liqueur made by the Benedictine monks that had, he assumed, the pope's approval. Alex laughed and said it was amazing how devout people found support in their religion for their indulgences but did not hesitate to criticise those with different tastes.

"Oh, yes," was the response. "As the poet put it, 'they indulge in things they are inclined to by damning those they have no mind to.' You will also hear that we encourage bad deeds because rascals can clear their guilt at their weekly confessions and then continue their misdeeds with a clear conscience. That is nonsense. No doubt your friend Marx commented on that."

"No, not that I can recall. He shared most religions' belief that one should help the poor and needy, but he wanted those in power to share everything. He saw hierarchies, such as our Church and Capitalists, as impeding that goal. The Russians are practising what they understand as his creed, but he did not support violence and it's questionable whether the ordinary person in Russia is any better off than in the days of the Romanovs. Now we have another evil, Fascism, opposed to Communism, and with respect, Christianity is floundering in the face of the two philosophies."

"Give us time. We have outlived one despot and evil ruler after another, and we will prevail. Let us leave the horrible world and discuss your future."

Alex admitted he was confused. He could return to logging, pass enough examinations to qualify for medical training, and then somehow work his way through university, but he was worried about Lithuania. Canada had declared war against Germany. He felt he should enlist to fight the Nazis, who had forced Memel to join Germany in March 1939. He had to decide soon and let the lumber company know, or they would not keep a place open for him. He would return to the farm to say good-bye and make up his mind there.

The priest advised him to pray. He assured him God would lead him to the right decision. Alex thanked him once again for all the help he had given him and promised to keep in touch.

At the farm, he discussed matters with Emile, who had decided to join the air force only to learn that it was flooded with applicants. He suggested that Alex take his time before joining up. Training facilities in Canada were rudimentary, and he would be wasting days when he could be earning good money logging.

Alex decided that he would take his chances in the army. He had been horrified by his brothers' description of the infantry. He thought that with his newly acquired mechanical knowledge and his experience in the logging camps using crosscut saws and axes, he would be happy in an engineering unit.

2
War

On November 1, 1939, Alex enlisted at a recruiting office in Montreal. He was cross-examined by a beribboned sergeant, who tried to enrol him in the infantry. Alex demurred, and said he would only enlist in the engineers. He was given a form to sign and told to wait for a doctor. He looked at the other recruits and wondered how the motley group would fare in combat. He was contemplating this when his name was called. An orderly took him to a room and told him to strip. He did so. He was examined by a white-clad doctor, who placed his cold stethoscope all over Alex's chest and back, made him cough, and told him to read some lines on an eye chart. He pronounced him fit for service. Alex became Sapper Alexander Greenus, number 678945, ready for training. He was given two days to wind up his affairs and told to report to the Fourth Field Company, a Montreal unit of 175 men.

He bade farewell to M. Bourassa, who agreed to look after his books and other possessions, and was blessed by Father Levesque. He returned to Montreal to say good-bye to Juozas, Nelle, and Giselle, who hugged and kissed him. She said she would pray for him and would always remember the happy times they had enjoyed. She was also thinking of joining the army as a nurse. If she did, she, as a registered nurse, would be an officer, and he would have to click his heels and salute her. He joked that it would be fun to make love to an officer and he looked forward to it. She laughed and told him he would be court-martialled if he did so. He should forget girls and concentrate on his training, she admonished. They hugged and kissed again, and she wished him well.

The engineers were stationed at an old school, which had been hastily converted to barracks. Alex reported there for duty. They took his name and told him to go to the quartermaster to be equipped. He was issued with the various pieces of a uniform (boots, shirts, and overalls), a kit bag, a mess tin, some webbing, a respirator, a water bottle, a small and large pack, and two blankets. He was directed to a building where thirty men slept under the eye of a noisy, grey-haired corporal, who was a Great War veteran. They were shown how to arrange their blankets and equipment for regular inspections by a retinue made of an officer, company sergeant major, and their platoon sergeant, one of whom invariably made a nitpicky comment.

On the parade ground, a shrill-voiced infantry sergeant drilled them. He said they were in an engineering field company and that meant they would be close to the front line and would have to defend themselves. He would teach them how to march, dress, and handle a .303 rifle. He said he despaired of making soldiers of the motley collection of tradesmen, loggers, and other odds and sods, but if they hoped to survive, they should listen to him and smarten up.

His vernacular was far from polite.

"Pick them up. Pick them up. Your legs, when you march! Left, right, left, right. Keep in step, and stamp your feet. Swing your arms. Pull your heads back and your stomachs in. You are in the army now! Look like men! Hold those rifles up. About turn. Halt. Listen. When I shout 'About turn,' I emphasize the 'About' as a warning, then I give the 'turn.' What could be simpler? We'll try it again. Come on. Come on. Quick march. You are like a brood of wet hens. You may have broken your mother's heart, but you won't break mine."

There were unprintable remarks about the recruits' ancestry. Alex ignored them. He was fit and move effortlessly through the drill sequences.

They learned rifle movements, marched, and countermarched in drill formation. They covered miles of countryside in heavy kit. Alex thought he had avoided the PBI, the "poor bloody infantry," but he soon learned he was mistaken, because all they did was infantry work. Imperceptibly, the recruits gradually improved, and at the end of six weeks, they marched with precision and upright bearings and knew how to fire a rifle.

Alex handled the training easily. After the logging camp life, the uncomfortable barracks and rough food that annoyed the others did not bother him. He enjoyed the physical training sessions and developed a fondness for running. At night, when others were in the canteen, he ran to a quiet spot where he could study the skies and ponder the future. His best friend was a man called John le Clus, a hefty electrician and the anchor of the unit's tug-of-war team. Engineering training was elementary because of the lack of qualified instructors, but they gained some experience in the use of explosives, bridge building, road construction, and mine lifting. At the end of the boot camp, Alex and John were made lance corporals to the amusement of their companions.

"You two are keen now, but you'll end up with all the dirty work, for which the sergeants will get the credit. You'll wish you were ordinary sappers."

The pair laughed and said they had only accepted the job because the pay was higher.

On December 21, the men moved to Halifax. Alex saw Pier 21 and the harbour in a new light. The dock area was crowded with men loaded with packs and kitbags, slouching on the ground awaiting embarkation. The harbour was full of naval and cargo ships. The bustle and apparent confusion contrasted with the orderly immigration procedure of earlier years.

His unit did not have long to wait before embarking. They were directed below deck to cramped quarters and shown hammocks in which to sleep. Soon afterwards, in spite of a snowstorm, their ship passed the harbour boom and assumed its place in a convoy. It was an uncomfortable voyage. They all feared the worst if they were attacked by U-Boats. They heard explosions, but their ship was not affected.

They docked in Greenock, disembarked on to a lighter, a flat bottomed barge, marched to a train station, and headed to Aldershot. Life there was a misery. It was a bad winter. The water closets froze; the barracks were cold, and the fire stoves were inadequate to dissipate the chill. Training was haphazard because of a lack of stores and instructors. Much of their time was spent improving the living conditions of other soldiers.

As the weather improved, their training progressed, and they participated in the protection of England as additional pioneer infantry. They were kept busy in the establishment of local defences. They were also committed to heavy works programs, mainly on the beaches, which they mined and straddled with barbed-wire entanglements.

In addition, there was individual and unit training, hut construction, and the preparation of winter quarters. At the end of 1940, they were at Caterham. Then followed divisional exercises, road clearing, mine laying and lifting, bridge building, and demolition exercises at Pangbourne.

Alex and John relished the physical work. Both were soon promoted to corporal. They went to London on leave. They were distressed by the damaged buildings and impressed with the locals' cheerfulness in the face of disaster. They ate well, walked through the parks, went to shows, eyed the girls, and left their departure to the last possible moment.

As they made their way to the Paddington train station, an air raid siren sounded, and they sheltered in an Underground station until the mournful all-clear was given. They walked past a bombed-out building and heard an air raid warden say, "There are people in there, but there is no hope of getting them out."

Alex asked him where the victims were, and the warden pointed to a pile of rubble.

He said, "They are further in there, but it is too late; the whole building will collapse any minute."

"Half a sec," said Alex, "I see an opening on the side." He put his pack down, grabbed the man's torch, and, pointing to some timber and bricks, said, "John, let's give it a go. Come here and help me clear this."

They started to move the rubble.

John said, "You're still a crazy logger, but I can't leave you to get buried alone." With that, he discarded his pack and helped Alex pull wood and masonry away, and they crawled through a narrow opening. They heard a cat meow and headed for it. Their hands were soon covered in cuts, and they had difficulty getting through the debris. There was a sudden release of pressure ahead of them, and they found themselves in the remains of a sitting room in which there was a young boy holding a cat and an unconscious woman trapped by a metal beam across her legs. John comforted the boy and told him not to worry because they would get him and the kitty out.

"What about Mummy?"

"We'll get her out too. We just have to move something first. What's your name?"

"I am Neil Gregory."

"And what's your kitty called?"

"Ginger."

"Ginger is a good friend; she led us here. We'll soon be out of this; just sit and watch us."

Alex examined the woman and gave the thumbs-up to John, indicating that she was alive. "As engineers, we know how to solve this one, don't we?" he said. "It's just a simple lever-and-fulcrum problem. Grab that piece of timber, and get it under the beam. I'll try and wedge this piece of masonry as you lift the beam and that should hold it in position without bringing the whole building down. How the hell I'm going to get this wedge across in this confined space remains to be seen."

"You're always talking of how you and your mates chopped trees, lifted logs, and solved all kinds of problems far from the madding crowd, so get moving."

"Look, at moments like this, we do not need reminding that although you are an electrician, you study literature and have a smooth way with words. 'Madding crowd,' indeed. Let's get the wood in place."

Alex turned and managed to move the wood towards the beam. It was a strenuous job getting it into place, and when he succeeded, he told John to heave.

"Yes, Corporal, here goes."

John took the strain, and the beam moved a little but insufficiently to release the woman. There was a movement of rubble, and Alex said, "We'll have to move fast. I'll help you lift the beam." Their combined efforts worked, and they eased the woman out.

She opened her eyes, moaned, and fainted again. Alex took his field dressing and applied a pad and bandages to her lacerated leg, which he said was broken. He made a splint with some pieces of wood that he tied with a bandage from John's field dressing and two handkerchiefs.

John was fascinated by his friend's unhurried attention to the victim but told him he had bad news. The rumble they'd heard was muck blocking their way out.

"*Tant pis, mon ami.* Let's scout around," said Alex.

He moved towards the boy, and the cat scurried away.

"I think we should follow that animal," he said and shone the torch in the direction of the cat's escape.

"There is a small hole here where the cat went. I'll open it up and pull the boy after me. You follow with the lady."

"Yes, Corporal. Anything to oblige."

Alex found the fallen material difficult to move and asked John to leave the boy and come assist him. They moved some of the debris and saw a distant light.

"We're going to make it," said John and then winced as a chunk of masonry fell on his right hand. "That was sore. Help me move this lot off my hand." Alex obliged.

When they had made further progress, they both shouted for help.

A voice shouted back, "Hang on! We'll get you out."

They could see activity at the source of the light, and the opening there grew bigger. They worked at their end and eventually reached the rescue team. Alex pulled Neil behind him and John the lady. One by one, they all reached safety. The woman was placed on a stretcher and then loaded into an ambulance, which took her, Neil, and Ginger to a hospital.

"You two need attention. We'll take you to a first-aid post— Crikey, look at that!" the air raid warden said as the whole building collapsed. "You just made it. Phew, that was close!" Then he looked at John and said, "You are a big blighter. How the hell did you squeeze through that small entrance?"

"That was the easy part. I am cut and bruised, and my hand is sore."

"It was great of you to rescue that woman and child. You Aussies are a brave lot."

"We admire the Aussies, but we are Canadians enjoying some leave after preparing your beaches for an invasion," said Alex.

"Sorry, mate. There are so many accents these days. We appreciate what you're doing. Canadians, eh? My wife wants to go to Canada."

John sounded like an Australian with his, "Good on her. We'd like to have you."

Alex realised he had a gash in his forehead, there was blood all over his uniform, and both their hands were torn and bleeding. They were taken to a first-aid post, where a nurse and a medical student were on duty. She asked for their pay books and noted that recently they had received TAB injections. She told the student that they need not worry about tetanus shots. She cleaned and bandaged their hands. The student cleaned the cut on Alex's forehead, froze it, and stitched it. The nurse told him to have the stitches taken out in a week's time and applied iodine to the cuts on their faces. She entered their names and numbers from their pay books in her report.

They were both visibly shaken by their experience.

"You have delayed shock," she said. "We see a lot of it among air raid workers. Drink this hot cocoa; it will help."

She handed them two mugs. They both felt better after drinking the hot liquid. They thanked the nurse and student for their attention and walked to the Paddington train station, where they waited for a train.

When it arrived, they found an empty compartment where they were joined by an immaculately dressed sergeant from an English infantry regiment.

"What the hell have you two been up to? No caps; torn, bloody, and dirty uniforms; damaged faces full of iodine; and bloody, bandaged hands. It must have been a hell of a scrap."

"You can say that again," said John, "but as they say, you should have seen the other guys."

"You are both NCOs. You are a disgrace and would lose your stripes if you were in my outfit. Engineers, are you? I don't know how you could behave so badly. You odds and sods colonial units are a pain in the neck. No discipline. No pride."

"Sarge, we are also now AWOL."

"I am 'Sergeant' to you. I suppose you filled yourself with wine. Just like the Itis and Frogs. You should stick to good English beer. Why they sent you lot to England, I don't know. You are always in trouble, and you steal our girls, wives too, whilst our boys are fighting overseas."

"Your General Montgomery said we had done good work, eighty miles of beaches mined and blocked with barbed wire. Hellish stuff. Ripped through our gloves. We paraded last week when he decorated one of our boys, who defused an unexploded bomb in a school yard," said Alex defensively.

"Who is General Montgomery?"

"He is one of your guys. Talks strange. We are in the First Canadian Division and fall under him. He is a terror and keeps everybody on their toes. He said, "Keep going, men. We will knock Hitler 'for a six.' What does that mean?"

"It is a term from cricket and refers to the six runs a batsman scores when he hits the ball over the boundary fence."

"Like our baseball guys hitting one in the stands for a home run?"

"I don't think much of that game of yours. We call it rounders here, a girl's game. Cricket is an historical game played throughout the empire. There are eleven players a side, and when one team is in, the other is out, that is, fielding. The bowler bowls at the batsman, who hits the ball past fielders if he can and then runs to the other crease. The side with the most runs wins."

"What do you mean by 'fielders'?"

"They are players placed to stop runs and to catch the batsmen out if they can. For example, there would be a mid off, a mid on, a point, a cover point, someone at fine leg, another at square leg, and probably someone in the gully and certainly some players in slips. When fielders move close to the batsman, they are called silly mid on, silly mid off, silly leg, and so on."

"Gee, that sounds stupid with those different legs and points and even men wearing female clothing in a gully."

"No, the slips are fielders behind the wicket but close to the line of flight of the ball in case the batsman snicks the ball when one of the slips will catch it and he'll be out."

"Sounds like lots of ins and outs. Slips? Silly men? So that is what Monty, as General Montgomery likes to be called, was talking about. He'll certainly confuse the enemy if he uses cricket techniques."

"Look," said the sergeant testily, "by the time you return to Canada, which your shoulder tags indicates is your home, you will have learnt a lot of things. One is not to wander around strange cities getting drunk and hurt. How did you get those bloody hands anyway? You were bullshitting about them earlier."

"Well," said John, "the truth is that we have been training at scaling cliffs by climbing up ropes. We saw two ropes hanging from a building, so we had a competition to see who could get to the top first. We were nearly there when an air raid warden shouted at us to get down and into a shelter. We got such a fright we slid down in a hurry and lost a lot of flesh on our hands. With the bandages on, we can't wash and that is why we look dirty."

The sergeant snorted and looked away. "The truth? Poppycock. I suppose you fell on your faces and messed them up. You have been in a brawl, and as I said earlier, you are a disgrace."

Alex switched to French and asked why John told such ridiculous stories.

"Well, that guy strikes me as a spit-and-polish bullshitter, and with his paunch, he couldn't climb a rope. So I thought I would indicate we were fit and would see action. I doubt if he will. He's probably a drill sergeant and always looks smart. He has no power over us and should keep his lousy opinions to himself."

The sergeant smiled and kept quiet.

When the train reached their station, John said, "Good-bye, Sarge. I would like to see you in a gully in those silly slips. Do you wear yellow ones?"

"You are badly behaved stupid idiots. How can we win a war with people like you?" the sergeant retorted.

It was a long walk from their train station to the barracks where the guard asked for their leave passes. He looked at them and said they were "Ay-woll" and would have to stay while the orderly sergeant decided what to do. The sergeant took one look at the hatless, untidy pair with bandaged hands, raw faces, and bloody uniforms. He said he was surprised and disappointed that two NCOs could get in such a mess and also arrive late. They were on a charge, and it was the guardroom for them. They were escorted to the guardroom where they wondered about the future.

"Well," said Alex, "it looks as if our good deed got us into trouble. I apologise. I pulled you into this. I'll tell the company commander that and say we were only trying to help."

"We have no proof of what we did. No one will believe us."

"Well, the worst that can happen is that we will lose our stripes and suffer some pack drill. Pity. I was looking forward to being a sergeant. But there's lots of war left, so we can get them back later."

The next morning, they were marched to the regimental orderly room.

"It looks like big trouble if we're going before the commanding officer instead of the company commander," said Alex.

"Shut up, you two," shouted the smart regimental sergeant major, who had taken charge of them. "You are a bloody disgrace, and you don't have caps, you idle men. I will march you into the orderly room, halt you, and give the command 'Right turn.' You'll turn, stand to attention, and wait until you are spoken to. Is that clear?"

"Yes, sir," they said.

When they stood facing the Colonel and the adjutant, they realised how unsoldierly they must look against the perfectly uniformed officers. The colonel said, "You are two NCOs who have behaved disgracefully and were impertinent to a British sergeant. He correctly took you to task for your behaviour. He reported you to his commanding officer, who passed his comments to Canadian Headquarters. There are too many complaints of the bad behaviour of our men, and it is time an example was made. You returned to camp in a disgusting state, and you look like a pair of desperados. Because of your rank, I, and not your company commander, am dealing with your misconduct. You have the choice of accepting my punishment or facing a court-martial at which an officer would be appointed to defend you. What is your choice?"

"I will accept your punishment, sir," said John.

"So will I," said Alex, "but, sir, it was my fault entirely—"

"Corporal, you will have a chance to explain after the adjutant has read the charges against you."

A phone rang, and the adjutant answered it.

"Good morning, Brigadier, sir. You refer to two of our men? Check their numbers? Yes, sir. One minute, 678945, A. Greenus, and 786543, J. le Clus. Are those your numbers?" he asked turning to John and Alex, who nodded. Alex assumed they were really and truly in trouble.

"Yes, sir, those are our men. Well, thank you, sir. Yes, they are excellent soldiers. No, I am not surprised to hear what they did. As you say, sir, a real credit to the corps. Yes, sir, I'll tell the CO. Thank you, sir."

He turned to the Colonel, asked to have a word with him, and gestured to the RSM to march the two men out.

"You two, right turn. Quick march. Left, right, left, right. Halt. Left turn. Stand at ease. It looks as if you are up to your necks in it, and they are deciding how to punish you. I think losing your stripes and a spell in the glass house would sort you out. What the hell were you up to?"

He was interrupted with a shout from the adjutant.

"Sar' Major, bring those men back."

"Yes, sir," he responded, and to Alex and John he shouted, "You two! Attention! Left turn. Quick march. Left, right, left. Halt. Right turn. Stand to attention."

"Stand at ease," the Colonel said. "The phone call you heard was from our brigadier congratulating the unit on having two heroes in its ranks, namely you two. He wants a full report so let me have that *tout de suite*. The chief warden of an air raid rescue team informed Canadian Army Headquarters that you saved two people in a building on the point of collapse. He has recommended you for decorations.

"The report said that you declined to give your names to the local air raid warden saying you were in a hurry and had to catch a train. A conscientious, alert nurse at a dressing station, who knew what you had done, took your names and numbers from your pay books. That is how you were traced. There will be no charges. Instead, congratulations. You are to proceed to the regimental aid post to have your injuries checked, then to the quartermaster stores to get new uniforms and boots.

"Corporal le Clus, you are the division's heavyweight champion, are you not? Due to box in the divisional championships next week? Will you make it?"

"Sir, I doubt it. Something fell on my hand, and I felt a crunch. It is still bloody sore. I beg your pardon, sir."

"That's all right. I'm very proud of you both. Dismiss. Report for duty in two days' time."

"Attention!" shouted the RSM. "Right turn. Quick march. Left, right, left. Halt. Left turn. Dismiss. Congratulations, and good luck to you two. I look forward to seeing you in the sergeants' mess one of these days."

"Phew," said the Colonel to the Adjutant, "I nearly put my foot in it. Thank God for that phone call. I would not have believed their story had they offered it as an excuse. I planned to strip them of their stripes and give them some field punishment. Pity about Le Clus's hand. I was looking forward to seeing him in the ring."

"Yes, I sensed you were angry. They certainly looked the worse for wear. That's not surprising after hearing what they did."

Three weeks later, the Colonel paraded the unit and announced that Corporals Le Clus and Greenus had been awarded the George Medal for bravery during the blitz on London. They would be going to Buckingham Palace at the next investiture.

After the parade, the two men were ragged by their mates and interviewed and photographed by an army public relations team.

The English papers publicised the awards, and the Canadian papers picked up the story. Alex and John were embarrassed by the publicity and refused interviews at the investiture. This led to further headlines and stories:

Modest Canadian Blitz Heroes

Corporals John le Clus and Alex Greenus, decorated for rescuing a woman and her son from a wrecked building in danger of collapse, declined to discuss their adventure. "We happened to be there at the right time. Many other air raid heroes have gone unrecognised," said Greenus.

"C'est vrai," said his friend, a native of Quebec.

They received a letter from Elizabeth Gregory, the woman they had saved. She thanked them for rescuing her, Neil, and Ginger and congratulated them on their decorations. She had moved to Cullompton in Devon to be with her sister. Her leg was healing well. Neil had recovered from their ordeal, and Ginger had settled down in their new surroundings. Her husband, who was serving in the Royal Navy, asked her to express his thanks to them. She said she tried to trace them but failed until she saw a newspaper article that stated they were from a Canadian engineering unit. She vaguely remembered them pulling her out. Neil had given her further details of the incident. They were welcome to spend time in Cullompton. Her sister's house was large, and she would be glad to have them.

Sergeant Paul Johnstone, who had spoken to the two men on the train, whistled when he read of the awards. "I knew they spun a cock-and-bull story about sliding down a rope. One of the first things one learns is to use one's legs as a brake and, in any event, that did not explain the stitches on one of their foreheads. They were true heroes, because they didn't boast about what they had done. They seemed more concerned about being AWOL than anything else."

He wrote and congratulated them on their awards and apologised for taking the Mickey out of them. In a postscript, he wrote that he had a French mother and was familiar with her language so, despite their strange accents, he knew what they had said about him. They should have spoken Russian or Chinese to deceive him, he said. They were right; he was a spit-and-polish maniac and for a sound reason—it was good for pride and discipline. They were wrong about his paunch; when he stood up, it disappeared. He was fit and had taken commando training. He had done a lot of mountaineering before the war and in two commando raids had climbed cliffs using ropes. On one raid, he had scaled the cliff with a rope, fixed it at the top of the climb, and as his mates reached the top, he pulled them over the edge of the cliff. He had been shot in the thigh and now worked in his brigade's battle training exercises.

Alex laughed and said Johnstone was one up on them.

"He has hit us for a six. He is right we should smarten up."

Alex wrote and apologised for their remarks. He said the sergeant mentioned Russian, so he had written in that language. They had watched a cricket match. Despite his tuition, they could not make heads or tails of it, but one batsman hit a six. They now knew what that was. He was wrong about the wine because neither of them drank or smoked. He would be pleased to know that they had smartened up to the puzzlement of their mates. He was right; they felt better when everything was spick and span.

Those two never give up, Johnstone thought when he received the letter. *Now I have to find an interpreter for this Russian stuff.*

On their next leave, Alex and John decided to go to Cullompton where Elizabeth Gregory greeted them and introduced them to her sister, Vera Smythe. Both were attractive, blue-eyed blondes. Vera told them to put their feet up and relax. She showed them their rooms in the large home she had inherited when her husband, a bomber pilot, was killed over Germany. Ginger purred and rubbed against their legs, and they felt at home in the comfortable surroundings. Neil was at Clifton, his father's old school, and had fully recovered from the bombing ordeal.

Vera told them that Cullompton was an old market town consisting of one street on the western side of the Culm River and its name probably came from that and the Saxon "tun" meaning town—hence Columtun. It was well known for its farmers' market, where one could buy cheeses and meats, such as ham and beef. With the wartime food restrictions, however, it was no longer held.

They wandered through the village and countryside and helped around the house—tidying up the garden, repairing paths, and painting several rooms.

One evening, they attended an impromptu dance at the village hall held for the entertainment of the American soldiers in the area. Alex had learnt a few steps from Giselle but held back until Elizabeth pulled him onto the dance floor. She was easy to dance with; she moved close to him and smiled. He later danced with the extrovertish Vera, who was as light as a feather and persuaded him to try a cross chassis.

John was an accomplished ballroom dancer, and the next day, he showed Alex some more steps. He had him lead, much to the amusement of Elizabeth, who then took John's place until both were satisfied with their pupil's progress. John said he would be the gigolo of the logging camp. Alex said that women in the camps were as scarce as hen's teeth. In any event, he did not plan to return to lumberjacking, but his newly acquired dancing knowledge might prove useful elsewhere.

One Saturday afternoon, they all wandered into the meadows alongside the riverbanks. It was hot, so when they came to a long stretch of river held back by a weir, Vera said, "Hey, Liz, this is our swimming spot!" She stripped and dived into the water closely followed by Elizabeth. They shouted to the men to join them. The sight of two beautiful female bodies after years of only masculine company motivated them, and they stripped. John dived into the water and swam to the two ladies.

Alex slid into the river and dogpaddled around until Elizabeth swam to him and told him he should lie flat and kick his feet up and down. She held him up while he did so. Her closeness excited him, and he thrashed hard until he was tired. He climbed out and dressed while the others cavorted in the water.

On the way back, Elizabeth held his arm and said how much they appreciated their company and all the work they had done. They would miss them when they returned to their unit. Alex told her she did not understand what a joy it was to be with them in the beautiful valley. If there was anything else they could do, she only need ask. She smiled and said there was something. She would tell him about it later.

After supper, Vera and John visited the local pub, while Alex and Elizabeth, who was a schoolteacher, discussed his impending A-level examinations. He explained that he hoped to study medicine after the war and had some matriculation subjects to his credit. His unit's education officer had arranged for him to write the English and French examinations. He read a lot and enjoyed the prescribed books *Vanity Fair*, *A Tale of Two Cities*, *Richard II*, and a modern anthology of verse.

Elizabeth informed him it was the practice of examiners to ask questions about key characters. She questioned him about Thackeray's Becky Sharp and Dickens's Sydney Carton. As far as Shakespeare was concerned, they often chose an elderly minor character, such as John of Gaunt in *Richard II* and Polonius in *Hamlet*.

Alex confessed he found poetry hard to absorb. Elizabeth encouraged him to concentrate on the Romance poets and Milton. She then read some of Keats's work, and he realised how different the words were when spoken. Elizabeth suggested that whenever he could find an isolated spot, he should read aloud, taking care to follow the punctuation, which she illustrated.

She then said that she wished to talk about another matter, as she had indicated during their walk. It would probably surprise him. She said she had not fully recovered from the bombing incident and a psychiatrist had told her to be active, try to forget the ordeal, and to obtain some occupational therapy. She had not been successful in doing so, but when they had danced and when she held him in the water, she knew the answer. She told him to come with her and led him to her bedroom. She told him to hold her. When he did, she said that she would never forget him; when he had pulled her from the fallen debris, she had woken briefly and seen his earnest face, bloodied from a cut. She had then passed out. She felt attached to him, and the past few days had cemented that feeling. She now wanted him to make love to her.

Alex was surprised and delighted but asked about her husband. She said that he had been away for eighteen months. They had agreed, knowing what wars were like, that if either strayed, there would be no questions asked. She had often been tempted and had flirted a little, but as she explained, her contact with him had really stirred her. She started to undress him. He again admired her beautiful body as he slowly caressed her. She urged him on, and they enjoyed their first lovemaking experience. She clung to him and cried a little. When he asked why, she said they were tears of joy, and she thanked him for relieving her tension. In the early morning, he returned to his room. They had heard John and Vera return, but John's room was empty. Alex thought how lucky both of them were.

The next day, Vera, who was a nurse, left for work, and Elizabeth said she had to go out shopping. The two men exchanged confidences. John commented that their action in the bombed building had earned them medals and the favours of two charming ladies. As far as he was concerned, Vera was better than any decoration. Alex agreed and said it was a pity their leave was so short and that ultimately they would be sent out of England. John said they must make hay while the sun shone. He found Vera attractive, lively, and educated. She had told him that he was the only man she had been serious with since her husband was killed and she was grateful to him for rescuing her sister and nephew.

In the few remaining days, Elizabeth summoned Alex for "occupational therapy," using Shakespearian phrases like, "Once more unto the breach," "Come, give us a taste of your quality," and "Commit the oldest sins the newest kind of ways."

When it was time to part, she gave him, *The Complete Works of William Shakespeare*, edited by W. J. Craig of Trinity College in which she inscribed, "With best wishes to my beloved therapist, from Elizabeth." She had the good luck to find a copy printed in small type on thin paper, so he would be able to carry the book throughout the war and afterwards. She had marked all the quotations she had used to remind him of their days together. He thanked her. She had opened his eyes to Shakespeare's genius. He would cherish the book and memories of her always. They hugged and parted.

On the journey back to their camp, John said that he and Vera had reached an understanding that after a month, they would meet again and would decide whether or not they should marry. She had hesitated because of her bereavement and did not fancy being a widow a second time. Alex said he and Elizabeth had been very close. They knew that a permanent relationship was out of the question, but the two weeks in Cullompton had been the best of his life. He was grateful to the two ladies for making that possible.

Elizabeth wrote and thanked them for the jobs they had done at a time when tradesmen were impossible to find. In particular, she was grateful to Alex because her bombing nightmares were a thing of the past, and she had returned to teaching. She reminded him of his promise to let her know how he fared in the A-level examinations. He was pleased to tell her that her tuition had paid off, and he had passed both subjects.

Life was interesting as they moved around Britain and took part in manoeuvres. They practised landing on beaches and became used to getting wet and handling their equipment in awkward conditions. They expected to land in France, but for Alex, it was not to be. On July 4, 1941, he was told to report to the adjutant, who told him to pack for a transfer to an unknown destination.

"But, sir," he said, "I am happy with the unit, and we have an important role to play. Where are you sending me?"

"Corporal, you know we think highly of you; in fact, you are next in line for promotion. Unfortunately, we have no alternative but to obey the order to move you. It is a secret mission, and we have been told nothing. But you have to go."

"I see. What if I refuse?"

"In that event, we are instructed to place you under an armed guard, who will escort you to an unknown destination."

"It sounds funny to me, sir. Can't you get more details?"

"Corporal, the Colonel failed to get the order rescinded. You have to go."

"Thank you, sir, for trying," Alex said.

He left to break the news to his friends. They guessed about his future.

"You are the mysterious logger. I know what it is; they are short of lumber and want you to cut some trees. You may be cutting wood for huts in the Shetlands. I hear they're sending a lot of Wrens up there. Lucky you!" one said. "What else have you got? Ah, Russian, you are going to establish a rest centre for Russian sailors or perhaps a British general favours borsch and thinks you can make it."

"It's your medal!" another suggested. "You're going on a recruiting tour."

"It could be those exams you wrote. You are going to be an information officer. You speak French. You're going to teach de Gaulle something," another speculated.

Alex bade farewell to his friends and said to John, "I cannot for the life of me imagine why I am being pulled out of a job I like and understand and away from fellows whose company I enjoy. You are all as curious as I. I'll let you know what it's all about."

"You may be sent to a hush-hush unit, the lips of whose members are sealed. You know a great deal about trees and could land in a good branch. I hope I'm not barking up the wrong tree when I suggest you are heading for our forestry battalion."

"John, those English classes you are attending have sharpened your timbre. You no longer beat around the bush. I twig your meaning. I'll miss your wit. Good-bye and good luck!"

3
The Arctic

The next morning, a truck took him and an officer to the nearest train station. The officer gave him a first-class ticket to Peterborough, winked, and wished him luck. There was a British major in the compartment, who raised his eyes when a Canadian corporal joined him.

The privileges of rank have gone to hell with all these free-thinking colonials around, he thought. *I wonder what this devil is up to. He has a medal ribbon. These colonials and Americans get them for crossing the Atlantic.*

He offered Alex a cigarette, which he declined with a smile.

"Sir, I have been sent to Peterborough. Do you know anything about that town?"

"I know very little. Baker Perkins is located there. They are famous for marine motors and ovens. There are rumours that they received orders for huge ovens from Germany. You are not a specialist cook, are you?"

"No, sir. I am in the engineers. I was a lumberjack in civvy street."

"That accounts for your muscles. I am curious. I do not recognise your medal ribbon. Do all Canadians get that for coming to England?"

"No, a friend and I helped some air raid wardens. To our surprise, we were decorated."

The major's attitude changed. "Congratulations. I can't help you with Peterborough, but whatever it is, good luck."

"Thank you, sir. I will soon find out."

Alex was met at Peterborough by a British Army captain. He said Alex had been chosen for a secret and important mission, the details of which he would learn later.

They drove to a country estate where he was shown into a comfortable room and told to rest until supper. He was still puzzled. Instead of resting, he strolled the grounds, but they did not provide any clues about the establishment.

The evening meal was served in a dining room with officers and other ranks eating together, and that struck Alex as unusual. He asked one of the other NCOs what the establishment was all about and was told he would soon find out.

He was enlightened the next day when he was directed to an elderly major, who surprised him by greeting him in Russian. He switched to English and said that before he went any further, he had to warn Alex that what he was about to hear was highly confidential. Any breach of security would, despite his being a Canadian, result in punishment under the Official Secrets Act.

Alex said that in that case he did not want to hear anything. He demanded to be returned to his unit where he was needed and where he felt at home. He was told unfortunately that was not possible. He could accept the task for which he was chosen or be sent to aerodrome maintenance work in Aden.

"Sir, this is blackmail, and I intend to contact the Canadian authorities about it. There will be a real rumpus when they learn of my mistreatment."

"Sorry, Corporal, that won't work. Your people are in on the game and have written you off. In any event, there is no way of communicating from here. Security is as tight as an oyster. Now what do you say?"

"I have no option but to listen to you."

"Good. The fact that I greeted you in Russian should have given you an indication of the direction the wind is blowing. The Russians are desperately short of equipment, and there are moves afoot to supply them with massive quantities on a regular basis. It would take too long to use the relatively safe route via the Cape of Good Hope and Persia, so a calculated risk will be taken to supply them by sea to Murmansk, a port within the Arctic Circle open year-round and to Archangel to the southeast. The Russians are unfamiliar with much of the equipment, and it is necessary to send linguists capable of handling the tanks and weapons to explain and demonstrate them and also to write appropriate manuals. You speak Russian and are invited to take one of the jobs with immediate promotion to sergeant."

Alex smiled and remembered that that rank had been within his grasp in his old unit.

"Sir, you said invited, but is it not as the English say, Hobson's choice?"

"You're dead right. I am surprised you have that knowledge of the English language. Your records show you spent several years in Quebec logging camps. There could not have been much English there."

"Sir, there was a motley crew of men, including some well-educated types, who guided me and to whom I am eternally grateful. Whether I have enough background to write manuals remains to be seen."

"That is where we come in. We have language experts here who will help. Then we will test the results on some Russian military men, so it should go well. You will leave tomorrow for a tank-training course. You will learn every activity associated with the tanks—driving, gunnery, maintenance, battle directions, transportation, and the rest. You will make notes for manuals. Your cover story is that you are the first in an experiment to establish whether it makes sense to give tank crews detailed training in all aspects rather than in developing specialists. You will be there as Sergeant Alex Street. You will have to remove your ribbon and

Canadian identifications. Sorry about that. Your full cover story is in this folder. Study it. You will be grilled on it this afternoon. I am sure you will pass muster."

"Thank you, sir. I'm a little bewildered. I have not used Russian much since leaving Lithuania and hate the Soviets for their mass deportations of Lithuanians. But I hate the Nazis more. To my disgust, I hear that the bastards were greeted by some Lithuanians as liberators because they had chased the hated Russians away."

"Sergeant, I appreciate your feelings. You will find out that little pleases the Russians. But they are our Allies and are holding out against Hitler. If he had moved against us instead of attacking Russia, we would all be speaking German now. Good-bye and good luck."

Alex learned that the fictitious Alex Street was a plausible character who had served in the Royal Engineers in the Shetland Islands and bored with the job had asked for a transfer to the Tank Corps just at the time they were looking for guinea pigs. It was a new experiment in the intensive training of all tank activities. It was hush-hush. He was not allowed to give any details of his background. He had special permission to sleep alone in the single quarters.

That afternoon, three NCOs asked him to repeat his cover story and then proceeded to blow holes in it. One said his tunic looked funny as if he once had a medal and shoulder badges. Another said he had a strange accent. One wanted to know if the old lighthouse at the northern tip of the Shetland Islands was still working. They told him to get a new tunic. He was to say he had moved around a lot as a child and picked up changes in dialects and that there never was a lighthouse at the tip of the Shetlands. He should study the guidebook they gave him. They said in his job at the tank training centre, he was to be friendly and cooperative but to remain distant.

He was given a rail warrant to get him to Lulworth, where he was welcomed and given a room. "Special treatment, you lucky man," said the trooper who showed him around. "Your first meeting is tomorrow at 0800 hours at Hut Number Four, where you will get instructions. The sergeants' mess will welcome you as a guest. They serve good food. Good luck, Sergeant. Not everybody enjoys the courses here. But they'll make a man of you if nothing else."

"Thank you, of that I have no doubt."

He stripped and changed into his gym clothes. He jogged around the camp to the amusement of others. He showered, read his cover story once again, and reported to the sergeants' mess where he was welcomed. His fellow NCOs were not curious, no doubt because they were used to birds of passage. Alex asked about routines and camp rules and found they were standard. He excused himself early, wondering what the days would hold.

They started with an interview with a tank corps captain, who said that they had been told to give Sergeant Street special attention. "You will be taught routines until you are sick of them. The purpose is simple: to make everything automatic so that in action, you will not have to think and will act like a robot. You will find the training in armoured tanks in this hot weather a challenge."

Alex said he appreciated the officer's comments and he would work hard.

The course at Lulworth consisted of learning about engines, starting with the Valentine tank's. The next day, there were lessons in driving and the functions of the five forward and one reverse gears were explained. It was hard work learning how the engines worked, how to change gears, and how to steer. They zigzagged at first and then straightened out. Next, they had to practise steering the tank over longer distances. That led to some amusing moments.

Once they were proficient in handling gear changes, they went to a practice ground where they drove the tanks to and fro. They were then taught how to solve basic maintenance problems. Hour after hour, they drove the tanks, first in small troops and then as a squadron, the formation they would use in their passing-out parade.

Alex had to repeat the course with the Mark II Matilda tanks designed to accompany the infantry. Unlike the petrol-powered Valentines, the Matildas had twin diesel engines. The trainees were warned that starting in cold weather could be a problem and that there was a device for warming the fuel before trying to start the engines. Alex paid particular attention to the device because he knew the tanks in Russia would often operate in subzero conditions. He found the smaller Matilda easier to handle than the Valentine.

Alex's fellow pupils left for their units while he trained in gunnery at Bovington. Both the Valentines and Matildas were equipped with two-pound antitank and Vickers machine guns. They were taught to aim at the vulnerable parts of the enemy's armour. They fired first at a range and then from inside the tanks. They then had to strip the Vickers machine guns. Soon, Alex had had enough of bullets, shells, and their noises.

The final course was training in a tank commander's job. He found this easy after the other sessions. He felt that the time spent on tactics was wasted on him, because he was certain the Russians had their own ideas on tactics. The instructions to the rest of the crew and communications between tanks were informative. He was surprised that only one member of the crew knew the communications drill.

I wonder what they will do when their leaders are killed or wounded? he thought. *It has been a productive three weeks, but I'm glad I will not have to fight in tanks. I think I have become claustrophobic.*

The officer commanding the training unit congratulated him on passing the courses and said, "Sergeant Street, there are few secrets here. The instructors knew you were something special, and they took every opportunity to trip you up. There is a universal opinion that you are unflappable and will do well in action. I suggest that if you ever get tired of what you are doing, let us know. We'll grab you like a shot, and you would keep your rank."

"That is kind of you, sir. I will bear it in mind. I have a suggestion; I think you should train crews in all the trades as I have been trained. That could be done in their idle times, and it would pay off in battles when deaths and injuries are inevitable."

"Thank you for the observation. We already give comprehensive training but not as intensive as yours. You went through the complete mill and handled everything well, so we know it can be done. I'll discuss this with my superiors. Good luck in whatever mission you are engaged." This last comment was accompanied by an un-officer-like wink. Alex smiled, saluted, and left.

He returned to the mansion near Peterborough where he slogged away at preparing manuals. He had kept the British ones from the tank course and translated them, adding his own observations as he went along. A Russian military man read his work and suggested some changes. The manuals were then printed in English and Russian.

On August 10, Alex was told to report to the naval base in Liverpool, where he was welcomed by a chief petty officer. He was told to make himself comfortable in Room 204, where he would find Captain Hytaniuk who was in charge of the Russian-speaking army personnel destined for the Arctic.

The captain was a tall, bronzed man with thick black hair and a military moustache. He came from Melville in Saskatchewan where his grandparents had settled amid incredible hardships. He worked his way through university where he studied mechanical engineering. He welcomed Alex and switched to Russian, saying they had better get used to thinking in the language because that was all they were likely to hear for the next few years. He introduced him to the other sergeants in the room as Alex Greenus, the team's tank expert from the Canadian Corps of Engineers. He had been appointed the Murmansk group's senior NCO. The captain told them he had joined the army straight from a logging camp, and after surviving that existence, he was not a man to argue with.

The others in the room were Fred Frey, Stephen Natashyn, Joshua Fryburg, all Canadians of Ukranian descent; Moses Bloomberg of the Royal Corps of Engineers; and Maurice Navid, a South African infantryman. Frey was a tank driver/mechanic; Natashyn was from the Service Corps; Bloomberg was a motor mechanic; and Navid was a weapons specialist.

Hytaniuk said the team's job was to offload and service tanks, guns, and vehicles at their destination and to train Russians in their use. When required, they would assist in handling aircraft, guns, ammunition, chemicals, food, rubber, and aluminium. He said they would face hardships and meet uninterested Russians, who would insist that the foreign servicemen sent to help them had visas. They would find these in the kit they would collect later.

They were told that the Murmansk convoys were Churchill's idea. The Royal Navy was not enthused. Its officers had to investigate the Murmansk facilities for the discharge of ships' loads, the refuelling of escorts, and local labour facilities. They were not impressed. Murmansk was only a few minutes' flying time from German planes at Petsamo, and it had been badly damaged by bombs. Its anti-aircraft defences were feeble, and at the port, the largest crane was incapable of handling tanks. The Russians needed help to improve the port facilities, and a British Naval presence would be necessary despite the poor holding ground in Vaenga Bay.

The navy's negative report left Churchill unmoved, and against professional advice, he ordered convoys to be established. While it was still free of ice, Archangel would be used. That port would be the destination of Dervish, the convoy in which they would sail.

Murmansk received the last movement of the Gulf Stream, which started in the Gulf of Mexico, flowed past Florida, the British Isles, and the North Cape, and thus the port was able to remain open the whole year. Captain Hytaniuk said that the presence of the benign current should not mislead them, because they would be sailing in some of the roughest and coldest seas in the world. They were fortunate that the violent autumn winds had not started. They would take orders from the ships' captains and were to share watches with DEMSA (Defensive Armed Merchant Ships) gunners. They would be protected from the cold weather with standard Arctic clothing to be issued in room 312 when the meeting ended. It consisted of a fur-lined duffle coat, two pairs of heavy woollen long johns, a white submariner's polo-neck jersey, thick mittens, heavy sea boots, and thick stockings. They would travel on three ships. The captain read out their assignments. Alex was paired with a smiling Maurice Navid. He shook his hand and said he was pleased to share his company.

They drew their clothing and walked to the docks where their ship, the *Llanstephan Castle*, was moored. She belonged to the Union Castle Line and weighed 10,786 tons. It was designed for service in Africa, but the exigencies of service dictated that it should operate in Arctic waters. It was the commodore ship of the six-merchant-ship convoy that was accompanied by the aircraft carrier *HMS Argus* from which Hurricanes were to fly to Kola. One of the ships carried fifteen Hurricanes in crates.

The ship's captain and convoy commodore was a blue-eyed, red-haired, elderly, powerful man with a string of medal ribbons on his tunic. He greeted the two army men and said he welcomed the help they would give to the gunners. He warned them that it would be cold later, particularly between Jan Mayen and Bear Island, where the wind came off the polar and Greenland ice caps. He said they were lucky it was not winter; otherwise, they would have to chip ice off the decks and rigging. They would have to keep the anti-aircraft guns warm, or the workings would freeze and render the weapons useless.

They had comfortable quarters. The crew and DEMSA gunners were friendly and said that with a Canadian and South African aboard, they were like the League of Nations. They were asked to help in the galley, and Alex was reminded of his first logging job. He surprised the cook by trimming a carcass and suggesting some dishes to prepare. He was reminded further of his logging days when one of the seamen slipped and broke his leg. Alex was nearby and checked the break before applying a dressing and splint. He made the sailor comfortable, and the man thanked Alex, who said he would look at the leg in a few days. He expected the bone to set without complications. It did, as was confirmed by a doctor in Reykjavik, Iceland, where the sailor was put ashore.

Maurice Navid was ebullient and made one Yiddish joke after another. During the watches he and Alex shared on the Oerlikon anti-aircraft gun, he recounted his life story. His parents had come from a *shtetl*, a small Jewish village in Latvia and spoke Russian, which he picked up easily. His father was a tailor and gave good service, so the family survived in the gold-mining city of Johannesburg. The wealthy Jews there had supported their less fortunate brethren. He went to Jeppe Boys High School where the many Jewish boys were tolerated happily by the school's Gentile pupils. He was a good cricketer and was chosen for the Transvaal Schools team, which excelled in the interprovincial schools' week.

Alex said that he did not understand the ins and outs of cricket and was told that the game originated with shepherds and its first rules were established in the 1700s. Maurice thought it was a pity they would not be able to play in the frozen north; otherwise, he would illustrate the finer points of the international game for him. He had gone to Witwatersrand University, where he studied literature, much to the annoyance of his father, who favoured law. He had a flair for languages and longed to explore the work of all writers. English and Afrikaans were compulsory subjects, but he mixed freely with the natives and also learned Zulu.

When war broke out, he and a group of his friends joined the First Transvaal Scottish, which was affiliated with the Black Watch; that was why he wore a bonnet and hackle. It was quite a joke—he was a Jewish Jock. His comrades teased him, calling him Maurice McNavid. They also had a number of Afrikaners. They were great guys but hardly Scottish, with names like Van den Berg, Le Roux, and Sonnekus. The regiment was part of the First South African Brigade, and after a couple of months training at

Premier Mines, they were off to Kenya where they walked miles carrying their equipment. He was a Vickers machine gunner, and they struggled in the heat then and throughout the campaign that knocked the Italians out of Kenya, Somaliland, Abyssinia, and Eritrea.

He nearly died at Massawa on the Red Sea where they embarked for Egypt. He was told it was 90 degrees Fahrenheit and 90 percent humidity. He passed out and spent the voyage in the sick bay. He hated Egypt. "Flies, filth, heat, beggars," he said. His regiment was sent to Mersa Matruh on the Mediterranean, where they dug defensive positions. He got some leave and made a long train journey to Palestine. He visited a kibbutz where General Smuts, the South African prime minister, had planted some trees. Smuts was popular, being one of the backers of the Balfour Declaration that guaranteed a home state to the Jews. The Arabs did not like that, and there was unrest in the country.

In June, he was pulled out of the line and sent on a Vickers instructor's course at Helwan, a suburb of Cairo. Bit of a joke, he said, because he knew the bloody gun backwards, but it was a break from the desert. When the course ended, he was told to report to an office in Kasr el Nil, Cairo. He said he wanted to return to his unit but was told to obey orders, so he did.

At the barracks, he was passed to a Pommy colonel who spoke Russian, and he responded. That cooked his goose, because the officer said, "You'll do. You are assigned to a special job and will spend the night here. You can hand in your rifle and webbing. Get a receipt. Be at my office at 0900 hours tomorrow and you will be flown to England." He protested that he was happy with his unit and didn't know England. He was told it was top-secret stuff and orders had to be obeyed.

He thought of slipping back to his unit, because it would be easy to get on a train to the desert. Lots of guys stuck at the base did that, but the Colonel read his thoughts and said that if he was not there at the appointed time, he would be posted as a deserter with dire consequences. He said he would report as ordered but wished he knew what it was all about. He was told, "Corporal, it will be important work. I wish you luck."

The next day, he was taken to Heliopolis airport. The flight from there was hilarious because his fellow passengers were senior officers who looked at him superciliously. He heard one mutter that a colleague, a colonel, had been bumped from the flight for that nondescript South African private. Maurice said loudly in Russian, "I would prefer being in the line than flying with these stuffed shirts."

"As I thought," he heard one whisper, "that man is a phoney. Bloody colonials. Probably doesn't speak the king's English."

One of the officers asked why he was wearing a Black Watch bonnet. Maurice explained about the Transvaal Scottish.

"Of course," the officer said, "I served in the 51st Division. Surrendered at St. Valery-en-Caux. No option. I escaped. Heard your men did well in East Africa. What brings you to England?"

Maurice said he wished he knew. It had something to do with his speaking Russian. He should have kept his mouth shut and not mentioned his knowledge of languages when he enlisted. He was happy with his pals and was now heading for some God-forsaken place called Peterborough.

"A polyglot in Peterborough. How interesting. I have an idea of what you're in for, but my lips are sealed. It will be a contrast to the heat of the desert."

How right he was, and now, after an intensive weapons course, he was at this gun heading for the Arctic Circle. "What is that expression about the cold and a brass monkey?" he asked.

Alex told him it concerned the animal's genitals. Maurice said Alex would be okay in the Arctic having lived through Canadian winters, but his blood was thin and he already felt cold.

Alex knew nothing about Africa and was fascinated by Maurice's experiences there. He often questioned him about the countries he knew. In his pursuit of knowledge, he had ignored geography and welcomed a chance to broaden his knowledge.

Between them, they read most of the books in the ship's library. Maurice wanted to discuss one Shakespearean play after another, much to Alex's delight. His companion was intrigued by the inscription in the book Elizabeth had given him. He learned the story of his liaison with her following the bombing episode. He told him he was a dark horse and modest for not wearing his GM ribbon. Alex just said he was lucky and left it at that.

It was a cold and rough voyage. Alex and Maurice shivered when they had gun duty. On one occasion, they fired bursts at a German reconnaissance plane and claimed to have seen smoke coming from it.

On August 31, they docked in Archangel. It was a cheerless-looking place in a snow-filled valley. Alex wondered what dangers lay ahead and how the Arctic Circle might change his life.

His men disembarked and, along with other army and air force personnel, were taken by truck to the outskirts of the town. They were shown to two large buildings where they were given sleeping bags and the familiar palliasses to be filled with straw and used as mattresses. They were told to make themselves comfortable until a camp was established.

The next day, the men destined to stay in Archangel gathered and were addressed by a smartly dressed naval officer in upper-class English.

He said, "I am Commodore Forrester, Senior Allied Officer in Murmansk and Archangel. Welcome to some interesting times. You are all aware of the importance of the work you will do—namely, to speed the movement of war material and in some cases, trained soldiers, to the Russian battlefront. A number of you are Russian linguists, and you should guide your unilingual comrades. The locals are touchy, and you are to abide by the instructions in the information folder you were given.

"Your commanding officer is Lieutenant Colonel Taylor, who served with distinction in Murmansk in the Great War. He is a mechanical engineer with a thriving business in Plymouth, who stayed in the Territorials. Although in a reserved occupation, he is in uniform again. He is well equipped to direct your activities and to handle problems. His adjutant is Captain Porter, Dragoon Guards, who will keep you on your toes. Normal discipline will be relaxed, but you may have to parade from time to time for important visitors and anniversaries, and you should then look smart and soldierly.

"A German airfield is only a short distance away, and their army, under a formidable general called Dietl, with two mountain divisions, is within 40 kilometres of Murmansk. He is determined to capture it. I hope you will not be involved in the fighting, but remember that while we are in comparative safety, the Russians are fighting fiercely and suffering heavy casualties. Good luck to all of you."

Maurice noticed the jerboa rat badge on the adjutant's blouse and commented to Alex in Russian that it was a pity to have a Desert Rat Guardsman here who would make their lives a misery. Porter overheard him and said in Russian that the Corporal was correct. He had been pulled out of the Seventh Armoured Division, promoted, and given the Archangel job. His main task was to help them and shield them from the vagaries of the Soviet officers. His father had been in the Diplomatic Corps in Moscow during the adjutant's childhood, and he had learned Russian then. He had remained bilingual, although he was inclined to regret it as it had brought him to the cold and inhospitable Archangel. He then said in English that he had been addressing a fellow Eighth Army soldier and had told him that as the adjutant his job was to help them in their relations with the Russians.

Colonel Taylor said their first task was to erect the prefabricated huts they had brought and the sooner that job was done, the sooner they would leave their dilapidated buildings. He then called on a regular Royal Engineers company sergeant major to dismiss the men.

"Russia or no Russia, we still have the army bull. That Porter will have us on the parade ground if we don't look out. I know the type. They think they are God's answer to a maiden's prayer," moaned Maurice.

"If we work hard and keep our noses clean, he'll leave us alone. There must be some order and discipline," said Alex.

"I thought I was working with a relaxed logging man, and now I find he is someone who welcomes order and discipline. Sounds like the poor bloody infantry all over again. I thought I had seen the last of the PBI."

The next day, Colonel Taylor showed them the open ground he had secured before their arrival and the plan for the huts. They did a quick survey and marked the areas for the foundations and concrete floors to which prefabricated huts would be fixed. When that was done, a team of engineers cut foundation trenches to a depth below the freezing level and filled them with quick-drying concrete onto which was laid slabs of concrete to provide floors. Alex relished the hard work and was impressed with the forethought in bringing the huts, concrete ingredients, and equipment for the job. Counter-sunk bolts in the concrete were used to anchor the wooden prefab buildings, and before long, the site was filled with workmanlike structures. Colonel Taylor had obtained access to the town's electricity and water systems but was refused a sewage connection. He ordered a large hole to be dug, in which a septic tank connected to the latrine and wastewater outlets was made. Two large workshops took longer to erect with their steel structure and RSJ's (Reinforced Steel Joists) on which lifting gear ran.

The work was finally completed, and the training of tank crews began. The Canadians were surprised at the limited amount of insulation in the buildings and reinforced the walls with whatever material they could find held in place by wood from packing cases in which aircraft had been shipped.

Tanks were offloaded from ships onto railway flatbeds and shunted to a siding where they were inspected, and when crews were trained, they were sent with them to the battlefront. Alex liaised with Lieutenant Alisa Volgymko, who was in charge of the Russian trainees. She was a blue-eyed blonde of medium height.

She was also athletic and conscientious, and Alex worked well with her. His men trained the Russian base staff in the use of tanks and their weapons. They then assisted in training Russian novices, who were willing but rough and hasty. Alex persuaded Volgymko to slow them down and ensure they followed procedures. It would be scandalous if tanks were wrecked before they reached the battlefront.

Alex and the Russian lieutenant shook hands when another batch of tanks with trained crews left Archangel. As the days went by, their grips lingered longer. She acknowledged that change with a smile and wink.

In their free time, the pair discussed modern Russia and life under the Soviets. Alisa was a convinced Communist, and when Alex suggested the revolutionaries had misinterpreted Marx's dogma, she laughed and trotted out some standard Soviet slogans. Alex said he understood that all Soviet fighting units had political commissars and wondered why. She said that there was one in Archangel, the man in a captain's uniform who hung around occasionally. He was there to ensure that she and other officers stuck to the party line.

"Do you mean to say that you have that political guy breathing down your neck all the time?"

"Yes, but not looking at my body, as you are."

Alex laughed and said he would like to see her without the bulky winter clothes when he would have a better appreciation of her as a woman.

"At the moment, you are as stiff as one of your Moscow drill instructors," he added.

She smiled and said, "In the spring, perhaps you'll see more of me. I must warn you that we have been discouraged from fraternising with you people. On that account, we had better part. The commissar is looking at us. I look forward to hearing more of your distorted views on Marx and his ideas."

When next they spoke, Alex said he wondered why the commissars did not fight instead of hanging around interfering with frontline officers and their troops. Alisa said they bore all the dangers of war and helped to keep up the morale of the troops by emphasising the glories of Communism and the evils of Fascism and Capitalism. They also reported inefficient leaders and encouraged a common spirit and a loyalty to Russia. She said the Capitalists, Churchill and Roosevelt, claimed to be fighting for freedom, but they were really defending bloodsucking industrialists' interests. They dragged the smaller Capitalists like Alex along with them.

Alex laughed and said that one of the weaknesses of Communism was to call all non-Communists, Capitalists. He, for example, was a humble forest worker and had about a hundred pounds in his bank account.

"My parents are poor farmers and have to give a portion of their produce to the Russian-influenced authorities. My family are Roman Catholics and oppose the clamours of the atheistic Lithuanian Communists that religions should be banned. Incidentally, if you are so certain of your cause, why do you fear religion?"

"Religious autocrats in their fancy dresses have exploited the masses for centuries. Do you ever see a thin priest or bishop? And why should one be subservient to some old guy in Rome? Why are there so many different religions, such as Christians and Jews and Muslims? They cannot agree about their gods, so we are right to condemn them all. They should not be allowed to pollute people's minds. No, the sooner there is equality for all and we all work for the common good, the better the world will be. We have to beat the Fascist pigs. I don't hear the Pope condemning them. We are told that he has an arrangement with the Fascists, called the Concordat, in which it is agreed that they will leave each other alone. We have been shown pictures of Catholic bishops standing with horrible Nazi leaders and all of them were giving the Hitler salute. How do you reconcile that with your Christian views?"

"You trot out the usual Soviet propaganda. You should remember that despite their differences, religions have a lot in common. For example Christians, Jews, and Muslims share a link with Abraham, a famous prophet. In Jerusalem, you will find edifices important to them. There is the Church of the Nativity, the Weeping Walls, and the Mosque of Omar. Our Bible is filled with guidance to acts of charity and kindness.

"You have a point about the Concordat. The Pope has a duty to preserve our Church; hence his negotiations with the Nazis. That does not mean we are anti-Semitic. Has your commissar not told you that there is pressure on Rome to drop the Concordat? You can understand the Pope's desire to preserve his Church, which has survived all kinds of wars. If we move from religion to talk of human rights, then the non-Communists win, because we do not believe in pogroms and purges."

"Sergeant, wake up. Your Christ was a Jew. The Nazis, including some of your bishops have concentration camps and are murdering Jews and other people they classify as 'undesirables.' Their *Einsatzgruppen* has killed your Lithuanian Jews. Our information is that SS Colonel Karl Jager reported that 136,000 have been executed."

"That sickens me, but the Nazis' despicable actions do not justify your atheism, pogroms, and the persecution of religious people—we who are helping you condemn the Nazis' concentration camps and their killings."

"We agree on some things. Let us leave it at that. You pray for me. I'll think well of you. I have good news for you. You are invited to a party we are holding tonight for your naval officers and air force pilots. A number of our nurses and female administration staff will attend. I know you like ogling women, so here is your chance. Also you can have a change in diet because we will serve caviar and fresh fish."

"You are right. I like ladies, but you and your colleagues are so covered in *shubas* and *papenkas* that you look like men. Unfortunately, I cannot accept. I am not an officer."

"There you go again with your Capitalist hierarchy. No, your rank will not be a problem. It will be a change for my friends to talk to someone who knows Russian instead of struggling with your proud officers who think everybody should speak English. Be at our mess at 6.30 in your best uniform, not in your overalls. We will wear party dresses, and you'll see that we are females after all."

Alex shaved and pressed his battle dress. Maurice whistled and asked what was on the go. Had he found a scarce local female? Alex said he had been invited to a reception. It was strictly business with the Russian lieutenant; there was a difficulty with one of their manuals that they would discuss.

"Really? And how manual will you get? I suggest an enfilade followed by a frontal assault, so that your arms surround her. At that stage, give her a squeeze for me. Are you contraceptically armed?"

"Maurice, the Russian women are discouraged from fraternising with us, and, judging from what others have said, their dinners are stiff and boring. It will be strictly business."

"Oy, oy, oy. Of course. It depends on the definition of business."

Alisa deliberately placed Alex away from her to avoid trouble with the commissar. He chatted freely with his neighbour, a nurse from the Ukraine, who longed to get home but realised it was a forlorn hope with the advances the Nazis had made into Russian territory. She said their hospital lacked supplies and hoped the British and Americans would help. She encouraged him to try the Russian dances that were in full swing now that the tables had been cleared away. He had dodged the free-flowing vodka that stimulated the other energetic dancers. He was alert and enjoyed dancing with the nurse.

He also danced with Alisa, who was most attractive out of uniform. Their closeness was exciting, and she asked what he thought of the Russian ladies now. He hugged her and said that should convey his feelings. She indicated she had received the message, but although she enjoyed their closeness, it was contrary to the fraternisation rules. Alex said that the rules were stupid, and he squeezed her tightly before releasing her.

He tried the energetic Russian dances but could not kick his legs in and out whilst in a squatting position. The onlookers cheered and encouraged him when the evening ended with a limbo at which Alex, who kept fit, excelled before collapsing exhausted.

He thanked Alisa for the evening, and she said she would invite him again. They shook hands, and the extra pressure she gave and the intimacy of their dances encouraged him to lean forward to kiss her, but she quickly withdrew. He turned to leave and saw the commissar glaring at him.

On his return to their sleeping quarters, Maurice questioned him. Alex stuck to his story about "business." He said his bilingualism had impressed the Soviets. Maurice and others probably would be included in the next social evening, provided they could dance. Maurice said that was one thing he could do. He grabbed Alex and waltzed him around the hut to the amusement of their comrades.

One remarked that they had not been away long and already two of them were dancing. They would probably kiss next and sleep together. Maurice declared it a good idea and hugged Alex before pretending to kiss him. That ended in a wrestling match, which Maurice lost.

Shipments of tanks were regular and included American General Lee M3Lee Ram tanks accompanied by instructors, none of whom spoke Russian. They were relieved to use the services of the linguists. It had not taken long for Alex, Maurice, and Fred Frey to familiarise themselves with the new tanks and weapons and to pass the knowledge to the Russians. When satisfied that their armour would be used effectively, the US team departed on a homeward-bound convoy.

One morning, Alisa said she had received an urgent call for help from the Soviet troops fighting to the Northwest of the town. Mortars and machine guns held them up, and they urgently needed tank support. None was available from the regular forces. She planned to use the six demonstration tanks, namely, two

Matildas, two Valentines, and two M3Lees. Alex and Maurice jumped at the idea and were told that they and Fred Frey, the driving instructor, would each command a tank, she another, and two promising recruits the others. The crews were assembled, and they set off in a snowstorm with Alisa leading.

Alex hoped she would remember the compass deviation in her tank. He recalled the scorn with which his insistence that each tank's compass be tested for deviation had been greeted. *This episode should convince the doubters,* he thought. He was relieved when the snow cleared and he could see army signs that indicated they were on track.

They were ordered to break formation and destroy the mortars and machine gun nests. As they passed through the infantry lines, exhausted soldiers waved at them, and they pressed on hoping there were no mines ahead. One tank was disabled by gunshot, and another hit a mine, but the remainder continued. Alex was pleased to be in a Matilda, which was noted for its effective armour plating and relished his command and the opportunity to practise the lessons he had learned and taught. He directed his gunner to a machine gun emplacement and was delighted to see it eliminated. He turned his attention to a mortar pit and ordered machine gun fire that killed the Germans manning the weapon.

When the enemy retreated, Alisa fired a red Verey light, and the infantry advanced and settled in the German positions, which commanded the country ahead of them. A Russian officer shouted his thanks. Alisa responded that the crews included two Canadians and a South African. He said he did not know that Communism had spread so far. He was told a team would retrieve the damaged tanks, whose crews clambered on the remaining ones for the homeward journey.

That evening, Colonel Taylor was startled to get a hearty thump on the back from a Russian colonel, who complimented him on the brave action of his men in their tanks in liquidating an important enemy position north of Archangel. The puzzled Britisher accepted the praise. Later, he asked Captain Hytaniuk if he knew anything about the incident. He said he had seen six tanks move out but thought they were on a training exercise. When he checked with Alex, he discovered the truth and questioned why he took such action without authority.

Alex reminded him that he had been told to respect Russian ranks and the lieutenant, his superior officer, had ordered them to participate in battle practice, which was of value to the trainees. The captain snorted and said if Alex received any further requests for help to obtain authority before acting on them.

"Sir, had I taken time to do that, we probably would have been too late to be of any use. The Russians are now friendlier, and I am sure our action will make our lives easier."

"Sergeant, you and your colleagues performed well, but I will give you a short-wave radio. You can check with me before you get into any more battles. I must congratulate you on your rapport with the Russian lieutenant. She strikes me as a hard-bitten Communist."

"You are correct. She is tough and totally imbued with Marxist beliefs. I have exposed some weaknesses in her beliefs but do not push my luck too far. We work well with her on tank training."

The next day, Alex and Alisa returned to the battleground with some mechanics and driver trainees to give them practical experience in tank recoveries. The tank damaged by a mine was beyond their ability to repair and was left to be collected. A damaged track on the other tank was mended on the spot and driven to the base camp.

Alisa alarmed Alex by saying that he, Maurice, and Fred had been recommended for decorations in view of their excellent work in training tank crews and for the battle action. He said they were in trouble for acting without orders and would prefer not to have attention drawn to them. She said the infantry commander had already sent in his report recommending the awards, but she would see what she could do. Following the tank exploit, as Alex had stated, there was a noticeable improvement in relations between the British and Russian training staffs.

A week later, there was another call for armoured help. Alex, as the senior training NCO, obtained permission from Colonel Taylor to help the Russians, and he and Alisa assembled eight tank crews. At Alex's suggestion, they advanced in two columns. Despite the earlier use of tanks, German intelligence apparently did not believe the Russians had armour, so there were few antitank weapons with their forward forces. The tanks again drove the invaders away without loss. Once again, the Russian colonel congratulated Colonel Taylor on the part his men had played in the operation and for the training of the Russians who had taken part.

Overcast skies, snow, and fog heralded the approach of winter, and Colonel Taylor instructed his men to prepare for a departure to Murmansk. Engineers had laid the foundations for the structures in that town and for most of their huts, which they would now have to disassemble. They loaded the dismantled buildings and their equipment on a ship, boarded it, and watched with interest as an icebreaker led them to Murmansk.

They were sad to leave for Murmansk, which they knew was subject to bombing, and were pleased to discover that their camp was relatively safe on the outskirts of the town. The Russians had accommodations nearby, and there were two large buildings that replaced the Archangel workshops. They traded cigarettes and alcohol for Russian fur clothes. In their new garb, it was difficult to distinguish them from their Allies to Captain Porter's dismay when he inspected them.

There were three miles of quays in Murmansk, but in many cases, the banks had collapsed either from bombing or neglect and were useless for berthing. Only a limited number of cranes were suitable. Until the navy supplied a heavy crane, it would be difficult to offload heavy tanks. The Russians were incapable of handling the flow of goods, and there were further problems because a rail link to the docks was not finished. Tanks were driven to the workshops and then taken to a ramp from which they were driven onto railway flatbeds.

The engineers improved the makeshift bomb shelters on the site. Apart from damage to one of the warehouse buildings, the bombers did little harm to the buildings, unlike the ships anchored awaiting their turn to offload their cargo at the inefficient dockside. The ships were attacked repeatedly, and some were sunk.

The town consisted of scattered huts and some brick buildings. The main road, Stalin Street, almost deserted because the inhabitants had fled from the bombing, had some tall, bomb-damaged buildings and a dilapidated hall of culture used as a cinema. It was a dreary place, and social activities were limited. There were official army nightclubs, known as Churchill Clubs because Churchill had organised them for the Arctic Convoy sailors he called "the bravest souls afloat." Beautiful, bilingual Russian ladies at the clubs provided comfort for the sailors in the so-called "friendship houses." It was suspected that the hostesses were KGB agents trained to extract information from their guests.

The Canadians organised a hockey team to play the Russians and that, along with sleigh rides and skating, provided some outdoor exercise. A building was set aside as an exercise room. Alex and Maurice wrestled there and encouraged others to follow suit. Their Russian contacts heard of the activity and asked to participate. Some were powerful, and after one tussle, a Canadian was heard to remark that he now knew what a bear hug was.

Alisa gave Alex some skis, and he joined a Russian party on a nearby slope. On one occasion, she misjudged a turn and fell. Alex slid into her, and they rolled together in the snow. He kissed her and said that at last he had achieved his goal. She responded warmly and told him she had invited him to ski because the commissar was out of town. She suggested that he come to her quarters for some hot cocoa. He hesitated. She said her roommate was on leave, and nobody would see him in the snow that was falling.

It was delightfully warm in her room, and the hot drink added to his pleasure. They resumed their discussion on religion, and she asked where the Russian Orthodox Church, which had given the Soviets so much trouble, stood in the religious world. Alex said it was really a branch of his Roman Catholic Church but an earlier leader had argued with the Pope and established an independent organisation. She laughed and said it seemed that Christians enjoyed arguments and fighting. He said that might appear so to a heretic such as she, but as he had said earlier, there was a link to a universal God.

She put her mug down and moved over next to him.

"Now look me in the eyes and tell me you are fully satisfied with your religion as I am with atheism."

He said that she had beautiful blue eyes. He would prefer to discuss them, but he admitted there were divisions among religions, although a common link was one of love for one's neighbour. That, applied correctly, had profound implications.

Alisa said, "For once, I share your religious views, because I am your temporary neighbour and love is a good idea. Since the dances and being close to you in the training of our soldiers, I have grown fond of you. As two soldiers far from home and with the danger of the Germans occupying Murmansk and the unknown consequences, we should use this moment for love. I faked my skiing fall to entrap you. You are so different from my Russian companions. Most of them are uncultured. You are educated, good-looking, and athletic. If we make love, there will be an added thrill for me. We would be one up on the commissar. So, my tank-training companion, get ready for a change of action."

As she started to undress, Alex moved towards her. He helped her to get rid of her clothes and was fascinated with the transformation from the stern officer in a drab uniform into the exquisitely formed naked smiling beauty. He hugged and kissed her.

"I hope you are prepared," she quipped.

He produced a condom and said they formed part of their official kit. They were obliged to carry them if engaged in amatory affairs. They always laughed in Murmansk, because the likelihood of their being used in the Arctic was remote.

"Remote, but you carried one. So you planned to seduce me, did you?"

"I was a Boy Scout, and we were trained to be prepared. Yes, I wanted to make love with you and sensed you were willing."

"You are lucky and should always keep a supply of condoms on hand."

"With that hint, I certainly shall."

She smiled and said, "You are a hypocrite. We were told that Catholics were not allowed to practise birth control for the simple reason that popes wanted large families and therefore more followers. If we continue, will you have to confess to someone that you have sinned?"

"There are subtle changes in religious practices that do not mar the essential tenets of one's faith. Large families are out, and surreptitious birth control is in. I am merely following a popular trend. Let's hurry; you have stirred my passion."

"Well, well. You appreciate that I have no concern for what you call the tenets of your faith. I do, however, have a concern for our delay. Get rid of your clothes, and let's start."

He obliged, and she pulled him to her. She took control, and there was no foreplay. He responded, and their two muscular bodies became entwined in exciting movements. He said Alisa was his Arctic connection, and he hoped they would connect often. She agreed but said they had to be careful of the commissar. They spent the rest of the afternoon together and wondered when they would again share such exquisite moments as they had just enjoyed.

Their opportunity for more lovemaking came when she received an order to proceed with an instructor to Volgoda, a big railway junction and the distribution point for the Murmansk tanks. There was a logjam, because an armoured division general had taken the trained tank crews to replace casualties and new tanks could not be moved. She ordered Alex to accompany her. He obtained permission to do so, and they caught a train on the Archangel-to-Volgoda line. En route, he stared out, shocked at the damage caused to the railway by German bombers and by the wreckage alongside the line. It took five days to reach the junction where they soon sorted out the shambles. They selected six men from the rookies hanging around and put them into nonstop training. They then used them to train others, and soon, the tanks and crews were moving to the battlefields.

They were given a large building for training purposes. It had two rooms in which they slept. When the place was deserted, they continued to play their love-thy-neighbour game unsure when their bliss would end.

Back in Murmansk and back under the watchful eye of its commissar, they resumed their formal public relationship and worked hard handling the increased flow of tanks and weapons.

Apart from the miserable cold and the dismal town, life was tolerable for Colonel Taylor's men. Their work kept them active, and supplies from the merchant ships ensured that their food was good. Some occasional game meat from the Russians provided a welcome change. Navy communications kept them informed of the latest news, all of which was gloomy. This, added to the closeness of the Germans trying to capture Murmansk and the constant air raids, cast doubts on an ultimate victory.

The biggest problem was the lack of hospital facilities for the increasing numbers of wounded and the survivors suffering from exposure. The Russians would not allow the British to establish their own hospital, and the existing underequipped one could not cope with the wounded coming in from the front line not more than 40 kilometres away.

The Kola Inlet looked like a naval base with destroyers, corvettes, trawlers, and an occasional cruiser anchored there. The soldiers received news from the naval crews, who found little to do on shore. Their stay was short, unlike that of the merchant seamen whose laden ships awaited berths and empty ships awaited the formation of homeward-bound convoys.

One afternoon, a naval lieutenant commander asked to see Sergeant Greenus, and when they met, he told Alex he was improperly dressed. Alex said he did not understand. The sailor said he was not wearing his George Medal ribbon. Alex wondered how he knew about the award and said that he had grown tired of explaining what it was so he had removed it.

"I know all about your exploit. I am John Gregory, and it was my wife and son you saved. It was a noble act for which I am most grateful."

Alex said that he and his friend had acted on an impulse and were glad they were successful. The sailor said he was too modest. He had read an official account of the incident from which it was clear the air raid warden felt it was too dangerous to move into the wreckage; yet Alex and his friend had done so. Alex laughed and said it was Ginger who should be thanked, because his meowing had led them to the entrapped pair and it was the cat who had found a way out after the entrance they had used was blocked. The sailor also thanked him for visiting the sisters and helping with the maintenance of the property. He said their presence was the turning point in Elizabeth's medical recovery and enabled her to return to teaching.

"I can claim some of the glory, because I gave Neil the kitten. I can never thank you and your friend enough. I have brought you something that I know is scarce around here." He gave Alex a carton of cigarettes. Alex thanked him and thought he, a non-smoker, now had something he could use to influence the tardy Russians with whom he dealt. Gregory told him that his friend and Vera were to be married. Alex told him that for security reasons that were beyond his comprehension, he was not allowed to write to his former comrades, and he was glad to hear John's news.

That night, Alex thought of the beautiful Elizabeth. He hoped the occupational therapy they had enjoyed would not affect her relationship with her husband. He hoped he would never hear of it. *It was all in the line of duty,* he thought, *and far away from this God-forsaken part of the world.* He thought of how Alisa's vigorous lovemaking contrasted with Elizabeth's gentle approach. Maurice and he often used her Shakespeare book.

He heard that HMS *Edinburgh*, Commander Gregory's ship, carried five tons of Russian gold. After it left Murmansk, it zigzagged ahead of Convoy QP 11 and was struck by two torpedoes from a U-boat. It tried to get back to Murmansk, but it had no rudder and there was heavy ice on the upper deck, which caused it to sink. Of its crew of 760, 57 died. Alex hoped Gregory was not one of them.

Convoys arrived with small losses, and it was not until March 1942 that German aircraft flying from Northern Norway and U-boats began to molest the convoys seriously. There was a drama in June 1942 when German bombers, although harried by Hurricanes operated from Murmansk, destroyed most of the town in a great fire. There was further grief when in the early summer of 1942, Convoy PQ 17 was destroyed. Its navy escort was withdrawn and the ships ordered to scatter. After the enormous losses, the navy pressed to suspend the convoys. That angered Stalin, and Churchill, to placate him, ignored the navy's advice. The ghastly losses on the Murmansk Run continued.

The Russians also pressed for the return home of Colonel Taylor's men engaged in the training of tank crews, claiming that they could now train their own personnel. The British acceded to their demands.

Colonel Taylor said he appreciated all the work the unwanted men had done and wished them well in their future activities. Alex asked if he could switch with one of the engineers and stay in Murmansk. The colonel found it difficult to understand why he did not seize the opportunity to leave such a dull place. The Russians had made it clear which soldiers had to leave, and trainers such as he were on the list. There was nothing he could do about it. They were given a copy of the Colonel's report on their activities.

On the day of departure, Alex told Alisa he had to go, but commissar or no bloody commissar, he was going to kiss and hug her. He did so and thanked her for her help with the tanks and crews and for the great times they enjoyed. Amid tears, she joked that he was not to love many neighbours. He said that she, too, should not go wild and take the creed too seriously. She had a surprise for him and his friends. She had been unable to stop their gallantry awards but had kept it quiet. Now they must take the decorations they earned. She gave him their Medals of Valour and citations.

He thanked her and said they enjoyed being able to help at critical moments. Alex gave their medals and citations to Maurice and Fred and thanked them for their friendship. He wondered if he and Fred would meet Maurice in the inevitable future battles in Europe. He then joined the other Canadians on a ship in a westbound convoy that took them to Boston.

Alex thought of the days in Archangel and Murmansk and was proud of what his group had achieved. He was heartened by official stories of how vital the Arctic convoys were and how important the supplies were to the Russians.

It had been an eventful experience, and he wondered what the future held and whether he would ever see his beloved Alisa again.

4
Training and Promotion

The voyage to Boston on an American ship was uneventful except for the ship's tasty food, which was a pleasant contrast to the Arctic fare. Alex and his fellow travellers did not linger in the historic city and caught a train to Ottawa. There was nobody to meet them there, and after bidding farewell to his companions, he persuaded a reluctant RTO (railway transport officer) to get him to the engineering base camp. He had to wait for transport.

He reported to the orderly room and handed his papers, including a report of his activities in the Arctic, to a corporal who said they knew nothing about him. Alex said he was sorry to be a nuisance. He could be found in the sergeants' mess.

The atmosphere in the mess was friendly. Several of its members fired questions at Alex about the notorious Arctic convoys. He said he had been a landlubber with only two voyages in the northern ocean to his credit and could only tell them what the seamen had told him. It was an unhappy story of rough, icy seas; danger; and the loss of many men and ships. He was glad to be back in Canada.

A regimental sergeant major told Alex that his arrival was unexpected. He would be grilled on his experiences with the Russians by an intelligence officer, after which he would be given leave. A steward handed Alex a message that required him to report to the station adjutant at 0900 hours the following morning.

Alex was given a bed but slept fitfully. He wondered what lay ahead. After a tasty breakfast, he made his way to the orderly room and from there was taken to a sparsely furnished office. He was interviewed by an Intelligence Corps major in what Alex thought was a waste of time. The officer did not speak Russian or French, and Alex had nothing secretive to divulge.

"Sergeant, you have come from Russia. What were you doing there?"

"Sir, it is all in the report I left in the orderly room."

"I have not seen it."

Alex paused and thought it sloppy for him not to have already read it.

He said, "A team of Russian-speaking soldiers in which I was the leading NCO trained the Russians in the operation of the tanks and weapons supplied by Britain and America, those that survived the hazardous trip to the Arctic. A few Russians were ungrateful for the supplies that were delivered at such a high cost in ships, lives, and injuries. We rubbed along with the rest happily."

"Heathen bastards," snorted the officer.

"Sir, I generalised. The Russians lost over 15,000 men in preventing the capture of Murmansk and in holding the western approaches to Archangel. I admired them and those with whom I was in close contact."

"It sounds that they made a Commie of you, Sergeant."

"No, sir. I kept my faith and am looking forward to my first Mass in months."

"Oh, so you are a Catholic, are you? How do you justify your Pope's Concordat, his agreement with the Nazis? Did the Commies explain their atheism?"

"I had some discussions on the subject, but we agreed to disagree. We concentrated on the training of men. In two instances, we were in action with our tanks."

Alex remembered the pleasant days when he and Alisa argued about religion and Marxism in measured terms, unlike the snide remarks of the pompous base-wallah who was interviewing him.

"Well, Sergeant, you have had an interesting and pleasant time away from Canada. Now you will have to get down to some hard retraining. It is unfortunate that wartime conditions have made life uncomfortable here, but you'll just have to get used to it."

Alex was irritated and responded, "Sir, I would like to put the record straight. I served in England. It was not a holiday—with the bombers and rough work in mining beaches and in straddling them with barbed wire. My time in the Arctic was only interesting if viewed in the light of the Chinese curse, 'May your life be interesting.' We worked in subzero temperatures; we handled tanks, guns, and other equipment with inferior dock facilities; we lived in rough conditions; a German army was only 40 kilometres away poised to wipe out Murmansk; and we were subjected to day and night bombing. Despite all the hazards, we unloaded and serviced 1,200 tanks, taught their crews how to handle them, and trained Russians to take over from us. Three of us commanded tanks and in two sharp battles, dislodged advanced German units. The Russians decorated us. That is all in the report I handed in to the orderly room clerk when I arrived here. I was surprised to learn that you have not bothered to read it."

"That is insolence, Sergeant."

"No, sir, it is the truth. While you think you were suffering from the so-called war conditions in Canada, some of us were in action. A glance at my file would have confirmed that." Alex rubbed the scar on his forehead that reminded him of the London Blitz.

"You got a Russian medal, eh? I see you are wearing its ribbon. Have you permission to do so? You already face a charge for insubordination, now you will be punished for the unlawful display of a foreign award. You are in trouble, Sergeant."

"Insubordination? Permission? Unlawful? Foreign award? I suggest you study British medals. I was ordered to wear this

George Medal ribbon, because I am to be interviewed by the press. I shall recount with delight my treatment at the hands of a deskbound zombie whose sneers and innuendoes about our Russian allies and my religion rank with those of Goebbels, the German propaganda minister. Try to punish me if you wish. You have no evidence of our conversation. I see that you are Major Andrew McTavish. The media boys always ask for names. I shall tell them whom to interview to confirm your pompous attitude. How does the thought of your name and photograph in Canadian newspapers appeal to you? I can visualise the heading, 'Basewallah Major ridicules decorated engineer'. Good-bye, I hope you weather the rigours of living in wartime Canada. I saw a real steak and white bread for the first time in ages last night. Will you volunteer for the comfortable life of frontline soldiers that you assumed I experienced?"

Alex stood up, did not bother to put on his beret or salute, and stormed out.

The major ran after him and stopped him. "Sergeant, I apologise. It would be unwise to publicise our interview. I trust you won't reveal it to the media."

"Major, I accept your apology conditionally. I am entitled to receive a copy of your report on me. Provided I approve it, I will be reasonable. If I don't like it, I'll ensure the media splash your anti-Russian views and religious slurs."

"Thank you, Sergeant. I take your point. My report will favour you. You may relax. Enjoy your leave."

Alex smiled and shook hands with the discomfited officer, whose limpid grip nauseated him. He called in at the orderly room, collected his leave pass, and went to the city centre on an army truck. He proceeded to Montgomery Street, where he spent time with Juozas and Nelle. They discussed Lithuania and his army adventures. He called on the Bourassas, whose lives had changed, because Emile had rejected his deferment as a farmer and was training to be a pilot in Manitoba. Giselle had joined the Army Nursing Service and was in a hospital in Vancouver. They remarked on his thinness, and he said it was the absence of the good food cooked by Mrs. Bourassa that was to blame. She said dinner would be roast chicken and that should improve matters. He discussed farming and was interested to learn that due to the shortage of labour, local farmers had formed a cooperative and teams helped with ploughing, hay cutting, and other chores. Prices were good and the farmers could not complain.

On his return to the depot, he was interviewed by a pleasant captain who opened his file and complimented him on his excellent record and his British and Russian decorations. Alex smiled and said he was an ordinary guy who was lucky to have been noticed.

The officer told Alex he had four choices. He could return to his unit still training in England; transfer to the Intelligence Branch, which was impressed with his linguistic ability; join a tank regiment; or train as an engineering officer in Canada.

Alex did not fancy moving around England again, and the thought of a desk job made him determined to avoid the intelligence offer. He had had enough of tanks. He said he would like to attend the engineers' OTC (Officers' Training Course). He was told he would appear before a selection board. In his case, there should be no trouble.

But there was because one of the board members questioned whether Alex had enough technical knowledge. He was reminded of Alex's service with a field company, his practical logging and farming knowledge, and further experience in the Arctic plus his mathematics and biology studies.

The chairman of the board said Alex would be an ideal officer in a forestry company. It was always short of leaders with logging experience, and he was passed for the course. Alex was told he would probably be posted to a forestry company when commissioned. He wondered if he wanted to be involved with trees again but thought it would be more interesting than logging camp work.

He was given a rail warrant to Chilliwack in British Colombia. He enjoyed the trip across Canada. At the end of the journey, he was collected in a jeep driven by a corporal, who said Alex faced a tough six months at the engineering training camp where the cadets were pushed hard. Alex told him he looked forward to the activity and was sure he would survive.

Alex was welcomed by a major with Great War ribbons, who was in charge of training.

"Sergeant Greenus, you are now Cadet Greenus and should remove the stripes from your uniform. You have an outstanding record and are well acquainted with army procedures. Nevertheless, you will be treated like any other cadet. Some of them are straight out of university. Others lack experience. It would please us if you accepted the basic training in good spirit and exercised leadership in other activities."

"Sir, I am honoured to be on this course. I will strive at all times to be perfect."

"Thank you. I shall watch your progress with interest."

After the relatively slack discipline of Murmansk, being barked at by one drill sergeant after another irritated him, but he buckled down and enjoyed the course. He worked hard on the technical subjects. He was helped by fellow trainees, most of whom were engineering graduates. He guided them in practical work. His energy and strength were impressive. He excelled in weapons training and led the course in field tactics, the practice of which reminded him of Alisa and the tank attacks. On completion of the course, he was commissioned and posted to an officers' pool in Halifax. Fortunately, the reference to forestry in his file was overlooked. In June 1943, he was again at Pier 21 en route to England to join the Sixth Field Company.

The voyage was comfortable. He had a cabin this time and did not miss the hammocks of his earlier trip. He was welcomed by the commanding officer of the field company, who introduced him to his fellow officers and platoon sergeant.

The unit practised assault landings with the Seventh Brigade at Inveraray on the West Coast of Scotland. Alex was impressed with the Duke of Argyll's magnificent castle. He wondered what

Karl Marx would have thought of it. The unit moved around England, where there was a heavy demand for engineers to be trained for landings and the clearance of beaches. They trained with the versatile Bailey bridge, which replaced the heavy Inglis bridge used on the officers' course.

One day when his platoon was near Bristol, Alex called on Clifton College and met Neil Gregory, who was excited because he had been selected for the school's cricket eleven. Alex listened patiently to Neil's description of his spin bowling.

The boy said his father was at home at present and that his aunt Vera had a small boy. Alex was relieved to know the commander had escaped death in the northern seas and dropped his idea of visiting Elizabeth.

He took Neil and a friend to the school's tuck shop, where they gorged themselves on buns and soft drinks. Neil's friend said he was pleased to meet the hero who had saved his friend's life. Neil had often spoken about him and the medal he had received. Alex said another Canadian was involved, and their best reward was to meet Neil's family. He regretted he would not be around to see the youngster's appearance for the first team. He surprised the boys by saying he hoped Neil was not hit for a six.

He visited the Fourth Field Company, who were busy practising beach landings and the clearance of mines and obstacles. There were strange new faces, but the old RSM was there and gave him a smart salute. He took him to the Colonel, who asked about his mystery transfer two years earlier. Alex told him about Murmansk and training in Chilliwack and how he had been destined for a forestry company but ended up with the Sixth Field Company. He had licked his platoon into shape and was happy. The colonel told him that if he ever changed his mind, there would always be a place for him in the Fourth Field. Alex thanked him, saluted, said farewell to the RSM and found John le Clus. He was now a sergeant and greeted him warmly. He congratulated him on his commission. Alex did not tell him that he could have returned to the fourth as a sergeant but did not want to spend more time in Britain.

John said everyone was tired of England except him, because being there meant he had more time with Vera and their small son. Alex congratulated him on his marriage and child. He said he had brought him a wedding present, a bone carving of an animal he'd found in Archangel. John was delighted. He said Alex must have noticed that Vera was a collector of carvings and to have one from the far north would delight her. It would also be a reminder of their friendship.

John asked about Lithuania, and Alex said he hated the Nazis more than ever because they had now destroyed the Kaunus and Vilnius ghettos. Unfortunately, many Lithuanians were collaborating with the Germans. He hoped the freedom fighters would eliminate the vermin.

Next, Alex went to Scotland to search for two uncles who were coal miners. He only knew they worked near Glasgow. He called at the city's Mitchell Library in North Street for information and learned that Lithuanians were employed mainly in Bellshill and Mossend between Glasgow and Edinburgh. Bellshill was known as a centre for Lithuanian culture.

Alex took a train there and asked at a mining company's office about Lithuanians working there. He was directed to the last building in a row of miners' cottages. He knocked on its door. A charming lady, who turned out to be his cousin Rosemary, opened it and invited him in. He chatted with her and her mother. They knew they had relatives in Canada but did not know one was an officer. The mother suggested the two of them go to the Social Club for a meal and dancing. Alex smiled and thought of Maurice Navid. The dance was a success, and Alex silently thanked John, Elizabeth, and Maurice for their training. Rosemary saw his faraway look and asked if he was all right.

"My apologies, Rosemary. It has been some time since I danced, and I was thinking of my previous attempts."

"You dance well, and you would make those girls standing across the room happy if you invited them to waltz with you."

"That will be tough, but I'll obey your orders."

"Away wi' ye, and enjoy yourself. There'll be some Scottish dances soon, and that will enable you to twirl with all the lasses."

The lasses were willing, and although he found them difficult to understand, they were lissom enough and delighted in coaching him in the reels and other dances.

Alex returned from leave refreshed and intrigued by his Scottish relatives.

The Sixth Field Company moved to Southampton. They were sent to France shortly after D Day, June 6, 1944. In the battle areas, it was their job to make and mend roads, lift minefields, and maintain water points. They supported the infantry, and in one engagement, Alex was wounded in the chest. In hospital, he met a captain from the Fourth Field Company, who told him of their strenuous campaign when they had to clear the way for the infantry.

"The Germans left mines everywhere and were up to all kinds of tricks like putting one mine on top of another. We would clear the top one and then hear of a disaster when the second one exploded. The Huns are masters of defence and had Tiger tanks buried hull down. They created terrible damage. We lost a lot of men and had to train rookies sent as replacements."

Alex asked after John and learned he had been awarded an immediate Distinguished Conduct Medal for removing explosives from a bridge despite two wounds and was promoted to company sergeant major. He had recovered and was back with the unit. He was much respected. He had refused a commission because he wanted to stay with his men.

When released from hospital, Alex rejoined his unit. At one stage, he and his platoon were seconded to a forestry company to speed up the delivery of timber urgently needed for an important wooden bridge. He was comfortable with the *joual* and boisterous behaviour of the regular foresters from Quebec, whose activities were an eye-opener to those of Alex's sappers who came from Western Canada. He surprised his men by sharing their heavy work. He knew from experience that frequent rest periods resulted in higher productivity. He introduced them, and with his energetic example, his platoon helped to deliver the required lumber on time. The commanding officer of the forestry company thanked Alex and tried to persuade him to stay with the unit, but Alex preferred iron bridges to wooden ones.

His team built one bridge after another across canals and rivers. One was called Sniper's Alley, a forty-foot single bridge that enabled the Americans to destroy three tanks. Alex's platoon cleared routes for the leading troops by dynamiting steel-rail obstacles and used an armoured D-7 dozer to fill in ditches. At times, when explosives would have been dangerous to use, they cut obstacles with oxyacetylene torches.

On one occasion, a disabled tank blocked the approach to a vital bridge, and some engineers were about to blow it sky-high. They said two of the tanks' crew had been wounded and its commander, a sergeant, and the tank's gunner had taken them to a first-aid post. They said they would be back, but something had delayed them and the engineers could not wait any longer.

Alex told them to hang on.

He climbed into the tank and fired its 75-millimetre cannon at a deadly German 88-millimetre and put it out of action. He then fired at two machine gun nests before switching to the Vickers machine gun and spraying bullets on the opposite bank of the river. He climbed out of the tank, got into the driver's seat, and started its engine. He gestured to the infantry officer to follow him and proceeded across the bridge. His tank shielded the infantry that followed him. The Germans retreated. The bridge was secured, and Alex returned to his men.

The uninjured members of the tank were surprised to see it on the far side of the river, and its sergeant asked how it had got there. "Oh," said the infantry officer, "you missed the fun. An engineer officer got into the tank and knocked out an 88 and two machine guns and gave the Jerries hell with the tank's Vickers. He then drove the tank over the bridge thereby protecting my men who advanced behind it. The Jerries had had enough and left."

"Engineer officer?"

"Yes. He told me he had qualified in all aspects of operating a tank and certainly proved it. He said he had fought in tanks in the Arctic. He was a friendly, modest guy, but what a great soldier! I have recommended him for a decoration, because without his bravery and initiative, we would still be on the other side of the river. He said that his time at Lulworth, Bovington, and in the Arctic was not wasted."

"He must have received first-class training. Lulworth and Bovington are known for their strictness. But the Arctic? I wonder what he meant by that?"

"I don't know, but he growled that you should be court-martialled for abandoning a serviceable tank."

"Oh hell. I had to help my men and meant to get back quickly and paste the Jerries. I am pleased you got the bridge."

"Look, I will say nothing provided you move your tank to a position where you can defend us against a counterattack and stay alert."

"Thank you, sir. You can rely on us."

"That is a moot point, but don't let us down."

Alex was awarded an immediate Military Cross and promoted to captain.

His men wondered what unusual thing Alex would do next, and it was not long in coming. After ferrying troops across the Rhine, they resumed their bridge-building activities. One day, they saw two bedraggled men on the bank of a canal. Someone said they were Russians, so Alex went to them and asked if he could help.

They smiled wistfully and said just to hear their own language made them feel better. They had been captured by the Germans but escaped and had been walking for days. Alex arranged food for them. He then took them to a bathing area and scrounged new clothes from the quartermaster. He found a razor and toiletries, and by the time he had finished helping them, the men looked the officers they were.

One, Captain Nicholas Gromyko, said that he could help them because they had recently been forced to lay mines for the Germans. He said they were tiered pressure mines designed to destroy heavy vehicles and could be easily rendered harmless by snipping a wire leading from the top layer to the next. The Germans were systematic, and he sketched the details of the minefield. The mines were five metres apart, but those in the next parallel row started two and a half metres short from the edge so there were formidable obstacles in depth. The minefield started on the opposite side of the canal and covered a fifty-metre width.

Alex thanked him. He instructed his men to prepare some small stakes with which to mark the mines, and he took his mine-lifting specialist, Corporal Beldon, to find the first mine in the pattern. They had no trouble doing so, and Alex got some of his men to mark mines based on Gromyko's sketch with another team following to snip the wires and lift the mines.

They were busy on their task when a Corps of Engineers brigadier arrived to check progress on the important bridge, the completion of which was needed urgently. He was pleased to see it finished and was intrigued with Alex who was working with his usual energy. He did not see the senior officer, who shouted, "Who is in charge here?"

Alex saluted and said, "I am, sir, Captain Greenus."

"Greenus, I see you have the MC. I remember now; you were the man who secured a bridge by firing from a tank and then driving it across the bridge. I did not know my officers were trained on tanks."

"It was all in a day's work, sir. It was fortunate that I had done an intensive tank course in England and had fought in tanks in the Arctic."

"In the Arctic? I did not know we had fought there."

"I was involved in training Russians in Archangel and Murmansk. On two occasions, we knocked out some German mortar and machine gun nests."

"Remarkable. I have dined out on your exploit here with my armoured corps officers. I can now add flavour to my story. I must congratulate you on the speed with which you built this bridge, but how on earth did you discover the minefield? It would have created havoc."

"We helped two Russian officers, and they gave us the minefield plan. Cunning mines. The Jerries are always up to new tricks, but we were warned and we'll clear the area by nightfall. If you'll excuse me, sir, I would like to continue; we are working in teams, and my men are slowing down."

"Russians, the Arctic, tank fights—What next, Captain Greenus? Go ahead. It is good to see enthusiasm at this stage of the war. You said you were helped by two Russians, did you not?"

"Yes, sir. I speak Russian."

"You are surprisingly versatile. I would appreciate your report on those mines and how they should be defused and the name of the man who dealt with the first mine. You can give that to my ADC, Captain Rasmussen."

"Certainly, sir," said Alex.

He gave the name of Corporal Beldon, who had exhibited bravery on many occasions and was the platoon's mine expert. He was pleased later when Beldon was awarded the Military Medal presented to him by General Montgomery. Alex was mentioned in dispatches.

Just before the end of hostilities, he received a letter from Captain Gromyko in the Cyrillic script that must have puzzled the British censors. The Russian thanked Alex for helping them and reviving their spirits. His companion, Major Voroshilov, had returned to the tanks, and when he mentioned details of their escape to his colleagues, one of them said Alex had trained him in Murmansk. It was one of the war's amazing occurrences that such connections took place. He remarked once again how fortunate they were to have been seen by Alex, probably the only Allied Russian-speaking soldier within many kilometres.

At the end of the war, Alex obtained leave, borrowed a jeep, and headed towards Germany. His plan was to get to Lithuania to see his family. He got as far as Bremen, where he was stopped by some British soldiers, who took him to their commanding officer. The officer said his quest was hopeless. There was devastation everywhere, the railway systems had broken down. Alex reluctantly returned to his unit.

5
Studies and Lithuania

Because of his early enlistment, Alex was in the first batch of soldiers sent home. At the Montreal demobilisation centre, he applied for an education grant to study medicine. He received it and a warning that even if he passed all examinations, it would be seven years before he qualified as a medical doctor. Alex said he understood and applied for admission to McGill University. Its enrolment officer was sympathetic and said that the Quebec matriculation passes and the English A-levels would enable him to start his first year bachelor of science studies.

The university was full of ex-service people, most of whom worked hard to make up for lost years. Alex found rooms to share with a sapper he knew and managed to survive on the government grant and earnings from work as a waiter at a French restaurant. His companion was quite happy to leave the feeding arrangements to Alex, whose good cooking was augmented by occasional leftover dishes from the restaurant.

He joined the university's wrestling club and took part in tug-of-war and cross-country running. He visited the swimming pool regularly, where good swimmers showed him how to better his style. He thought he should write and tell Elizabeth he had improved but decided it would be unfair to disturb her. For relaxation, he read Shakespeare's plays from Elizabeth's gift book and remembered her John of Gaunt and Polonius.

He also remembered Maurice Navid, who quoted the Bard frequently. Ebullient Maurice, that keen cricketer, prankster, and stalwart friend, had been sent from Murmansk to England and then back to the Middle East. He fought with the Sixth South African Armoured Division in Italy and was killed leading a night patrol near Chiusi.

He explained cricket to me and said he hoped to have a long innings. I am sad that he was out before he could bat again.

Alex and John le Clus and some of their mates joined the Royal Canadian Legion and attended its Armistice Day parades. On one occasion, they were approached by a British major who wore the green beret of the commandos.

"Congratulations. I see you two have added to your GMs. How are your rope-torn hands?"

It was the former Sergeant Paul Johnstone, who had chastised them after the London bombing incident.

"Blow me down," said John. "How are you, Sarge?"

"I am well. What about you two? What happened to you in the rest of the war?"

Alex said he had ended up in the Arctic and the final battles in Europe.

"John bowled a maiden over, and his son was born in England. He saw her fine leg, and they took cover. They were nearly caught in the gulley. He had me stumped. I only found out about this later."

"I see you have not lost your sense of humour, but where did you learn those cricket terms?"

"My half section in the Arctic was an accomplished cricketer and insisted on enlightening me. He spun it out. I learnt that a leg break had nothing to do with a damaged limb; that a silly point was not a stupid grammatical expression; that a cover drive was not a hidden road; that a ton was not 2,000 pounds but 100 or more runs; and that it was not cricket to misbehave. It was strange jargon. What about you, Sarge?"

"There you go again. I was commissioned and on D Day again climbed some cliffs. I enjoyed my commando days. I stayed in the army and am at present an aide-de-camp at the British embassy. I may tell you one day what my true role is. It is under wraps at the moment. It is great to see you two and to know you survived. What are you doing?"

Alex told him he was a medical student and John was building a small fortune in his electrical business.

At the end of the ceremony, they shook hands and parted ways.

Alex's roommate helped him with calculus and physics. He found he could cope with biology and general and organic chemistry, and at the end of three years, he qualified to enter medical school.

***

In 1951, Alex decided to visit Lithuania. He obtained Canadian citizenship and a passport and travelled by ship to Copenhagen thence to Klaipeda by ferry. There Russian officials told him he would not be allowed into the country because he had no reason to be there. Alex told them he had been born in Lithuania and wanted to see his family. That did not matter. They did not want people like him to disturb others who were happy with conditions in Lithuania.

Alex protested that his mother was a widow, and he wanted to see her and improve her living standards. The official laughed and said they were not like his Capitalist friends who exploited workers and then let them suffer poverty in their old age. He was certain Alex's mother was being looked after adequately by the State.

Alex felt like providing the little information he could glean from the heavily censored letters he received that disputed that statement. Instead, he pulled out his Medal of Valour and said that he had earned that fighting in the Great Patriotic War. He was entitled to better treatment from the official and would like to see his superior. The official sneered and asked who the hell he thought he was making demands. He claimed that Russian medals could be bought, and there was no way a Canadian could have earned one. For dishonouring the decoration, he would be arrested.

Alex stiffened and thrust his citation and Captain Gromyko's letter in front of the man. He shouted, "You are an imbecile who has wasted time impeding the movement of a friend of Russia! You had better start looking for another job, because I am going above your head to sort you out!"

Alex heard someone say, "Who will you sort out?"

Without turning, Alex said, "This cretin who has insulted me. I who fought with the Red Army near Archangel, and I have given him proof of that. I want to see his superior officer and report this idiot, who should be fired."

"It is I, his superior, who asked the question. Come into my office."

He looked at the citation and letter and asked Alex about the incident that led to its award. He explained the circumstances, and his questioner apologised for the attitude of his official. He said they had to be strict with visitors because so many of them caused trouble. He would admit Alex, but the maximum stay he could authorise was six days.

Alex thanked him and made his way to the train station. He was appalled at the number of damaged buildings and people's shabby clothes. He had no trouble getting a train ticket.

At Mosedis, he sought a barber, thinking that like all hairdressers he would be a source of information, and for a while, their conversation flourished. The barber, a well-groomed, intelligent man, remembered the Girnius family but did not see any of them now. He said life was terrible. The Red Army moved through the country and took what they wanted. They were a barbarous lot, and he had seen an officer shoot one of his soldiers because he had been given a cake the officer thought he should have. Women were at their peril because the soldiers raped indiscriminately.

The Russians' collective farming program had wrecked the lives of small farmers. The whole thing was a failure, and farm produce was always scarce. The Russians lived well and did not concern themselves with the welfare of Lithuanians, many of whom were shipped to Siberia. If young and fit enough, they were conscripted into the Soviet army. Religion had been suppressed, and the local church was closed. Elsewhere, churches and synagogues were used for government offices. The country was full of spies.

"And here comes one now," he said just before a well-dressed, middle-aged man entered. He hardly acknowledged the barber's greeting and was soon absorbed in a newspaper.

Alex asked where the retirement home was and left to find his mother. He sensed he was being followed, and as he turned, he saw the man from the hairdresser move into the entrance of a building. Alex thought he would have some fun and retraced his steps. As he passed the man, he asked if he had decided not to have a haircut and if he knew where the retirement home was. He glared at Alex and told him that he already had directions and should be on his way. He shrugged his shoulders and moved off. Alex followed to annoy him and then returned to the barber to tell him he was right. His customer had trailed him.

"You can pick them out. They are traitors to their country. We'll get them one day. I am glad you embarrassed that twit, but they will not leave you alone because they hate emigrants who return and talk of a better life. You will have to be careful; a visitor from Australia disappeared the other day and was found beaten up. He claimed that the police were responsible, but he was ignored and kicked out.

"I am a qualified chemist but cannot get a decent job, nor can I get a passport to leave. I am stuck standing and snipping hair all day long. Our traditions are dying. The schools have to teach in Russian. Good luck. I hope your mother is well but be on guard."

Alex walked to his mother's retirement home, a dull, grey building with unkempt grounds. He knew he was followed but did not bother to elude the stalker.

Terese, a smiling widow of medium height with black hair and brown eyes, was with their mother. Both ladies hugged him and wept. His mother said she had thought she would never see him again. She thanked him for the money he sent and said it had saved her from disaster. His father, who had never recovered from the seizure of their land, would have been proud of him. Times were terrible, and she was lucky to have a room in the home and to have Terese nearby.

Alex and his sister redecorated their mother's room and bought new blankets and clothes. The effect was immediate, and his mother looked happier. She could not thank them enough and told him he was wise to go to Canada. He said he wanted to get her and Terese out of the dull and tedious Communist country that Lithuania had become. He instructed Terese to get passports for that purpose. He said St. Casimir's, a Catholic church in Montreal that had been kind to him, would find accommodation for them. Uncle Juozas and Aunt Nelle would keep an eye on them when they reached Canada.

When Alex asked Terese where his brothers were, she cried. She said Jonas had been wounded fighting the Germans, and Stasys was a worker in the underground resistance movement against the Russians. The twin boys, Algirdas and Kazys, had been conscripted into the Russian army and told horror stories of the sadistic training and humiliating hazing rituals they endured. Officers were never punished for beating recruits and living conditions were primitive.

Algirdas was now a security guard at a bank in Vilnius and Kazys a fireman in Kaunas. Accommodation was provided, and they lived quiet, uneventful lives. Sofija and Marija were married to workers in a brickfield; Janina was married to a sailor and lived in Klapeida; and Julija was a nurse in Alytus. He and Terese walked to their old farm. He was shocked to see their razed home and the neglected land, now part of a collective farm. Terese told him that his Jewish friends in Mosedis had vanished, victims of the Nazi occupation. Nowadays, locals who were involved in religious affairs or who were politically active were shipped to Siberia. Nothing was ever heard from them. Their church, which had been such an important part of their spiritual and communal life, was derelict. Fortunately, its famous stone wall, which had witnessed centuries of war and insurrection, was intact.

He was saddened by the news and the thought of gentle Father Staugaitis in the bitter wastes of Siberia upset him. He asked when the priest had been deported. Terese told him that he had escaped that fate because just before he was due to leave, he took one last look at the river he loved and heard screams. He saw a child struggling in the water, jumped in, and saved her. She was the daughter of a senior Russian officer. He cancelled the priest's deportation order and secured him a job as a schoolteacher. Father Staugaitis was still a wonderful spiritual guide. God must have destined him to stay and keep the faith alive. He now taught at the local school but still administered Mass at his home.

Alex bade a tearful farewell to his mother and sister. He went to the local school where the children were noisy and active, seemingly unaware of the miserable conditions in which they lived. The priest was delighted to see him and took him to his room adjacent to the school. It was sparsely furnished with a shrine in one corner. He saw Alex staring at it and said, "Yes, I still administer the sacraments. The police hate me for it, but tolerate me provided I keep things private. A small number of people take Mass knowing that their names are being recorded. But that is a way of life and God will protect them. I should not tell you, but we receive outside help, in my case from a parish in Australia. Money is sent to a friendly business and passed to me. This enables me to help families suffering the most. I am sure the KGB knows about it, but the authorities are so desperate for foreign currency that they have taken no action against my friendly company or me.

I am sorry about your father and brother Jonas and for all your Jewish school friends who vanished when the Nazis moved in.

"I am forced to teach a syllabus of indoctrination in Russian, but there are some excellent Russian poets and writers, and by being selective, I can use them to teach the children the reasons for past struggles that are similar to ours. I take a risk, but I always find one of our heroes and quote them in the same context."

He was pleased to hear that Alex was at a university studying to be a doctor and wished him well. Alex pressed some money on him. The priest said that would enable him to get food for a struggling family. Alex had meant the priest to use the money on himself but said nothing.

There were Russian troops everywhere, and life was gloomy with food shortages and queues of people hoping to obtain scarce supplies. He wandered to the Bartuva River now devoid of holiday cottages and wondered if the country would ever be free of foreign control.

He had asked Terese how he could find Stasys, and she gave him an address in Klaipeda. She said he must take care not to be followed. She had received the address against an oath of secrecy but felt he should have it. He should not be surprised if their brother had already left it. She said the KGB (Commission for State Security), the old NKVD were active and merciless with the underground workers. She thought the police would have followed him. He said they probably had and promised to be careful in Klapeida.

Alex knew that Lithuania had a tragic history of suppression by Poles and Russians. The Nazis invaded Lithuania in June 1941. They were welcomed by some Lithuanians and supported the underground group called the Lithuanian Activist Front, which had opposed the Russians. During the German occupation, a Soviet-sponsored underground group aided a Lithuanian anti-Nazi resistance group.

When the Russians evicted the Germans in 1944, the Soviets faced an armed partisan resistance movement and a fight ensued that resulted in more than 20,000 Lithuanian casualties. This brought an end to armed underground resistance, but the movement itself continued, supported by the Catholic Church, whose underground publication *The Chronicle of the Catholic Church of Lithuania* defied KGB attempts to uncover its printer. Stasys and his colleagues fought a desperate battle against the secret police, and many were arrested and imprisoned.

Alex went to the seaport and walked casually in the vicinity of the address on the note. There was nobody around, so he turned back and knocked on the door. A stranger asked what he wanted. Alex said he was Girnius. The man recognised him from his resemblance to his brother and shouted to Stasys to come. The brothers hugged, and Alex was pulled inside. He was told he was lucky to find them, because they were about to move to a new address. They did that regularly to avoid the KGB, whose ruthlessness had practically wiped out the underground movement.

They chatted about the early days when they worked through summer and in the autumn harvested corn, potatoes, onions, turnips, carrots, beetroot, and cabbage, which they pickled for the winter. They collected cultivated cherries and in the forest bitter apples, tiny strawberries, bilberries, and nuts, which they sold in the town. They cursed the lousy Russians who had destroyed that way of life. Stasys said their father, who was destined for Siberia with other unfortunate victims of Soviet purges, died suddenly after their land was taken away and so had been spared the misery of the tundra wasteland.

Alex told him of his life in Canada and in the army and how he hoped to get as many members of the family as possible to Canada. Stasys shrugged his shoulders and said he and others were making the Russians' lives a misery, but he knew their activities could not last. There were collaborators everywhere, and he planned to leave when the opportunity arose. It would be impossible to get to Canada. He said bitterly that one refuge of easy access was

Germany, a country responsible for the deaths of their Jewish friends.

Stasys told Alex that he had been conscripted and became a farrier in one of the Russian army's mounted units. One night, he and a friend overpowered the guard at their barracks and led two horses, whose hooves had been covered with pads in anticipation of their escape, out into the street. They had then ridden to the woods that surrounded the town. They contacted some of the Forest Brothers, an underground group that harassed the Russians in all the Baltic States.

He joined and fought with the group, which hid in the wooded countryside and in Lithuania controlled large regions. They harassed the Russian army and secret police, the KGB, with a mixture of captured arms and hampered the enemy with ambushes, sabotage, and underground newspapers. It was a dangerous life, and capture meant torture and most likely death.

"I was wounded in one engagement and ended up in an underground hospital in one of the bunkers the activists built. I was well looked after and had an affair with a nurse. When it became clear that open resistance was no longer feasible, I elected to work in the urban areas. Now I am fighting to the last."

"You should clear out while you have the chance."

"You are right, but there are some things I must attend to, one of which you could help me with."

He took Alex to a room where a man lay half asleep and moaning. Stasys explained that he had been wounded in a brush with the authorities and was in a bad way. He wanted Alex, with his medical training, to look at him. Alex examined a wound in the man's thigh and said a bullet had to be removed. One of the man's ankles was badly lacerated and full of pus. Alex cleaned it, put on a fresh dressing made from a torn sheet, and shook his head. "This is septic, and the poison is creeping into his system. He needs medication."

Stasys said they had no medical contacts and dared not take him to a hospital where he would be exposed. Death was the price the fighters understood they might have to pay for resisting the Russians. He shrugged his shoulders and said that their wounds were a bitter forfeit for ultimate freedom.

Alex said he would see what he could do and went to a nearby hospital where he spoke to a doctor. He told him he was a Canadian medical student with a problem. A friend's dog had been badly hurt by a vehicle, and the wound needed cleaning and stitches.

The doctor smiled and gave him a ready-to-use threaded surgical needle. He said that it would be best to anaesthetise the animal, for which purpose he gave Alex a small bottle of ether. He said, too, that the wound would need dressing and gave him some antiseptic powder, a bottle of painkilling tablets, and some rubber gloves. He told Alex to hide the gifts and walked with him past security guards to the exit where he shook his hand and with a smile said he hoped the animal was a patriotic dog. Alex grinned and said there was no doubt about that.

He applied the powder and a new dressing to the ankle and asked Stasys to boil the sharpest knife he had along with some tweezers and to lay them on a clean cloth next to the bed. He poured some of the ether onto a pad and told Stasys to apply it to the sick man's nose. Once he was under, he cut across the bullet wound and asked the third man to staunch the blood. He probed with the tweezers and luckily had no trouble extracting the bullet. He sewed the incision, applied a dressing, and told Stasys that the man should be given painkillers when needed. The ankle should be dressed daily with the antiseptic powder. It was the best he could do, and he hoped the man would survive. He learned later that his ministrations were successful and the man had recovered fully.

He managed to see two of his sisters, who were married to brick workers in Taurage. He then returned to Montreal and was relieved to hear a few weeks later that Terese had obtained passports for herself and their mother. They were cleared by the Canadian consul in Lithuania and, with fares paid by the Canadian Lithuanian community, would soon be in Canada. They arrived in Montreal three months later, and Terese, who had worked as a confectioner, had no trouble finding a position and earned enough to cover their living expenses.

***

Alex qualified as a doctor in 1952. After an internship at the Royal Victoria Hospital in Montreal, he spent eighteen months qualifying as a surgeon. He established a practice in Drummondville, where many of his patients were immigrants who appreciated being dealt with in their own language.

He could not forget Stasys and his friends, and after two years of practice, he again flew to Copenhagen and from there travelled to Klapeida by ferry. Just like the previous time, he was harassed by immigration officials and told he could not enter Lithuania. He demanded to see the official in charge and was taken to the same office as before where a scowling, fat, bearded man sat and glared at him.

"You caused trouble before, and you should not have returned. We know you write filthy propaganda against us, so you will have to return to Denmark."

The bully was startled when Alex asked him if he had fought in the Great Patriotic War. He said he had not; he was too young, but he knew that Canada, like Britain, had sheltered behind the brave Soviet soldiers who faced the main onslaught of the Fascist pigs.

Alex said that some Canadians of whom he was one fought with the Soviet troops.

"You fought with our brave soldiers? Nonsense. Get out before I throw you out."

"Before you do, read this," Alex said and gave him his citation and Captain Gromyko's letter.

The official was startled, said Alex should have spoken earlier, and gave him permission to stay for six days.

He called at the hospital where the friendly doctor still worked. He told him he was now qualified and that the dog had recovered. The doctor said it was strange that he had called because he knew of another dog that required treatment. If he wished to help, he would give him supplies to enable him to do so.

Alex took the supplies, and as he left the hospital, he noticed a Volpo car with two men in it following him. He quickly took a bus, and the car followed. He alighted at a shopping area and moved around in it. When he came out at another street, his followers had gone. He walked to the area near the address given to him, and when satisfied that all was clear, he called at the house. He said he was Doctor Girnius and had come to treat the dog. The man said he resembled Stasys, who had told him of the brother who had saved a compatriot's life, and let him in. The wounded man had a broken arm with a bone piercing the flesh. Alex sighed and said he should have been treated earlier.

He told the man who admitted him to apply the pad of ether he had prepared. When the wounded man was under, he reset the arm and hoped the bones would knit. He dressed the cut, applied splints to the arm, made a sling, and then attended to a slight bullet wound in the other arm. There was a heavy knock on the door. The man said it was Stasys, who had come to help remove all traces of their occupation of the house.

Stasys and Alex hugged each other. Stasys said they had to leave that night despite the curfew. They had to clean up the house so that the owner's story that he did not know they had been there rang true. The owner had been transferred to a mining town, but his spell of duty there would end soon. If interrogated by the KGB, the owner of the house would say someone must have been watching it, noticed that he kept a front door key under a rock near the entrance, and used that to gain entrance. If the house were raided before his return, the KGB would not find anything.

Alex discussed the situation in Lithuania. Stasys said he must have noticed that things were still bad under the Russians. If people did as they were told, they could eke out a living, but there was little chance of progress unless one was a collaborator. There were many Lithuanians who spied for the Russians, and although Alex might think that he had not revealed the safe house, the odds were that someone on the street had seen a stranger enter it. In due course, that would reach the KGB and a visit from three of them would follow. In this case, it did not matter, because they were planning to leave that evening anyway.

"We risk curfews and move around at night. It is a cat-and-mouse game, but we have our successes. We do not attack targets that would affect civilians, and in most cases, we get away with it. As you know, we suffer casualties and few doctors will treat them without reporting the gunshot wounds to the police. That means a visit by the KGB, and once in their hands, it is torture and possibly death."

"Don't you think it is time to accept that the Russians will be here forever and get out of the country? The rest of our family is settled. Could you not come to Canada?"

"I would love to, but it would be difficult. It is hard to believe, but our best bet for emigration is still Germany, but who would want to live there? We suffered enough under them to know we would not be welcome. It is tricky trying to get out of the country, as you know, from when you got away. You had some good breaks, but they are now rare. Sooner or later, one has to find a friendly ship's captain or be smuggled aboard by the crew. They demand money before they will do that. The ferries are the best means of communication, but they are loaded with plainclothes KGB, as some of my friends have discovered. There are roadblocks and checkpoints everywhere. The Russians require citizens to carry several documents without which one is dumped in jail unless one has a suitable bribe handy. When we are told to stop operations, I shall try to get into Spain, but in the meantime, I'll soldier on."

"Look, here is my address and a wad of US dollars I brought with me. I have had no trouble changing them, so they should help. Also, here is my watch, and that should realise a little. If you can possibly get to Canada, I'll sponsor you. If you do get away, let me know, because we must keep in touch. It upsets me that in a small way in the war, I helped the Russians beat the Germans and now they oppress my family and many others here. I was decorated by the Russians and carry the medal with me. That is the only way I have managed to get into the country. Even then, it was difficult because they know I write virulent articles about their despicable actions here, so this is likely to be my last visit. All the members of our family have my address. I must go now. Look after yourself. I will pray for you as I have always done."

"Alex, thank you for everything. I know you always sent money to our mother and that made all the difference to her life. Then you helped her and Terese to live in Canada. I was surprised they got passports, but Mother was a welfare case, so perhaps they felt they could save money and Canada could look after her. You will not hear from me for some time, but if I am lucky, I'll let you know immediately."

Alex returned to a hotel whence he was to leave for Canada and was surprised by a visit of three men who identified themselves as KGB agents. They asked why he, a Canadian, had come to Lithuania a second time in four years. Alex realised they must have a file on him and that he had been followed. He said he was born in Lithuania and came to see his relations. When they asked who they were, he gave them his sisters' names. They asked about his brother Stasys and wanted to know if Alex had seen him. He wondered how they knew he had a brother with a different surname.

He said he had no idea where Stasys was. They asked what his occupation was, and when he said he was a doctor, they asked if he had treated anyone in Lithuania. Alex said he was not licensed to do that, and as they could see, he did not have a doctor's bag with him. On his last visit, he had arranged for his mother and sister to leave the country and he hoped to help his remaining family to do the same.

They said they were not satisfied with his responses, and he had to accompany them to their office. Alex switched to Lithuanian and said they should remember that he was a Canadian citizen and intended to report their invasion of his privacy. He also said that he had been awarded the Soviet Medal of Valour, another reason to leave him alone.

They ignored his pleas and pushed him into a car, drove to a building festooned with red flags, and took him to a cell. They told him to await an army colonel's arrival. Alex bent his head in thought. He heard someone enter but did not move until he was hit across the head and an angry voice told him to look up. He did so and was shocked to see that the officer was Alisa. She hit him again and called him a traitorous pig.

She unrolled a sheet of paper on which was written, "This room is bugged. I am going to shout some more and will slap you. When you are released, go to this address." He took the paper and shouted that she was a nasty bit of work, for which he was again slapped. She stormed out of the room to the surprise of the guards because she was normally so controlled and unemotional. One of them followed her and said they had checked and the prisoner indeed had the Medal of Valour. She snorted and said, "Really? He is no friend of Russia. He writes scurrilous articles against us. Let him go. We don't need problems with his government. Free him and let him go to Canada where he can do no real harm. Make sure he can't return to Lithuania." Alex was surprised to be released. He was to leave the country and never to return.

He walked to his hotel puzzled by the confrontation with Alisa. After a bath and a meal, he went to the address in the note checking that he was not being followed.

I am becoming paranoid, he thought.

The building was in a shabby apartment complex. He knocked on the door of the number given to him and was told to enter. When he did, Alisa moved into his arms and they kissed warmly. She had never forgotten him and had never married. She ended the war as a major and stayed in the army. She had elected to come to Lithuania because of her connection with him. She had arranged for him to be collected when she knew from her KGB contacts that he was in Lithuania. Alex laughed and thanked her for keeping tabs on him.

She said they were wasting time talking. She had longed for this moment and started to undress him. He responded by removing her civilian dress, and they were soon lost to the world. After a second spell of energetic lovemaking, she said she had something to tell him. Either they had been careless or the Canadian condoms were of poor quality, because soon after they parted, she realised she was pregnant. She had given birth to a son, Ivor. He had grown into a fine boy with decided musical talent. Her mother, a Moscow teacher, provided a home for him, taught him music, and told him that his father was a decorated war casualty. Alex was overwhelmed by the news and asked how he could see Ivor.

She said a meeting with their son was not possible, but as a result of their discussions in the far north, the horrid army commissars, and Russian cruelty in Lithuania, she had become disillusioned with Soviet Communism. She had tolerated the wartime commissars until one was responsible for the unjust demotion of the commander of her tank regiment, who was a fine, brave soldier. The commissar spies upset army commanders, and that led to confusion. She also found the behaviour of the victorious Soviet troops in Europe when they raped not only civilians but also Polish and Russian women held by the Germans reprehensible, and she severely punished miscreants under her command.

At first, the army work had been instructive. Then she moved to the security services still retaining her army rank. Of late, she had become tired of harassing people, many of whom were not subversive but only trying to express their views as they would in an open society. She was looking for an opportunity to escape and, if successful, to get Ivor out as well.

Alex hugged and kissed her and said that was the best news he had ever heard. He was confident he could smuggle her into Denmark where she could be cleared for entrance into Canada as a refugee or, if they married, as his wife. It only remained for him to fix passages on the Klaipeda to Copenhagen ferry. He would check a timetable at the ferry docks. She agreed to his scheme, and they arranged to meet the next morning at the apartment. They hugged once more and parted.

He had no trouble in getting into the dock area and was told to enquire at the ferry office, where he obtained a schedule of sailings. They met as arranged. It was decided that she would tell her staff that she had to go to Moscow for a few weeks on a secret mission. She did so and was driven to the train station where she walked to the head of the line for tickets and demanded a ticket to Moscow. The ticket clerk frowned at her arrogance. Her uniform scared him though, and he complied. She then went to a washroom where she changed into civilian clothes, put on a blond wig and dark glasses, and walked to the line carrying her uniform in a bag. She stopped when she saw an old lady whose luggage was marked "To Moscow." She told Alisa she had been visiting her soldier son and wondered how she would get on the crowded train.

Alisa thrust her ticket into the woman's hands and said she had been called away urgently. There was no time to cash the ticket, so she would like her to have it. She turned before the woman could get a good look at her, brushed aside her thanks, and caught a bus to the docks. She dumped her uniform in a large trash container and found Alex. They had decided that only if challenged in the dock area would she reveal her rank. She would then say that she was investigating a smuggling racket.

Alex handed the ferry ticket clerk his passport in which he left a large banknote and ordered two tickets to Copenhagen. Before the clerk could ask, he said that his companion wanted to shop in Denmark and did not have a passport.

"That is all right," said the clerk, "but she will have to buy a return ticket; we don't want to pay her fare back if the Danes evict her."

Alex paid the extra money, smiling at the clerk, and they boarded the ferry. Alisa told him about her fortuitous discovery of a woman who needed a train ticket to Moscow. "That was a bit of luck, because if the KGB check on my disappearance, they will assume I went to Moscow."

The ferry left on time. At Copenhagen, Alisa stayed in the dock area while Alex went to the Canadian embassy to obtain Canadian entry papers for her. An embassy official said he would have to see Alisa. He and Alex went to the docks where he was satisfied that she was a refugee. They returned to the embassy, and the official gave Alisa a document that would enable her to enter Canada as a refugee.

Alisa told Alex that said she had thought about her arrival in Canada. She knew that there was a Russian mole in the Canadian immigration department, and her name would stick out like a sore thumb if she arrived as Alisa Volgymko, and that would have unknown consequences. It was essential that they married immediately, and then she would arrive as Marija Greenus, a name that the mole would ignore.

Alex agreed. They were directed to a Roman Catholic Church where they explained their dilemma. The priest said he understood, but his hands were tied. He could not marry Alex to an unbeliever. There was no time to educate Alisa or for her to convert to his faith. Their best bet would be to approach the civil authorities at the city hall.

Alisa was angry and said Alex's religion was a farce; the only time he asked for help, he was turned down on doctrinal grounds. He said she should know that in any hierarchical system, rules had to be obeyed. He understood the priest's attitude.

They walked to the city hall. They were taken to an office where a smartly dressed man smiled when they asked for help. They wanted to marry immediately. He said that normally banns had to be published for three consecutive months to give people who might oppose a marriage a chance to do so. However, there was a provision for emergency weddings for which a larger fee than normal was charged. He wanted identification, and Alex handed him his passport and Alisa's refugee document. The official laughed. He said he had guessed it was one of those matches.

"You are honest," he said. "We have so many rascals using our country that we have to be careful. We are always happy to help

Canadians. I can remember your soldiers giving us much-needed food at the end of the war."

He issued a special licence, took them to a marriage officer, and acted as witness at the marriage ceremony. They thanked him for his help and called on the Canadian embassy where Alisa received a new Canadian entry form in the name of Marija Greenus. She said Marija was her real first name. Her mother called her Alisa because she was fond of Sweet Alison, better known as sweet alyssum.

"You are my Sweet Alison," she used to say.

Everybody called her Alisa, but she should have the correct details when she entered Canada. The official thought that was a lot of specious nonsense. He was used to dealing with refugees, knew there was a real reason for the subterfuge, and let the matter pass.

The couple celebrated with a lunch at a smart restaurant where Alex said she was a smooth liar, no doubt conditioned by the secret police with whom she cooperated. He would have to be on guard in future. She smiled and assured him that she would never deceive him and could not thank him enough for getting her out of Lithuania.

He held her hand and said he had dreamed of meeting her again. He had wondered often if she had survived the war. The ferocity on the Russian front must have been frightening. She said she had been wounded twice but not seriously. He would be pleased to know that she had come across some of their Murmansk trainees, who had performed well in battle. He told her briefly of his war that followed their parting. He said that, thanks to help from the government, he had been able to train as a doctor. Nevertheless, it had been difficult financially, and he had worked as a waiter to make ends meet. The struggle was worth it, as she would see when they reached his home. He assured her she would be comfortable there and among friends.

They flew to Paris and then to Toronto and Dorval airport in Montreal where Alex hired a car and drove to the Eastern Townships.

6
Deceit

The KGB was concerned that Colonel Volgymko had disappeared. Three KGB agents checked Alisa's office but could find no reference to a special mission to Moscow and her superior there denied all knowledge of such an activity. They checked the train tickets from Klaipeda to Moscow issued on the day of Alisa's departure and all had been used. The train conductor could not identify her. He said the train was always crowded with women and he hardly glanced at them as he punched their tickets.

The KGB advertised a picture of Alisa in uniform in a Klaipeda newspaper and asked anyone who had seen her to report to them. There were two responses. The first was from a lady who said she had seen Alisa in uniform go into a washroom at the train station but had not seen her exit because she had to go to another platform to meet someone. The police assumed Alisa had followed her normal practice of changing into civilian clothes, because they knew she hated the baleful looks she got from Lithuanians when in uniform. The second response was from a ticket clerk who said he remembered her well for her arrogance in jumping the queue and demanding an immediate ticket to Moscow.

"So," said the agent in charge of the investigation, "our important colonel travelled to Moscow and disappeared on a secret mission. That is that, except that at our training school, that old toughie, Dimitrov, said that when the solution to a crime or mystery was too obvious, one should look for something else. What if Colonel Volgymko got off the train before Moscow?"

"No, that was not possible. The conductor told me he only collected tickets after the last stop before Moscow so she must have been on the train."

"Her ticket was on the train, but was she? Could she have given her ticket to someone else? There is no evidence of a secret mission, and she may have ducked out of the country. Her colleagues said she had expressed concern at some of the official policies."

"You are stretching your imagination. People travelling from Klaipeda to Moscow are as scarce as Christians are at Lenin's tomb, so it is unlikely that she could have found someone to take her ticket. She was a decorated, highly placed officer and due for promotion. She had a good life with all the special privileges we would all like to have. She would be a fool to give that up. However, we should go through the motions before some deskbound bureaucrat criticises us. We have lost track of her on the train. Let's check the docks. It is easy to slip into Denmark on the ferry."

The ferry ticket clerk said he did not recognise Alisa from the photograph of her in the uniform of a colonel the agents showed him. When asked if there was anything unusual in the passengers recently, he said that a Canadian and his blond girlfriend had taken the ferry. Because she did not have a passport, she had bought a return ticket, but it had not been used so she must still be in Denmark where locals liked to shop. He did not say there was a resemblance between the blonde and the Colonel, but in view of the bribe he was given, he said nothing.

The detectives looked at the duplicates of tickets issued and noticed Alex's name. "Here is that Greenus again. The colonel gave him such rough treatment that he must have left in a hurry. Good riddance. He is keen on getting people to Canada and probably smuggled a relative out on the ferry. But there is no sign of the Colonel, so she must have gone to Moscow. After that, who knows?"

A month after Alisa's disappearance, the following notice appeared in *Pravda*:

War Hero Mystery

Colonel Alisa Volgymko, a decorated veteran of the Great Patriotic War, vanished mysteriously a month ago. She left her headquarters in Klaipeda, Lithuania, boarded a train for Moscow and has not been seen since. Despite widespread enquiries, the police have been unable to trace her, and it is feared that in the pursuit of her duties, she was accosted by one of Moscow's notorious crime gangs and murdered. Her mother, a Moscow schoolteacher, said her daughter always phoned when she came to the city, but she had not heard from her.

Alisa's mother did not believe the official story, because whatever the circumstances, she knew Alisa would have contacted her. She told Ivor that his mother was on a secret mission somewhere. The KGB's contacts with the Moscow gangs said there were no stories about a female KGB agent being murdered. The investigating agents shrugged their shoulders, and Alisa's file was closed.

***

After leaving Dorval airport, Alex and Alisa stopped in Drummondville to buy toiletries and pyjamas for Alisa. She was amazed at the variety of goods for sale.

"Why do you have so many kinds of toothbrushes and toothpaste?" she asked.

"The manufacturers compete with each other, and that is to the benefit of the consumers," said Alex.

"But surely if only one kind of each were made, the cost of production would drop."

127

"Monopolies never work, and customers might not like the single products."

Alisa's eyes opened further when Vera le Clus, at Alex's request, took her shopping for clothes. Again, the wide range of choice amazed her, and so did Vera, who did not recommend the first suitable item they saw but said they should shop around. Some of Alisa's immediate needs were met at a thrift store, and she could not believe that the excellent contents came from donations.

Alex's home was neat but lacked a feminine touch, and he asked Vera to buy additional furniture. Again, Alisa was astonished at the choices available.

"What happens if things are not sold?"

"Then we have sales, and one can pick up bargains. If a manufacturer continues to make articles the public does not want, he will go out of business."

"It sounds like a waste of resources to me."

Alisa kept fit with jogging, swimming, and aerobics and soon felt at home among Alex's friends. There were two things she needed to do. The first was to improve her French, and the second was to change her status from refugee to landed immigrant. She handled the first by enrolling in a Berlitz course and by speaking French to Alex. Her French improved rapidly.

She told Alex of her activities after they had parted at Murmansk. When she discovered she was pregnant, she continued with her work until towards the end of her term when she obtained leave to Moscow where Ivor was born. She left the baby in her mother's care and returned to the Arctic Circle.

Because of the success of the two tank sorties, it was decided to form a tank regiment at Murmansk to support the army in its drive to get rid of the German forces. Alisa was promoted to captain and given command of a squadron of tanks. She took Alex's lessons to heart and ensured that all her crews were trained in all aspects of tank warfare. That paid dividends, because her squadron was the most versatile in the regiment. When the Germans retreated from the north, she was transferred to Marshall Zhukov's army and took part in its advance towards Berlin.

She had three tanks shot under her, was wounded twice, and promoted to major. While she was in hospital after the second wound, a doctor diagnosed her with battle fatigue and she was sent to Moscow to recuperate. She was approached by an officer of the security force, who asked her what she planned to do when she had recovered. She said she had always been a soldier and was likely to continue as one. He pointed out that the war would soon be over and that further promotions would be unlikely. Would she not consider joining the security force? It would need to expand fast to cover the conquered territories in the Balkans, Central Europe, and probably Germany. She asked what the work would be. He said essentially secret detective work and action against the underground forces that were likely to oppose and harass Russian occupation personnel.

As far as the outside world was concerned, she would be an army colonel helping the Soviet administrators. "You could wear all those hard-earned decorations when you chose to do so," he said. She would need to spend at least two years in Moscow as a trainee. That thought appealed to her because she could be with Ivor, and she agreed to be interviewed. She easily passed the required tests and entered training, which was intensive.

She revelled in it though, and upon her graduation, she chose to go to the Baltic countries. She established herself in Lithuania because of the interest in it that Alex had created for her. She established a network of spies and helped to eradicate underground members until the constant persecution of innocent persons began to revolt her. She knew that Alex's family name was Girnius. She created records of all of them and knew when Alex came to Lithuania, because immigration offices had an alert against the name Greenus. By the time of his second visit, she was ready to seek his help in getting out of the country.

Alex said his war had been relatively mild compared with hers. She laughed at his description of his interview with an intelligence officer on arriving at Ottawa after Murmansk.

"Yes, we had base-wallahs who pushed veterans around too."

She was intrigued by his meeting Captain Gromyko and the fact that as an engineer he had operated a tank in battle. He said his earlier attention to his studies paid off, and he qualified to study medicine, and that was where he now stood.

Arthur Naujokas was with the RCMP special branch, which he joined after his years in army intelligence. Alex consulted him about Alisa. Arthur said that if she exposed what she knew of Russian spying in Canada, he would recommend a change in her status.

When approached, Alisa said she was willing to help him provided there was complete anonymity even in his department, because a leak would lead to the Russians discovering her identity.

Arthur agreed.

She told him that when she was being trained in espionage, they were still talking of the exposure by the Russian spy Gouzenko in Ottawa. There was annoyance and handwringing and plans to re-establish a spy network. There had apparently been some success, because when she was in Lithuania, she had been surprised by the amount of information the KGB received on Lithuanians in Canada. She cited Alex's interrogations in Lithuania as an example.

She said that undoubtedly there was a spy in the immigration department in Ottawa, whom Arthur should make it a priority to unmask. She told him that the second and third secretaries in Ottawa were KGB agents and that in addition to the immigration mole, there was someone feeding the Russians military secrets. She said there were Russians who came to Canada and obtained citizenship status and passports based on dead people, whose details were easily cribbed from gravestones. It was a joke that

Canada was a soft touch and provided the best way to get into the United States. She was sure a few phone taps would reveal enough to expose the spies, but that was Arthur's province.

He thanked her. He said it would be unwise for him to clear her before the immigration mole was uncovered, because that person might see the application and blow Alisa's cover. She said that before long, she would have to appear before an immigration board to justify her staying in Canada. She would be exposed to public scrutiny, so he should hurry. He said her marriage to Alex should ease things. Arthur worked closely with the immigration department and told her it might be possible to twist some arms to get the landed immigrant status awarded privately.

He reported a week later that he had been successful by telling a friendly contact that Alisa had given some vital information, and if she could be processed quickly, she would divulge more material of national importance.

"There are trade-offs all the time, and this was an easy one. We have traced the spy in the immigration department. When I give the nod, you and Alex should report to Neil Carruthers in Room 15 of the immigration department in Ottawa, and he'll help you. As a quid pro quo, I would like some more information to back my case."

She said she could help if there were Russian radio interceptions to translate, and she could explain the Russian coding system, as the codes were changed daily. She paid weekly visits to a safe house in Ottawa where she read, translated, and analysed material collected by radio operators. She also read *Pravda* and other papers, from which she prepared economic and political reports. She had learnt English at the postwar training school and used it in the reading of English newspapers and other material.

One day, Alisa asked Alex if she could attend a church service, and he said he would be delighted to escort her. They attended Mass the following Sunday. The decorations, the incense, the hand-rung bells, the gowned priests and servers, and the music bewildered her.

Karl Marx was right; I feel drugged, she thought. *I am relaxed and now understand what he meant about religion being the opiate of the masses.* Despite her misgivings, the large congregation and their responses to the priest's graces impressed her.

She asked Alex why the priest and attendants wore so many different gowns. Why did they not wear the same clothes as other men? He explained that the gowns indicated what period of the year was being celebrated. Others denoted rank, making it easy to identify a bishop or cardinal. She was puzzled with the priests' titles. He said Roman Catholicism was a hierarchy with the Pope at its head, then next in order came cardinals, archbishops, bishops, monsignors, and priests.

"But where do the women come in? I came across nuns and convents in Lithuania but no female priests. As you know, in Russia, gender means nothing, and women can rise to top positions."

"You have raised an important point about women best left to the Pope and his cardinals to handle. You see Christ only had male disciples, and the Church has followed that example. He was unmarried, so priests have to take a vow of celibacy."

"I cannot understand that. Russian Orthodox priests can have wives, and that Church permits contraception, divorce, and some abortions. When will your Church modernise itself? Also, I cannot understand why you call your priests 'Father' and yet they are not allowed to have children. That is odd. How did that come about? Is that the same with all Christians?"

"No, other churches allow their priests and ministers to marry, and they have different titles."

"But if you all follow one God and all use the Bible, some of you must be wrong. If your God did not specifically say that priests had to be celibate, then it is just a rule designed by humans. You could change it without upsetting your God—assuming he exists. I am puzzled too, because I heard that Muslims and men in the Mormon religion can have more than one wife."

"Yes, it is complicated, and there are differences just as there are among people in the USSR. Despite its imperfections, I am satisfied with my faith, as I so often explained in our discussions in the Arctic Circle. It is so encompassing that I can assure you that the priest at our church will welcome you. He will not chide you for your Marxist beliefs, blunted as they are by your postwar experiences. You know that I enjoy arguing with you—your eyes sparkle, you look earnest, and then you laugh. I will not impose my prejudices on you, and I am the happiest man alive to be your husband. I should read you the story of Ruth, who was with strangers as you are and was described as 'Ruth amid the alien corn.' I should warn you, the Bible is flexible, and I'll be able to produce quotations to beat any of your arguments."

"You go ahead. As long as you continue to love me, you can talk all day long. I am intrigued with your religion. It is so powerful in Quebec. It has so many good people running it. Is it the same elsewhere?"

"Yes. One can attend a Catholic service anywhere and feel at home."

She continued to attend services and had long conversations with Father Masse, the local priest. Her religious discussions with Alex became less confrontational, and she asked what she would have to do to attend Mass as a full member. He told her that she would have to be baptised and receive instruction before her first Communion. He was delighted with her attitude and prayed that she would be converted.

In August 1958, Alisa was excited because the Moscow Youth Orchestra, of which Ivor was a member, was to tour the United States and Canada. It would perform in Montreal in September. She and Alex discussed the possibility of their son joining them and decided they would somehow meet him and ask him to make a choice. It was planned that Alex would contact Ivor during an intermission, give him a note signed by Alisa, and, if he agreed, he would take him to her.

At the intermission Alex approached Ivor and gave him Alisa's note, in which she suggested he follow the instructions the bearer of the note would give him. That would enable them to meet at long last. At the bottom of the note, Alex wrote, "At the end of the performance, go to the last cubicle of the nearest washroom and stay there when others leave. I will be there to help you."

The boy did as he was told, and Alex gave him a gaudy anorak and cap to wear. As directed, Ivor left the cubicle door locked, climbed into the next cubicle, and followed Alex out of the building. When the rest of the orchestra moved to their bus, the leaders missed Ivor.

One of the boys said he had gone to the washroom. The director of the orchestra found the door of the last cubicle locked and hammered on it to no avail. One of the boys climbed over the wall of the cubicle and said that the last one was empty. They searched everywhere but could not find Ivor. The director had been instructed at all times to guard against defections. He knew his days as director would be numbered unless Ivor was found. To avoid unnecessary publicity, he kept quiet but contacted the Russian embassy. They told him to do nothing until he returned to Russia where it was decided to forget the incident.

Alex drove to the restaurant where Alisa was waiting. She and Ivor hugged and kissed. She told him that he must have wondered at her long silence. He said he had assumed she was on a secret mission, but he did not know it was in Canada. She smiled and said she had left Russia voluntarily to marry Alex, the man who had collected him that evening. He should remain with them because his rescuer was none other than the decorated soldier, his father. The two males looked at each other for a moment. Alex hugged Ivor and said he had only known about him a short while. They felt they should stick together, but if Ivor decided to stay with the orchestra they would understand.

Ivor frowned and said everything was such a shock, but he was tired of public performances, travelling, and the constant propaganda they were fed. It was not believed in the countries they visited. He would stay with them. Alex and Alisa were delighted, and Ivor returned to Drummondville with them.

Alex had no trouble obtaining residence authority for his son. Ivor's general education had not been neglected, and, like many gifted musicians, he was good at mathematics. He was enrolled in the local school where his French improved rapidly and his initial hesitation to mix with the other pupils soon disappeared.

At the assembly one morning, the teacher in charge asked if anyone could play the piano, because the usual pianist was unwell. Ivor hesitated and then held up his hand. He was asked to play the national anthem and a hymn from the music provided. He studied the score and then indicated that he was ready and started to play. The teacher was astounded at his playing, and after the assembly, she called him over and asked where he had learned to play. Conscious of the need to preserve his anonymity, he said his grandmother had taught him. She tried to persuade him to join the music class. He said he preferred hockey, leaving the teacher puzzled.

When Ivor told Alisa about the incident, she said they should find a way for him to resume his playing. He said he longed to play the organ, but it had not been possible in Moscow, and he wondered if he could learn it locally. Alex said he would talk to Father Masse. The priest said it rested with the organist and choirmaster, who was himself a talented musician.

He agreed to take Ivor on as a pupil, and the boy was soon at home on the organ. Most of the music was religious, with Bach's work dominating his repertoire. The choirmaster was curious about why his pupil seemed so uncomfortable in the church. Ivor told him he was not religious and was unused to the Catholic symbols and statues, but he enjoyed the music.

One Friday, Father Masse came to the Greenus home with a favour to ask of Ivor. The choirmaster was unwell, and he wondered if Ivor would play the organ on Sunday. The boy said it was impossible, because he did not know the service and could not conduct the choir. The priest told him that was not necessary because the singers were well trained and would follow the music as they did when the choirmaster was playing. Secretly, Ivor was excited by the challenge but feared he would wreck a solemn service. To Alex's delight, Alisa, who realised it was a great opportunity for her son, urged him to accept the invitation.

Ivor arranged to practise the music the following morning with the proviso that if he felt uncomfortable, he could withdraw. He studied the order of service and was puzzled by everything except where music was indicated. He practised his part twice and decided he was comfortable with his performance. He then selected some Bach music he had brought and began to play.

He relished the moment and was so absorbed that he did not notice that the priest and two others had entered the church and were standing fascinated by his playing. When he paused, the priest waved to him and asked if he would be there on Sunday. Ivor said yes, but he would need signals during the service, because he did not understand the Latin words still used in that church. The priest told him to watch his face and he would be fine. On Sunday, he was to join the choir in the robing room, where he would be given a cassock. Ivor looked puzzled until the priest explained it was a gown that members of the choir wore.

On Sunday, after playing the introductory music, Ivor sat bemused by the service; suddenly, he noticed the choir looking at him, and with a start, he glanced at the priest who gave him a slight nod. Ivor returned to the music and did not again falter. In the changing room, the singers told him they had enjoyed his playing with its slight variations, which even reminded one of them of a concert pianist's style. Ivor smiled and thanked them for following him after his initial hesitation.

The priest was delighted with Ivor and asked him to be at the church the following Wednesday when a specialist would be present to tune the organ. He had been an accomplished organist, who, on retirement, devoted his time to servicing church organs.

Ivor told the visitor that some notes were out of tune and that one of the pedals was defective. The man thought Ivor really must have a musical ear and mischievously asked him to run through his testing music to see if he still thought it needed attention. Ivor played for a bit, stopped, and pointed out what he thought was wrong, and the tuner laughed and said he was right. When he had finished tuning, he asked Ivor to play something of his choice, and the boy selected some of Bach's organ music. The listener was impressed. He said that if Ivor intended to study further to let him know. The tuner told Father Masse there was a mystery about the boy, because his musical knowledge was profound and he had a polished touch. The priest offered no explanation. Alex had explained Alisa's and Ivor's backgrounds to him.

Ivor had grown into a tall, athletic youth, whose delicate fingers belied his strength. He was an enthusiastic hockey player. Alisa became that mother beloved of other hockey mums—someone with a car willing to take players endless kilometres to play teams in the various leagues. Ivor's team did well and won the local league and then the regional. Ivor was a fast skater with excellent game sense. Invariably, he would pass the puck to a teammate in a better position than he, unlike others who looked for the glory of scoring goals.

His hockey match play ended after a game his team lost. The coach, like many of his contemporaries, was a loudmouthed bully. He started in on Ivor, haranguing him for not scoring the winning goal and instead passing the puck to a teammate who fluffed his shot. He had heard the coach upset at his teammates before and had discussed this with Alex. He told Ivor to maintain his cool. Hockey was not the end of the world, and he should not allow the coach to rattle him.

Ivor stood up and said he did not agree with the coach. He had trained them to pass the puck to fellow players who had a better chance of scoring. That, he asserted, was what he had done. He said he was sick and tired of the coach's bullying and his ridiculing of players in public. He glared at the coach and told him he did not intend to be the victim of more abuse and had played his final game.

Ivor's teammates tried to persuade him to stay, but his mind was made up. Alisa was angry with him, because she supported the coach's vigorous, direct approach. She felt it was good for many of the boys, who took life too easily, to be shouted at and brought to task. She enjoyed the travelling, meeting new people, seeing new places, and watching her son performing well on the ice. She was annoyed that those days would be over. Alex agreed with Ivor, and the matter ended.

The following spring Alisa, who often stayed away for days at a time, presumably on her foreign affairs work, was not at home when Alex returned after a week's absence at a conference. He wondered what had happened. He found the answer in a priority post letter on his desk.

It was from Alisa and shocked him.

> *Good-bye, Alex. I have returned to Russia.*
>
> *I leave Canada with many regrets and have a confession to make. I was an army colonel, but as I told you, I served in the NKVD and later the KGB. I remain in its service.*
>
> *We kept a file on you and knew all about your brother Stasys and your visits to Doctor Makauskas at the Klapeida Hospital. He has been sent to Siberia for his treachery. Surely, you wondered why you were allowed to enter Lithuania a second time after all the condemnatory articles you published?*
>
> *You collected a lot of information on your first visit and copies of the spiteful stuff you wrote are in your KGB file. Our immigration officials were instructed to advise me immediately any Greenuses or Girniuses entered Lithuania, and on your second visit, we tailed you everywhere. You gave us the slip after leaving the hospital and that told us you were suspicious. We found you easily enough later when you were arrested, and we made our plans to escape.*

It was not difficult to make love with you. I enjoyed it and felt patriotic in encouraging you. You fell like a ton of bricks in helping me to escape. You may be surprised to hear that the old lady at the train station was an agent of ours. She enjoyed the unexpected opportunity of going to Moscow. I thought you would be suspicious of someone coming all the way from that city to Lithuania to see a son, but you weren't. And do you think that normally we would have accepted your feeble story to the ferry ticket clerk? He was one of the thousands of Lithuanian patriots who work for us. You probably call them collaborators, but that is your choice. Anyway, we were allowed out by design.

It was a wonderful break for me to meet Arthur with whom you cleared the way. There was a mole in your immigration department. I betrayed him, and that improved my image. It did not matter much, because he was about to be fired by us—he was a gambler and kept asking for more money.

The easy access I had to the RCMP offices made my spying easy. It is amazing what one hears when accepted as a loyal person. In Ottawa, I used to read Soviet newspapers and your country's agents' material. I reported their level of knowledge of Russian affairs to my superiors. They were pleased with that and to have leads to your agents in Russia. I think three were eliminated.

My main job was to collect information on Canada's nuclear activities and links with the US research. Did you know you have some brilliant scientists? There was material everywhere. You may have wondered why I was keen on all those long hockey trips with Ivor and his teammates. I made notes of everything I saw and *heard. People open up to visitors, and it is surprising what an intelligent questioner can elicit.*

I was not really concerned about the bullying coach who caused Ivor to resign from the hockey team. I was cross because of the ending of the trips for which I volunteered that provided me with opportunities for fact gathering. I recruited agents for our spy ring and have been promoted because of my work.

I know you had hopes of converting me to Christianity. I kept that alive by occasional church visits and conversations with you and your priests. I must confess I was impressed with them and their devotion to duty. I learnt of many of their kind acts. They opened the door for Ivor to resume his musical bent. They were good to him. I sensed he would abandon Communism for Christianity. In my guise as an escapee from Russia, I could not disabuse his mind of the fallacies of your faith.

You told me about St. Paul seeing the light on the way to Damascus, a definitive point in the Christian mythology. At the NKVD training school, there were religious scholars who taught us to debunk the fallacies of all religions. St. Paul might have seen the light, but he remained a Jew. He did not convert to Christianity because that did not exist. He was also a married man, as were many of your Popes, so where your celibacy fallacy came from, I do not know. I must admit I have seen Christianity in a new light and will continue to study it.

That is all. By the way, I regret deceiving you. Were you not surprised that I, associated with what to you

*is a repressive regime, suddenly recanted and fled with
you from Lithuania?*

*It was my patriotic duty to do so. It added to my
credibility as a reformed woman when Ivor joined us.
I am sad to leave him but know you will take good
care of him.*

*I told you one of my reasons for leaving Lithuania
was the despicable action of the commissar who caused
the demotion of the colonel of my regiment. That was
rubbish. The commissar praised him, and the colonel
was promoted only to be killed by a Fascist shell as
we advanced to give freedom to the people of Eastern
Europe.*

*It has been tense for me lately. You noticed this when
you asked if anything was wrong. Your diagnostic
senses were correct. I was caught looking at some secret
files. I knew my excuse would not last long, and my
superiors told me to get out.*

*You must think I am one awful, deceitful bitch, as
indeed I am in your eyes but not in Moscow's. I must
thank you for the kindness shown to me and Ivor and
hope my betrayal of your and others' trust does not lead
you into trouble. Do not think only evil of me.*

*I prevented the deportation of your two sisters and
their families from Taurage. I used their husbands'
occupations as an excuse—they make much-needed
tiles and bricks. Did you not wonder how your mother
obtained accommodation in a retirement home while
more deserving cases were turned down? Again, I was
responsible. I ensured that emigration papers were
issued to your mother and sister. I also saved your
Father Staugaitis from deportation. The river rescue*

141

of that child was staged. It was known that it was his habit to walk to the river in the late afternoon, and when he was seen approaching the river, the screaming started and the girl moved into the water. Had he not saved her, he would have been sent to Siberia, but she was in no danger. She is a good swimmer and would have reached the riverbank with ease. I was also easy on your brother Stasys. Your partisans were careless and no match for our professionals. They have been wiped out, and resistance has ended. It was our practice to send the families of known underground dissidents to gulags in frozen Siberia as a warning to others. You and Stasys, with your illegal activities, exposed your family to that treatment. I kept all the files of members of the Girnius family and saved them from that.

You are an innocent and did not question the series of coincidences affecting your family and your friend, the priest. By the way, he will have to be careful, as I can no longer shadow him. I am not returning to Lithuania. Do not come to Lithuania again on the strength of your Medal of Valour. Because you obviously side with Soviet enemies, the award has been revoked. I know that in the eyes of your Church you are not married, so go ahead if you find a suitable wife. I hope you do and that she is worthier than I.

I dearly wanted to stay in Canada and learn more about your Church, but certain forces made that impossible. I quietly read much of your Bible, and forgiveness is frequently mentioned. If I was fully convinced that your religion is correct and embraced it, I could take comfort in the Lord's Prayer: "As we forgive those that trespass against us." Will you ever forgive me? I shall never know. I must suffer in silence.

I shall never forget those Arctic days and those we enjoyed in Canada in memory of which you have Ivor, the symbol of the love we shared. I know you will look after him.

Farewell.
Alisa

Somehow, the betrayal did not surprise Alex. It explained her long absences. He wondered what the forces were that caused her to leave. He was saddened. He would miss her energy, dynamism, and love, but he was not bitter. On the contrary, he felt sorry for her and hoped she knew what she was doing. Her sudden rejection of Communism had puzzled him. He often wondered what role she had played in the Soviet's brutal treatment of the Baltic people. Now he knew; she was part and parcel of the obnoxious regime, and she had led him by the nose. He remembered with sorrow the lunch in Copenhagen when he said she was a polished liar and she said she would never deceive him.

He phoned Arthur and told him Alisa had gone. He was told not to worry; his department had been suspicious from the beginning that a high-ranking Russian officer, known to have been active in the merciless interrogation of Lithuanian activists and in the mass deportations of innocent citizens, should suddenly want to escape from Lithuania and had done so easily.

"You were the dupe, Alex, but we said nothing to you because we wanted to see how she worked. She was under constant surveillance and, no doubt due to what she thought was our slackness, became careless. We were about to act when she left. She led us to her contact, and he has been declared *persona non grata* and kicked out. We gave her the names of three of our agents in Russia and that led her to believe we had swallowed her story.

What she did not know was that we had discovered that they were double agents, and we were glad to get rid of them.

"I am sorry she deceived you and that I could not warn you. I am sure you understand that."

"Arthur, thank you for explaining things. I realise your hands were tied. I was indeed surprised when Alisa said she wanted to escape from Lithuania but forgot my qualms by loving her. It is obvious she was trained to lie and deceive, and I swallowed the bait hook, line, and sinker. You know that the Russians have done terrible things in our old country, and she must have blood on her hands, but love blinded me. We were attracted physically and were lovers in Archangel and Murmansk, but war conditions often lead to unreal assumptions. She had an enquiring mind, and we always enjoyed our discussions. We were often at loggerheads, but she never dropped a hint of what she was doing. I shall miss her, and I regret the path she has chosen."

"Alex, I understand, but forget the sorrow and get on with your life. You told me you have plans to buy an old logging camp. Why don't you go ahead? I would enjoy cutting and sawing trees again with you. Immerse yourself in that, and pray for the freedom of Lithuania."

"You're right. I'll do something to fill the gap caused by her departure. Fortunately, I have Ivor, who declined to accompany her, to educate. I look forward to that. What classical condolences can you quote this time?"

"I told you when we first met that books hold all the answers. You can start with Otis and his alliterative admonition: 'Destructive, damnable, deceitful woman!' I wonder why he didn't make a job of it and used 'dame' not 'woman.' Milton asks: 'Hast thou betrayed my credulous innocence, With vizor'd falsehood and base forgery?' You should again read Shakespeare's Iago and Brutus, classic deceivers. Finally, think of Henley's 'My head is bloody but unbowed.' By the way, we were helped in our efforts to trace Soviet agents by an acquaintance of yours, Paul Johnstone. He used to laugh his head off when he recounted your flippant attitude to his admonitions after your narrow escape in a bombed building. He taught criminology at an English university before the war and the British secret Service, MI5 grabbed him at the end of hostilities. He is familiar with German and spent some time rounding up nasty Nazi bastards. He was sent to Ottawa to follow clues on Russian spies, and that is how we met. He masqueraded as an army officer. He told me you knew a lot about cricket, whatever that is. He said you bowled him over with your knowledge."

"In the war, he persuaded John and me to smarten up. We met him in Canada. He postured as an aide-de-camp but indicated he was on a hush-hush mission. I am glad he helped you. We misjudged him. He is a brave man."

"He has been transferred to Washington. I do not envy him his job. Britain is in bad odour there after the Burgess and Maclean scandals."

"Tell me, had Alisa stayed, would she have been prosecuted?"

"Yes, she was a Canadian citizen; the penalties would have been severe. She would certainly have been jailed."

"Well, she escaped that disgrace. Good-bye, Arthur, and again, thank you."

To himself, he said, "That is the end of my Arctic connection."

7
A KBG Colonel

Alisa had enjoyed her days in Canada where her intrigues added spice to an otherwise uneventful life. She could not believe how naïve everyone was, including the high officials with whom she dealt. She regretted her betrayal of Alex and the loss of Ivor, but she had long ago decided to sacrifice whatever was necessary to promote Russia's interests and her career.

She returned to a warm welcome by the head of the KGB's First Chief Directorate, Marshall Ivor Gorbachev, a squat, muscular man, whose face bore the scars of a shrapnel burst.

"Comrade Volgymko, you performed well. Our Canadian records are up-to-date, and thanks to you, we have good moles in place. You know my directorate deals with foreign espionage, and we valued your services in that activity. You deserve a rest before your next assignment.

"It will be with the Seventh Department that deals with the surveillance of Soviet nationals and foreigners. You should find that easy with your knowledge of languages. It has been decided that you should frequent international gatherings in Russia to uncover subversives. It is simple for undesirable people to enter a country with delegates to international events.

"We are certain our enemies use that method to spy on us. Their representatives must be rooted out. You will have unlimited power to apprehend and interrogate subversives. You have an excellent reputation for that work. It must have been traumatic to abandon a husband and son, and you deserve a rest. Take a month's leave and relax. After that, report to General Sergei Sikorsky, and he'll brief you in detail."

"Thank you, Comrade Marshal. I look forward to being myself once again, not a poseur about to become a Christian. You have no idea of the power that religion has in Quebec. Old Karl Marx was right with his 'opiate of the masses' phrase. He made an unwitting pun, because it was one Mass after another in Canada. Do you think religion will make a comeback in Russia?"

"We allow some religious observances, but this generation has abandoned religion for the greater benefit of the people. It has no hope of a resurrection."

"The Catholics believe in life after death and talk of the resurrection."

"There is no proof of their belief. What is evident is that there is trouble in their ranks. Some of their priests and bishops are sexual predators. What can you expect with celibacy? Other religions believe in reincarnation. The Greeks worshipped the sun. Some Indians burn widows. Others leave food in coffins. Some believe there is a devil. Dante was famous for his description of hell. And they talk of miracles! It is all a lot of stupid nonsense designed to control people's thoughts and actions just as the Romanovs did. I am pleased you were not deceived. Read our latest directives. You will soon be in the groove again, free of the Christian mythology."

Alisa wondered if she would have that freedom. She could not avoid an admiration for Father Masse and other well-educated men devoted to the service of others. Something mystic inspired them.

She spent a month with her mother, who bemoaned the loss of Ivor.

"He is a Russian and a gifted musician. You should not have left him in Canada, a country without a cultural background and full of Capitalists who exploit people."

"Mother, I did my best to persuade him to accompany me, but he was well into the Canadian Christian way of life. He enjoyed his father's company. He played church music. He regularly sent his love to you. Losing him and abandoning a man I love are sacrifices I have made for our country."

"Be careful you don't carry your patriotism too far. You have a high rank and many honours, and you could stir up jealousies. Your next step would be to general. That would be unusual even in the Soviet. Here one is promoted on merit, not on who you know, as in the West. There are no biases against women. Nevertheless, there is always jealousy."

"I know and will be careful. I was praised for the clever way I got into Canada and into the heart of its security system. I even pretended that I would convert to Christianity and nearly did. The Roman Catholic religion is very powerful in Quebec, and my conversion facade made contact with people easy. I am now proficient in English and French, and my future work should be free of danger."

"I was told in confidence that you were in Canada married to your Murmansk lover. I smiled because I knew you were up to some mischief. I am pleased that your new work will be peaceful. I shuddered during the Patriotic War when you fought in the tanks. You were excused frontline duty after you were wounded but insisted on returning to the fighting. I know you have been involved in rough work. A friend told me you are known as the 'Iron Maiden.'"

"I am hardly a maiden with a son to my credit. I am a disciplinarian and stand no nonsense from weaklings. I do not use the torture of the type the original Iron Maiden inflicted. Nevertheless, there are times when one must be vigorous in the examination of traitors and subversives. I do not object to the title. It puts fear into my victims. Sometimes, they are relieved with my mild treatment. In order to avoid the cruel activities for which I am unjustifiably notorious, they confess readily."

"Alisa, please relax during your leave. There are a series of excellent piano recitals this month, and you should accompany me to them. You could lose your stress and lessen the sadness of Ivor's absence by listening to performances superior to mine. If at any time you want me to play your favourite pieces, you only need to ask."

"Thank you. I will gladly go with you to the performances. You can play Rachmaninoff at any time."

"You have always liked Sergei. His preludes are always a joy to play."

Alisa enjoyed listening to music with her mother. *Russia really has an artistic soul,* she thought. *We have our music, and the Bolshoi Theatre still leads the world. There is the Pushkin Museum, the Hermitage, and the Moscow Circus. Our artists' work is in demand everywhere. Our Marxist ideologies are accepted in all parts of the world with China leading the way. Our armies beat the Germans and enabled us to free most of Europe. Unfortunately, American and British Capitalists, the real warmongers, are promoting anti-Soviet feelings. We have stood firm in the so-called Cold War. We are confronted with human rights activists, who publicise wrong accounts of our activities in Hungary and other occupied countries. We have to keep order and deal with underground organisations. Our actions are mild compared with America's treatment of its black people and the cruelty of South Africa's neo-Nazi government. All in all, it is great to be a Russian.*

She attended the gymnasium for senior army officers and after workouts swam until tired. She cycled in the city, and when the time came to report for duty, she was fit and eager to start her new work.

Her controller, General Sergei Sikorsky, was a slim, athletic, and bronzed man with sharp blue eyes and blond hair. He held degrees in engineering and psychology and spoke several languages.

He had been a fighter pilot with an impressive number of victories and had a reputation for looking after his workers.

He greeted Alisa warmly and welcomed her to her new activities. He explained what they were and handed her a dossier that contained the full details of her duties, staff, and contacts. She was to attend international conferences in Russia to clean out unwanted delegates and to monitor the activities of Russian attendees. She was told that if she needed backup support, she should contact the nearest KGB office and, if necessary, produce the authorization she would find in the dossier he had given her.

"Do not hesitate to obtain help in tracking and detaining subversives. Your work will be discreet. You will pose as a member of Russian delegations, so that you can move freely among those attending conferences. There is a list of planned conferences in the dossier. The scientific ones are important. We will let you know if there is a particular assignment on which you should concentrate. Keep an eye on our delegates. Some of them may have ideas of leaving the country with their specialised scientific knowledge. They could use contacts at a conference to pave the way for their departure."

Alisa thanked the general and said she was pleased to be working with him. He laughed and said it might be difficult for an accomplished tank officer used to driving hard at the opposition to be passive and discreet. Her Canadian episode, however, had indicated how smart she was, and he was certain she would be successful in unearthing unwelcome characters.

Her first conference covered the ecological and evolutionary aspects of animal behaviour. She read the background material and could follow the reference to Pavlov and his dogs but little else. This did not worry her, because the genuine Russian delegates would carry the day with her and her staff in the background.

Her team was provided with biographies and pictures of all the delegates. Only two of them attracted her attention. One was an American who was absent from several sessions. He was tracked to a brothel where he was secretly photographed. The films would be handy for possible future blackmails. The other was suspect because he had frequent sessions with a Russian scientist. Their rooms were searched, and their phones bugged without any results. An agent heard them discussing snakes and thought it was a code word until another agent heard them discussing a snake lovers' club in India. It transpired that they were ophiologists who shared an interest in snakes, hence their discussions.

"So they were not slippery culprits after all," said Alisa.

"They were mathematicians. Good adders, I suppose," her deputy responded.

"Not snakes in the grass, as we suspected."

Alisa's subordinates were used to her wit, and her deputy smiled.

"Colonel, we win some; we lose some," he said.

She smiled. "We'll keep digging and will unearth some idiots before long."

Subsequent conferences followed a pattern similar to the first. Alisa and her team discovered several undesirable foreign characters. They were persuaded to leave before the end of the conference concerned. Alisa's team were alerted to a scientist who planned to defect and was overheard speaking to an English delegate on the subject. Alisa interrogated him, and after some persuasion, including pictures of him arm in arm with young boys, he admitted he wanted to leave Russia. He was stripped of his academic position and sent to Siberia to ponder his stupidity.

Alisa enjoyed visiting the cities in which conferences were held, and she learned more about Russia. Her work became routine. It offered little excitement until she enrolled at a conference in Tbilisi on wine production. She was interested in wine and attended several sessions and a formal dinner.

She paid little attention to the guests until she saw the person opposite her looking at her. She was startled and asked in Russian, "How is Ivor?" She received a blank stare, and the delegate, a Spaniard named Felipe Jiminez, asked his companion in French, the language of the conference, what she had said.

"She asked how Ivor was."

Jiminez shook his head and said he did not understand. Alisa apologised in French for her action and said he reminded her of someone she knew.

Alisa was upset with her lapse at dinner. The Spaniard's discomfort at her question was noticeable. She could not believe how much he resembled Alex. It was unusual for a Spaniard to have blue eyes, and his nose and teeth reminded her of him. The uncanny features of the Spaniard kept her awake, and she relived her happy moments with Alex and Ivor. At the dinner when she saw the Spaniard, her mind had drifted to them, hence her question. She realised that a connection between her former husband and an accredited Spanish wine farmer was a remote possibility. However, she remembered one of her KGB trainers, Josef Dimitrov, a tough, no-nonsense investigator, had impressed upon his students the need to consider all possibilities, no matter how remote.

She told an assistant to get their Spanish agents to check on Felipe Jose Jimenez. The next afternoon, she received their report, from which it was clear that Jimenez was a grape farmer in the area in which he was born. He was known for his enterprise in introducing new vines to the region. He was friendly with a Catholic priest and was married to a noted equestrian and trainer. An agent told her he had searched Jimenez's room and papers he had left in a hotel safety box and had found nothing incriminating. His phone was bugged, but it too revealed nothing.

I need not worry after all, she thought. But she did miss Ivor and wondered if she had done the right thing in leaving him in Canada.

Her staff noticed that Jiminez was friendly with a Russian delegate, Stephan Gromyko, and mixed most of the time with the Russians. An agent spoke to Gromyko. He learned that he was interested in visiting Spanish wine farms to examine the country's successful defeat of the phylloxera, a devastating disease. Jiminez had promised to help him.

Alisa was recalled to Moscow after a successful two years attending conferences and weeding out undesirables. She was given a job in the city interrogating a variety of people detained by the KGB. Her tough tactics strengthened her reputation as the Iron Maiden.

She had not forgotten the incident in Tbilisi. She had encouraged Gromyko to go to Spain, where he was to check on Jiminez's background. His report confirmed Alisa's suspicion that the Spaniard was a phoney.

Gromyko established that Jiminez was an immigrant with an excellent knowledge of horses and farrowing. He showed Gromyko where he claimed to have lived as a boy in a village. It would have been impossible to have trained horses or to have shod them there. By chance, Gromyko saw a war memorial in the village inscribed with Jiminez's name. "He died a hero fighting for General Franco."

"I see it all now. Jiminez is Stasys Girnius, who served in the cavalry and then practised subversive activities in Lithuania. He somehow escaped to Spain and became involved in the wine industry. He would have learnt Russian at school, so he was sent to Tbilisi to spy on us. He has been a little too clever because Gromyko said that Jiminez would be attending a session at the famous Anapakian Zonal Experimental Station of Viticulture and Wine Making in Anapa. If he does, we'll nab him there and send him to Lithuania to face a trial for his illegal activities."

She arranged for Jiminez's arrest at the end of the session in Anapa and was delighted to receive news that he had been caught and was on his way to Moscow.

Gromyko had taken Felipe to the airport. The Spaniard thanked him and bade him farewell. He obtained a boarding card and headed for his plane, but three men stopped him and told him to accompany them. He shrugged his shoulders and indicated he could not understand what they were saying. They said he would find out soon enough. Each grabbed an arm and pulled him towards them.

Felipe sensed that he was in trouble and would have to guard his words. He was taken to a room, where the three men identified themselves as KGB agents. One said in French that they were suspicious of his actions in Russia and wanted to question him about them.

"I am a Spanish wine farmer invited here to study valuable experiments in producing grapes in cold conditions. You can check with the Anapskian researchers who invited me to Anapa."

"May we see your passport?"

Felipe handed it over, and it was opened at the page with his photograph and name.

"You are Felipe Jimenez born in Penaranda, Spain?"

"Yes."

"We don't believe you. We think you are a Spanish spy, who started his evil work at a Viticulture Conference in Tbilisi in1965," said the investigator. He switched from French to Russian and said, "I am right, am I not?"

Felipe said he did not understand and asked to phone the Anapskian Experiment Station.

"You are not calling anyone. Our instructions are to send you to Moscow where our colleagues will get the truth from you. Take him away," the interrogator said.

Felipe was moved to a military aerodrome and flown to Moscow, where he was bundled into a car and driven to the downtown area. He hoped he would not be incarcerated in the notorious Lubyanka prison. It seemed that one of the guards had read his mind, because he told the driver to take the next turn on the right to the KGB Lubyanka headquarters.

"I hope our Spanish friend behaves himself; the boys can get rough in there," he added.

Felipe was dispirited by the comment and wondered what lay ahead. He was marched into the building past a guard point and down a long, dark passage at the end of which he was pushed into a room. He was told to stand until an officer arrived. It was Colonel Volgymko, who entered with two burly men. She was an imposing figure in her uniform with its rows of medal ribbons. She smiled at Felipe and in Russian said, "So we meet again."

He did not reply, and she continued, "You know if you had responded to my question at the viticulture conference dinner, I would have thought no more of your remarkable likeness to your brother, my former husband, who writes scurrilous articles about our activities in Lithuania. But I wondered why you spent so much time with the Russian delegates, even though you bluffed that you did not speak our language.

"My training makes me suspicious, and we persuaded Gromyko to keep close to you, obtain an invitation to Spain, and then invite you back to Russia. That is what happened. Poor Doctor Gromyko, he rather likes you and did not want to work with us, but when he heard it was that or his rebel father being sent to Siberia he had no choice. He is quite good with a camera, and here is a shot he took of a war memorial in Penaranda. As you see, you were killed fighting for the nasty Fascists against our Communist comrades. Of course, Christians like you believe in resurrections, but we do not and knew something was wrong.

"Here is one of your humble homes you pointed out to him. You could not have ridden horses from it as a boy, as you told Gromyko you did. Here you are replacing the shoe on a horse in an expert fashion. You did not learn that in Spain. Then before you rode a horse at the viticulture institute, you used more Russian words than those Gromyko gave you. You obviously know Russian, as our long-distance microphone then proved. The concierge on your floor of the hotel could not stop telling people that one of the foreign guests spoke good Russian. You are a Spanish spy, but what you could learn about our wine industry that you could not have found in the literature on the subject puzzled us. So you must have been up to something sinister. What was it?"

In French, Felipe said he could not understand what she was talking about and demanded to see a Spanish consul.

"You can demand all day long, but you will not be allowed any concessions. We know you are Stasys Grinius, and it was bad luck for you that I attended the viticulture meetings. I was on duty in Georgia when I heard of it, and because of my interest in winemaking, I attended a few sessions. We knew Spain had a phylloxera outbreak several years ago, and it was I who suggested you might be helpful in our research on grape diseases. It would have rested there, but because of my suspicions at the dinner, I kept your wineglass and our experts had no trouble obtaining some clear fingerprints. Our team in Lithuania matched them with yours from your army records. So you entered Russia twice illegally with a forged passport; you spied on us; and you are wanted in Lithuania for subversive activities. So, as the English say, your goose is cooked. You can stop that French nonsense and respond in Russian. What were you spying on?"

"You have a vivid imagination. I am a wine farmer and was a member of a Spanish delegation. My farm is on high ground, and we have early winters, so the Russian experiments with grapes that might mature in a short season interested me and other Spanish grape farmers. It was not spying; it was fact finding. We reciprocated by showing Gromyko everything he wanted to see about our industry. I did not mix with the French delegates because we are close to them. It is relatively easy to obtain information about their vineyards and wineries, but they do not have the special knowledge of the Anapa institution."

"Grinius, that was a nice try, but it was rubbish."

Felipe knew his cover was blown and said the Colonel was right. He was born in Lithuania but was now a Spanish citizen. "A year after I landed in Spain, I was given a new name, a standard practice there. There is nothing subversive about me, and there is no evidence against me in Lithuania concerning antigovernment activities. I left my home country, because I could no longer tolerate the vile Marxist regime under which our farm was taken from us, leading to my father's early death and my mother's forced relegation to a rotten home for old people."

"You will be sent to Lithuania and will see that we have a case against you. We do not have to be fussy about laws. There is no nonsense such as reasonable doubt in our system. If we think you are guilty, you will be guilty."

Felipe could not restrain himself and said, "You are a cunning and ruthless bitch working for the swine who wrecked our family and the lives of thousands of Lithuanians. Many were tortured, and over three hundred thousand were deported to Siberia. Your ego as a KGB officer in a smart uniform, full of medals, is such that you abandoned a husband and son who loved you. What sort of animal lurks beneath your beautiful face?"

She nodded to one of the guards, who hit Felipe viciously in the face and sent him spinning to the floor where he lay in pain. She walked up to him and said, "You are lucky that more important business beckons me; otherwise, you would see something of the hidden animal you envisaged. I'll advise my colleagues in Lithuania to stand no nonsense from you, but here is something to remind you of me." She kicked him.

He groaned and spluttered, "Bolshevik bitch, bastard, bully," and spat at her.

She kicked him once again and shouted, "Idiots like you think you can get past the KGB, but we are ahead of you! Never forget that!" she shouted and left the room.

Alisa went to the officers' quarters where she poured herself a large vodka.

I did not enjoy that. I felt I was dealing with Alex. How could I have been so rough? Stasys is Ivor's uncle, and one day, my son may learn of my harsh treatment of our enemies. But duty is duty. Thanks to me and old Dimitrov who told us to follow our hunches, another enemy of the state has been caught and will be punished. It is pity Josef is dead; he would have been delighted to have heard of my success.

8

Russian Intrigue

When Alisa left, Alex's first thought was for Ivor. He called him aside and discussed the sad news that she had gone back to Russia. Ivor said he thought she would because she had told him confidentially that she planned to do so one day. She said she could take him with her if he wished. He told her he was shocked to hear her comment and had no intention of leaving his father and friends. Alex hugged him, thanked him for his loyalty, and said he might have some good news for him. Because Alisa worked for the Russians, they obviously knew about Ivor's past and there was no need now to conceal it any longer. He could return to piano playing if he wished. As his son, he could also become a Canadian citizen.

Ivor wanted to do both of those things.

Alex told Ivor he had come across something interesting, but it might come to nothing. He had spoken to an old friend from the Fourth Engineers now in charge of the City of Montreal stores. He complained that he had been landed with worn-out and discarded furniture and other objects. The latest annoyance was a big, battered piano. His friend said it was some kind of "Stein" model; he could not read the name.

Alex suggested he and his son Ivor look at it. They visited Alex's friend and examined the piano. Alex said it could be a Steinway, but it was in a sorry state. He asked his friend what he wanted for it.

"Would $500 be enough?"

"Enough? For that junk? You must be joking. I'll have it delivered to Drummondville for $200."

"It's a deal," said Alex as he winked at Ivor.

On the way home, they stopped to buy sheet music. Alex said it should be easy to clean the mess inside the piano, and he and his friends would strip the woodwork and revarnish it. Ivor noted that the keys were dirty and the pedals were stuck, but he agreed that restoration was possible. He could not wait to play seriously again.

"You once said you had had enough."

"Yes, but remember, it was the constant travelling, the concerts, and the Communist brainwashing that got me down. Now I can play for pleasure."

Alex put the piano in his workshop, and he and a friend cleaned all the woodwork. revarnished it, and then cleaned and polished the keys. A piano tuner almost cried when he saw the neglect but patiently restored parts and retuned the instrument. He claimed it was back to its concert recital standard, and Ivor agreed. It occupied the pride of place in the living room, and the boy's beautiful playing thrilled Alex.

Alex registered Ivor for Canadian citizenship, and that was recognised at a ceremony in Montreal.

Ivor played the organ for church services and weddings when needed and became familiar with the services. He started to ask questions about Roman Catholicism. On a day that was memorable for his father, he said he wanted to be baptised as the first step towards Communion. Alex was delighted. So was Father Masse, who had developed a strong friendship with Ivor. He had been answering the boy's questions without trying to convert him. In due course, Ivor became a member of the Church with Bishop Levesque officiating at his first Communion.

Alex followed Arthur's advice and bought an old logging camp with 600 acres of clear-cut land. He, Arthur, and John le Clus, who ran a successful electrical supply company, renovated the log buildings and improved their insulation. The office was converted into a home for Alex and a storage shed into a bungalow for visitors. One of the big bunkhouses was divided into two separate dormitories. The cookhouse was modernised. Another bunkhouse was restored as a museum in which photographs, booklets, saws, axes, and other tools associated with the old logging days were displayed. The smithy was used as a workshop. The grounds around the buildings were cleared and planted with shrubs and flowers to beautify the area. Hydro and telephone connections were established. Alex encouraged his friends, environmental groups, disadvantaged children, Boy Scouts, Girl Guides, and his Royal Canadian Legion friends to use the facilities without charge.

The rules were simple. There was to be no smoking; no molesting of wild animals; no picking of plants; wet garbage was to go into composting bins; other garbage was to be put in bins for recycling; assistance in the camp's maintenance had to be given; and disclaimers had to be signed absolving Alex from any claims for injuries. He explained that the rules were to enable everybody to enjoy safe stays in a natural setting and to ensure that work was shared. The response was always excellent, and he had no trouble with approved visitors. Inevitably, some trespassers arrived to disturb the pleasant atmosphere, but they were speedily evicted.

Police advice notices warning trespassers were displayed. Alex was friendly with the local police chief, who had served in tanks in World War II. Alex gave him keys to the buildings and told him he and his staff were welcome to use the camp's facilities whenever they wished, subject to letting Alex's secretary know when they intended to do so. Consequently, the property was under almost constant surveillance and did not suffer from break-ins, as many summer cottages did.

Alex worked with Forestry Department officials on an afforestation plan, and visitors were encouraged to help with the planting of trees. In the area near the buildings, he removed tree stumps, and those that were too big to lift, he ground to a level below the surface. In no time, the whole camp area was clear. He engaged a former Outward Bound trainer to establish a training circuit that included canoeing on the lake adjacent to the property and to supervise the use of the walking trails that served as cross-country ski routes in winter. An environmentalist taught visitors navigation, a necessity when they wandered into adjacent wooded Crown property. Alex explained first-aid procedures.

He continued to write articles condemning the Russians in Lithuania. He obtained information of conditions there from the local Lithuanian network, from Arthur who had access to official research material, and from letters. A heavily censored letter from his sister Julija indicated, as he was pleased to note, that his relatives were well and grateful for the money he sent them but that their singing friend had gone.

He was upset. He knew she referred to Father Staugaitis, because they often sang a duet about a Lithuanian hero. He remembered Alisa's hint that the priest should be careful. He had written frequently to the Father, but of late, there had been no response, so he assumed he had been deported. He cursed and prayed that the priest would survive, as some deportees did.

He was at the camp one Saturday when the storekeeper from the nearby village phoned to tell him two strangers had asked for directions to the logging camp. Before directing them, he asked why they wanted the information. They said they wished to meet Doctor Greenus. Alex thanked him and phoned his friendly police officer. He asked him to visit the camp with a fellow officer; there could be some excitement.

He collected John le Clus, who had been busy on some electrical work, and they hid in trees near the camp entrance. A

Volvo approached and stopped; two men got out and walked into the camp. They were startled when two powerful men moved from the trees and asked what they wanted. They said they wished to look over the camp about which they had heard so much. Alex said he was the owner and only allowed visitors by invitation, as indicated on the notice at the entrance. Trespassers, such as they, were subject to prosecution.

He suddenly shouted in Russian, "Attention, you bastards!"

The intruders stiffened and one said, "Don't call us names!"

"As I thought, you two swine are Russians. I want to know what you are doing here on a Saturday afternoon. John, frisk that guy while I watch this one."

John discovered a revolver, and Alex told him to check the other trespasser, and another weapon was found. Alex cocked it and fired it into the air.

"Loaded. How interesting. Who the hell are you wandering around here with loaded weapons?"

"We are visitors to Canada and heard about your restoration of an old logging camp and plan to do the same in Russia."

"It is strange that you did not make an appointment to see me. Search the bastards, John."

"I must warn you," said one of the men, "we have diplomatic immunity."

"Oh, one minute you are visitors; now you have diplomatic immunity? Rubbish. The car's number plates do not have a diplomatic sign on them. In any case, you are trespassing with loaded weapons."

"We were told there were dangerous bears in the camp."

"The only bears are you Russian bears, and you have interesting things in your pockets," he said looking at what John had found. There were credit cards, drivers' licences in the names of Victor Slavinsky and Georg Rabin, and pictures of Alex.

Alex told the Russians he knew they were liars.

"If you have pictures of me, you must know all about the camp and its visiting conditions. You were armed, and I know you were looking for me. That is sinister, and you are under arrest. No, don't argue. Unlike your rotten country, citizens here can arrest people."

The pistol shot had attracted a crowd of children, who were boggle-eyed at the sight of Alex and John both with revolvers guarding two un-Canadian-looking men. They were further excited when a police cruiser arrived into which the strangers were bundled by a police officer after a quick chat with Alex. Alex gave him the weapons and the Russians' car keys and papers and told him that the intruders spoke English and probably French. He wanted charges laid for trespassing and for wandering around with loaded weapons. The police officer winked and said he would attend to that.

Alex phoned a newspaper friend and gave him details of the incident, which made the national media. One article read:

Strange Visitors

Dr Alex Greenus, the noted conservationist and philanthropist, received strange visitors at his restored logging camp on Saturday.

They were two Russian-speaking men armed with loaded revolvers. Both carried his photograph. They claimed they wanted to see his camp, because they planned to restore a similar one in Russia. They were armed because they had heard there were dangerous bears in the vicinity. When they were searched by John le Clus, a friend of Doctor Greenus, he found photographs of the doctor. He arrested the men and handed them to the police despite the intruders claiming that they had diplomatic immunity.

Doctor Greenus, who is a harsh critic of the ruthless manner in which the Soviets govern Lithuania, where he was born, said people could form their own opinion of the incident.

The Russians decorated him for his part in a tank action north of Archangel in World War II when he spent a year in the Arctic handling tanks carried by ships in the ill-fated Arctic convoys. Both he and Mr. le Clus were awarded the George Medal for bravery during the bombing of London.

Alex sent his friend some pictures taken of the incident by children, and there was a follow-up.

The Mystery Remains

Enquiries at RCMP Headquarters about the two armed Russians arrested for trespassing on Doctor Greenus's property failed to reveal if the men would be charged. They claimed to be diplomats, but a Russian embassy spokesman and the press attaché at the Canadian Foreign Affairs office declined to comment. It would be interesting to examine the passenger list on the next Aeroflot flight to Moscow. Our guess is that the names of two men in the picture below taken at the logging camp will be on it.

The head of the Russian embassy was furious with the two men, whom, with the help of Arthur Naujokas, he extricated from the police. They were ordered to return to Moscow, and as far as he was concerned, that was the end of the matter.

The media, however, was short of news, and both the central police station and the Russian embassy were monitored. Two men answering to the descriptions John and Alex provided were seen leaving the police station and arriving at the embassy.

At the airport, a press photographer took random pictures, including pictures of passengers to Moscow, from which the men were identified and media coverage continued.

Trespassers Identified

Despite silence from the Russian embassy and our Department of Foreign Affairs, it has been established that the two armed trespassers on Doctor Greenus's property were employees of the Russian embassy. They were released from police custody presumably at the request of the Foreign Affairs Department and taken to the Russian embassy. They then left on the next Aeroflot flight to Moscow. Why they visited Doctor Greenus's camp armed and carrying his photographs is not known. He is a virulent critic of Russia's administration of Lithuania, his country of birth, and claims the Russian occupation of that country is illegal.

If the pair intended to eliminate or intimidate him, they were clumsy in the extreme—they did not know the way, advertised their intention, and used a traceable hired car.

Doctor Greenus said the men obviously had evil intentions. It was a practice of the KGB to eliminate undesirable elements. He was certain he fell into that category.

"The men had loaded weapons. They trespassed. They lied to the police. Canada should not be kind to people like them. They should be punished severely as a deterrent to others. I resent my rights to prosecution being arbitrarily blocked by diplomats."

A few days later, Alex received a large envelope marked "Confidential." In it was a letter from the Foreign Office also endorsed "Confidential."

Dear Dr. Alexander Greenus,

We refer to the unfortunate intrusion by two Russians on your private property and the media and parliamentary commentary that followed.

The two men were employed by the Soviet embassy, whose ambassador assured us they were acting unofficially. They have been reprimanded and have returned to Russia. We deemed it expedient to help the Soviets resolve the matter subject to their sending you a letter of apology, which is enclosed.

Our action was taken in the best interests of our country, and we trust you, who have proved your devotion to Canada, will agree it was correct.

Yours truly,
Vincent Pelletier
Minister of Foreign Affairs

The Russian letter was written with understandable restraint:

Dear Dr. Alexander Greenus,

We refer to the unfortunate incident when two of our staff trespassed on your property. We offer our sincere apologies for their behaviour, which did not have our approval. They have been suitably dealt with.

My government is deeply conscious of your excellent work and bravery in Archangel and Murmansk with our forces in World War II and regrets the inconvenience our employees caused you.

If there is anything we can do to redress the wrong you have suffered, do not hesitate to ask.

Yours truly,

Ivor Gorbachov
Ambassador

To the Soviet Ambassador, Alex wrote:

Dear Ambassador,

Thank you for your letter about the unwarranted action of two of your employees. There are two things you can do to redress the matter and thereby avoid my taking legal action against you for your servants' misdeeds.

The first concerns my activities in Archangel for which I was awarded your Medal of Valour. My former wife, Colonel Alisa Volgymko, a KGB spy in Canada, told me that the award had been revoked. It should be reinstated. The second is that I would like a visa to visit Lithuania.

I trust you are able to meet these simple requests.

Yours truly,

Alex Greenus

The ambassador exploded when he read the letter. He had been rapped on the knuckles for the Greenus incident and now the upstart was threatening legal action. What on earth was the Canadian foreign minister doing? He should have settled with Greenus ages ago.

He acknowledged Alex's letter and said he would write in detail later. He advised Moscow to meet Greenus's demands, and when they agreed, he informed Alex his medal had been restored and enclosed the required visa.

Alex consulted his lawyer and at his suggestion wrote the following letter:

Minister of Foreign Affairs

Ottawa

I thank you for your letter referring to the Russian trespassers.

I do not agree that your actions were in the best interests of Canada and now seek redress for your department's unwarranted blocking of my legal rights to sue the miscreants. As you correctly surmised, I am devoted to Canada and am aware of the freedoms we enjoy, one of which is access to a decent legal system. You had no right to prevent my seeking redress for what was an attempt on my life. You could have deferred assisting the Russian embassy until its criminals had been tried.

The matter was discussed in Parliament when your answers to questions did not allay my concern.

I hereby give notice of my intention to sue your department. Its deviousness will be revealed in its response to my lawyer's discovery request.

Yours truly,
Alex Greenus

Alex spoke to Arthur about the incident and was told that, for once, he could not comment except to say that Alex's letter had caused a flutter in the dovecote.

"Always the intellectual, but your boss will eat humble pie before the matter is over."

"We'll see, my litigious friend."

The minister regretted Alex's response and said his department would defend any action he took because they were satisfied the two Russians had diplomatic immunity and could not be prosecuted.

Alex responded that it was strange that the minister had not said so from the beginning and at that stage had not demanded the expulsion of the miscreants. Instead, he had connived with the Soviets to suppress his rights. He intended to pursue the matter.

He did this by talking to his journalist friend, who was delighted with the story that unfolded. Alex told him about the Soviet concessions and that the visa was valuable to him. He agreed to the journalist saying that he had accepted an apology from the Soviet ambassador. He spoke to his MP, who was a member of the opposition and jumped at the chance to embarrass the government. Media that publicised the House of Commons debates picked up the newspaper story.

The effect was immediate.

Arthur asked Alex to see him and said he had been authorised to settle his case. The department's legal advisers were adamant that Alex did not have a case, but the harassed minister wanted to close the matter. Alex laughed and said he hoped that future ministers would look after Canadians' interest instead of appeasing foreigners. Arthur assured him that the lesson had been learned and asked what Alex wanted in return for letting the minister off the hook.

"What does letting him off the hook mean?"

"The origin of the expression comes from the old telephones, the earpiece of which rested on a hook. In your case, it would consist of a simple letter of which I have a draft saying that in view of the explanation you have been given you agree with the department's actions."

"But I don't. I was let down."

"Alex, there was a trade-off. We gained an important concession from the Russians for our action. I cannot tell you the details, but you have my assurance on that point."

"All right. Pay my legal fees and $5,000 to the trustees of the logging camp, and I'll sign."

"It's a deal. I can now tell you it was I who negotiated with the Soviets and got the Russians released and that, with your decision today, probably means the promotion I seek will be obtained."

"You stupid idiot, why didn't you mention that earlier? We could have saved the preliminaries. I would have followed St. Matthew's, 'Agree with thine adversary quickly, whilst thou art in the way with him.'"

Alex signed the letter and a press release, shook hands with Arthur, and left.

He returned to Drummondville in a pensive mood. He wondered if he should not have stuck to his guns and sued the government and the Russians. He owed a lot to Arthur and reflected that on balance he had acted wisely in his friend's interest.

He was soon absorbed in his medical practice.

He often placed his patients in a Montreal hospital whose surgical facilities were better than those in Drummondville. During an operation at that hospital, Alex asked for a clamp and a nurse handed it to him saying, "Here it is, Alex." He frowned. He was not in favour of familiarities or conversations during an operation, and he did not respond. At the end of the procedure, he turned and asked the nurse what she meant. To his surprise and delight, he saw it was Giselle.

"What are you doing in Montreal?" he asked. "I thought you were in British Columbia."

"I returned to be with my family. Why are you not at the hospital in Drummondville?"

"I perform operations at this hospital. How did you know my practice was at Drummondville?"

"I looked in the register of physicians and surgeons in Quebec and found your name."

"You are as bright as ever. I would like to hear all about you. Can you have lunch with me?" asked Alex.

"Sure, but it will have to be in the hospital coffee shop; I am on duty."

It was like old times, and they talked about her family and each other. She had served with the Canadian Army Nursing Service in Europe, where she met a young doctor to whom she became engaged only to lose him in one of the last bombing raids of the war. She was demobbed in Vancouver, where she stayed until her father died and she felt she should be nearer her mother. She was a senior surgical nurse and lived comfortably.

He told her of his engineering and Arctic days and said he was once married and had a son. He had restored an old logging camp that had given pleasure joy to many people. He said it was a joy to see her again and asked if she was involved with anyone.

"Involved? If you are asking if I have a lover, the answer is 'No.' Incidentally, you never gave me the opportunity of court-martialling you."

He laughed. "So you remember that. I ended up as a captain, so had we met, I would not have been in danger, my dear Lieutenant. I often regretted what I missed."

"No doubt, you warm-blooded medic. But you are wrong. I was the equivalent of a major, so you would have been subordinate to me."

"Really? Well, now I am a doctor, and you, a nurse, have to listen to me."

"I would like to listen longer, but I must fly. Keep in touch."

He sat for some time and savoured the meeting. His thoughts wandered to the early days, and he wondered if their relationship could be renewed. He went to the hospital registry, identified himself, and said that he had to contact Nurse Bourassa after hours about a medical matter. He would appreciate her phone number. He received it, and he mused that old Alisa had taught him deception and wondered how she had fared. The Russian mind was difficult to fathom, he decided.

Alex phoned Giselle and said he had been delighted to meet her. He would like to pursue their acquaintanceship. She welcomed that. He said he was going to Lithuania and would contact her on his return.

Alex worked with two other doctors, and it was easy for him to obtain time off to visit Lithuania with the newly acquired visa. He planned to visit his relatives and persuade them to leave. He would see how the country was faring and obtain material for his crusade against the Russian occupation.

He flew to Copenhagen and continued on by ferry to Klapeida. As he expected, an immigration official harangued him. Alex listened patiently and then produced certified copies of his medal citation and Captain Gromyko's and the Ambassador's letters. He suggested that the official would be embroiled in an international incident if he continued his harassment.

"I am doing my duty. We don't like ex-Lithuanians who return for visits. Wait."

He phoned his superior who told him that Greenus was dangerous but should be admitted. "Warn him he will be watched."

"You are admitted for six days. You are under surveillance," the official told Alex.

He was not concerned about being shadowed. He wondered if Alisa still monitored his family's activities. He knew that he would have to work fast in the allotted time.

He drove to see Sofija and Marija and their families and tried to persuade them to emigrate to Canada. They thanked him for the suggestion but said they enjoyed a reasonable existence and were reluctant to leave. He asked if they knew why they had not been deported for their religious activity. They said they wondered why they had been left alone and assumed it was due to their important work. They had been warned about the punishments for practising religious rites openly, and for their children's sakes, they celebrated Mass and prayed secretly.

He learned that Stasys had escaped and now worked for a wine farmer in Spain. He was pleased to hear that he was safe and wondered if Alisa had taken the pressure off him. Sofija took Alex aside and told him that Stasys's escape had been dramatic. On his way to the coast, he was lucky to meet Jonas, who was working for the security forces. Jonas directed him to a friendly farmer and learnt later that he had passed him on to a friend, who took him to Klapeida. Somehow, he got to Spain because Jonas received a card with a drawing of a soldier on a bridge with his arms around a tramp.

He found Algirdas in Vilnius and was impressed with his alert appearance. Having done his army service, he was quite happy to continue as a security guard. He could ski, play hockey, and enjoy the urban social life. He showed Alex where the Nazis had razed the ghetto, and Alex was shocked. He noted the poor condition of most buildings and the continued presence of Russian soldiers. All signs were in Russian, and he despaired that his old country would ever be free again. Although his brothers were not collaborators, they worked with the oppressors. He knew they had little choice.

Kazys in Kaunus was delighted to see him. He was now the town's fire chief and content with his wife and two sons. Although they professed to the faith, they were not actively religious. When Alex said he was interested in what was happening in the country, Kazys said he should meet a journalist he knew.

The next day, he introduced him in a small restaurant whose owner was openly anti-Russian. Alex asked the writer if conditions were improving. The journalist said if Alex looked over his shoulder he would see a man in a grey suit. He was a security policeman who had followed him. He was a Lithuanian collaborator and probably could lip-read. The police harassed people all the time. He suggested they speak about trivialities and he would meet Alex later and gave him an address for a rendezvous. They chatted about the weather and Canada. Alex smiled at the policeman as they left and was rewarded with a scowl.

That evening, Alex and the journalist had a long discussion from which it was evident that the Russian oppression continued. Men were still drafted into the army, living conditions had not improved, and religion was suppressed. The Russians were tolerant towards art and music, and some artists and composers produced good work. Armed resistance had faded, and the only hope for an improvement in conditions was a change in the Soviet government.

Alex thanked the writer and said that if he ever managed to get to Canada, he would look after him. If he approached the Canadian immigration authorities, he could be quoted as a sponsor. The man thanked him, and they parted. Alex left the country depressed by its condition and upset that he could not persuade more family members to leave it.

On his return from Lithuania, Alex phoned Giselle, who agreed to have dinner with him, and they spent a pleasant two hours reminiscing. She was still vivacious. Alex was surprised that no one had snapped her up. She agreed to spend a weekend in Drummondville where she would meet Ivor.

Alex was pleased to receive a letter from Stasys advising him that he had been given a permanent position on a wine farm in Spain He had an interesting story to tell him about Alisa.

Two weeks later, Giselle arrived in a dashing sports car. Alex had an emergency call and suggested that Ivor and Giselle go swimming. Both agreed that was a good idea. They raced each other in the water, and Ivor had to work hard to beat her. Afterward, they sat on the edge of the pool, and he answered her questions about his life.

Their concentration was broken by a loud splash and shout, and they saw an elderly woman flailing in the water. They dived in and swam towards her. Working together, they pulled her out. She was spluttering something about a child as they wrapped their towels around her. Giselle said she would fetch a blanket from her car and left to do so.

The woman repeated, "The child! The child!" and pointed to a child with floats drifting to the deep end of the pool. Ivor swam across and pulled the little girl out of the water. The woman said it was her grandchild. When she had started to float from the shallow end, the grandmother had leant forward to collect her and fallen in. Giselle covered the woman with a blanket and asked if she had transport. When she heard that she and the child had come by bus, she drove them home and told the woman to have a hot bath. The relieved and grateful grandmother thanked her.

They told Alex the story later, and he was impressed by their easy friendship and humorous description of the incident. He said he had pressed the authorities to have a lifeguard on duty when children were swimming. He thought the incident might lead to that. He would report it to the town officials. To stir them to action, he described the incident to a friendly reporter, whose story had the desired effect.

The weekend finished with Ivor driving Giselle's gearshift car. She explained the use of the clutch and the configuration of the gears and took him to a vacant plot to practise. His coordination was good, and he enjoyed driving through the town. He hoped some of his friends would see him, and he was rewarded with a shout and whistle from a group of them.

He told Alex that he enjoyed Giselle's company and hoped he would marry her.

"What makes you think I have that in mind?"

"It's pretty obvious that you love her, and she told me you have been friends for ages. She is a nurse and could help you in your practice."

"You're always practical. You would make a good factory manager. By the way, it's your last year at school. What do you plan to do?"

"I would like to study music, and subject to a satisfactory year end pass, Queens University in Kingston, Ontario, has accepted me."

"That's great. I'm sure you will enjoy that campus. After Queens, what will you do?"

"I'm not certain. I'll probably become a teacher. One can combine a degree with a teaching diploma. We'll see."

Alex smiled at the thought of Ivor's remarks about Giselle, and when next he saw her, he mentioned the boy's observations. She said she was surprised it took an observer to state the obvious. If it were given, she would entertain a proposal of marriage. He grabbed her, kissed her, and asked her to marry him. She laughed and said it was a shock to contemplate marriage at her age, but if he insisted, she would give it a try. He assured her she would not regret it.

They were married in St. Casimir Church by a fit and cheerful Bishop Levesque, who was a frequent visitor to the logging camp. In the winter, he enjoyed nothing more than a game of hockey on the frozen lake. He and Ivor were great friends and usually opposed each other on the ice.

The wedding guests included Ivor; Arthur and his wife, Frances; Alex's mother and Terese; Giselle's mother; her brother Emile, now a prominent farmer; Father Masse; John le Clus and Vera; and Alex's partners and their wives.

John made a brilliant speech in which he said how much he valued Alex's friendship. At one stage, he had thought it would come to a sudden halt when they were trapped in the rubble of a bombed-out building in London, but they were saved by a lovely animal, who showed them a way out. Now Alex had been saved from the dangers of bachelorhood by another lovely creature, Giselle, who was sure to lead him in the right direction just as the animal had done.

The couple spent their honeymoon in Cuba and returned bronzed and bubbling with life. Giselle brightened the lives of Alex and Ivor, and, as Ivor had predicted, she was helpful in the practice.

One day, Alex jokingly said he had a confession to make; he had married her solely on the advice of his accountant, who had said that by employing Giselle, he could shift income to her and save income taxes. It was known as income splitting and was quite legitimate.

"You are a most attractive rebate; I'll say that."

"You are a most calculating beast," she said and threw a cushion at him. She continued, "Anyway, I should tell you that you gave me the excuse to leave hospital work. It exhausted me. By the way, I want an increase in salary."

"Only if you hug me and ask nicely."

"So that's how you run your business! No wonder you only employ attractive receptionists and why they get frequent salary increases. Oh, all right '*Da mi basia mille*.'"

"Kiss you a thousand times over. With pleasure but when did you read Catullus?"

"You underlined those words in one of your books. You were probably thinking of hiring a new secretary."

"No, it was after the first morning on the farm when you showed me how to milk a cow. I dreamed of kissing you, and I now realise that I have been in love with you ever since. I marked those lines and often read them."

9
Stasys

Alex told Giselle he planned to go to Spain to persuade Stasys to come to Canada and would like her to accompany him. She said she would be delighted; she had seen a lot of Canada but little of Europe. She would love to see real flamenco dancing.

"I know your brother is in Spain, but the Franco regime has a sordid history and it and our church has blood on their hands. The civil war was atrocious. And what sort of people are they to witness bullfights?"

"We will certainly not see a bullfight. I think it is a barbaric, murderous activity. You're correct about the civil war, but there were atrocities on both sides. If Stasys is happy there, it can't be too bad a country. We'll be careful. I'm sure we will have a great time."

He wrote to Stasys and told him to expect a visit from them. Stasys phoned and said he was delighted that he and his wife were coming to Spain. He said he was now known as Felipe Jiminez. He gave Alex the phone number of his employer Senor Cervantes.

They flew to Madrid, where they spent two days exploring museums and art galleries, including the royal palace of Madrid, the Teatro Real, and the Prado Museum.

They then headed for Seville to see the architecture of the Moors, who occupied the city for 800 years. As the artistic, flamenco, and cultural capital of Southern Spain, Seville attracted composers, like Bizet, whose famous opera *Carmen* was based on the city. It was also famous for its flamenco dancers and bullfights.

A guide explained that flamenco originated with Gypsies, who were hounded from place to place, and their songs were sad and reflected their sufferings. He said the dancing was unlike ballroom dancing, and the women relied on body movements not their arms to convey their message.

Alex and Gisele were fascinated by the dancers, especially their clicking castanets; *zapateados*, the clicking of the heel and toe; and *palmas*, hand-clapping.

They enjoyed evening meals in the cafés that featured flamenco dancers. A friend had recommended Jerez, where they visited the Café-Bar Damajuana, famous for its food and dancers. Jerez was a city of palm-lined squares and was well-known for its sherries and the Royal Andalusian School of Equestrian Art, which they also visited to see the famous dancing horses.

Alex phoned Senor Cervantes and asked for Senor Jiminez. He was told he was busy. Alex left their hotel phone number, and shortly afterwards, an excited Stasys called and asked when they could meet. Alex said they were free to see him at any time. Stasys told Alex the nearest airport to the farm at Aranda de Duero was Valladolid. They could catch a flight to land there at eleven the next morning. They agreed upon the arrangements, and Stasys said he would collect them. He had a fascinating story to tell.

They arrived on time, and the two brothers hugged. Stasys shook hands with Giselle and said he must remember to speak French. That would be a little strange after having spoken Spanish for so long.

He drove them to the farm and made them comfortable in the house in which he lodged. His maid served a Spanish lunch of gazpacho, seafood paella, roast lamb, and sorbet.

"Lunch is the big meal in Spain and is conducive to the traditional siesta," explained Stasys, when his guests insisted on small helpings.

He asked for their news, in particular about Ivor. When told he was a student of music, Stasys said he should take a holiday in Spain where everyone seemed to sing or play a guitar.

"Ivor is a concert pianist and now is studying the organ. He would be fascinated with flamenco music and its origin. He must finish his studies before he ventures abroad though. I will mention your suggestion that he visit Spain.

"Stasys, as you know, I have been conducting a crusade to get our family out of Lithuania and into Canada. Why don't you leave Spain and join us? I would be your guarantor and would help you find work."

"Alex, a year ago, I would have jumped at the opportunity, but conditions have changed for the better. I have been in charge of this extensive wine farm for a year, and there is the prospect of owning Senor Cervantes's brother's farm. Also, I was selected or, one might say, *ordered* to undertake a secret mission for the government. It was based on my knowledge of Russian. It is the source of the exciting story I said I would tell you.

"The Spanish wine industry has never really recovered from the Moors, who forbade the production of wine, although they winked at the profitable sherry trade Spain had with England. For centuries, the wine Spain produced justified its description of plonk. Lately, however, there has been a serious attempt to produce good wines for the export market, and there has been some success. This has irked other countries in the international wine trade, one of which is Russia. The Spaniards suspect that country is intent on wrecking Spain's vineyards.

"To cut a long story short, they selected me to attend a wine conference in Georgia as a full-blooded Spaniard, who only spoke Spanish. I was to hide my knowledge of Russian and to eavesdrop in the hope that I would uncover the Russian plans for Spain. I was drilled by government agents in advanced Spanish and in viticulture terms. I had to agree in order to protect the grant to me of Spanish citizenship. I was accompanied by a scientist, with whom I was to swap notes at the conference.

"Everything went according to plan. After the first day, we thought we had stumbled onto the Russian schemes. During one of the intervals between the presentations of scientific papers, I heard a uniformed Russian talk of phylloxera and Spain. I assumed that they planned to infest our vines with that dreaded disease that earlier had brought the French wine industry to its knees. I asked about the soldier and was told that she was a colonel on vacation and being interested in wine, she had asked to attend the conference. That seemed a tall story to me.

"Anyway, at the banquet that evening, I sat opposite the Colonel, who stared at me and suddenly asked, 'How is Ivor?'

"I was puzzled and asked my table companion to whom I had been speaking in French what the woman meant. He said that it sounded as if she knew me and asked how Ivor was. I told him I did not know what she was talking about. The colonel recovered and apologised to me. She said I reminded her of someone, but her memory had played her false.

"It had not, because as you know, Alex, we were often taken for twins. She did not know that though. I checked her name on the table card and saw she was Alisa Volgymko. Obviously, she, your former wife, thought it was you opposite her.

"Alisa must have been suspicious and must have ordered an investigation of me. There was evidence that our room had been searched and the papers I had left in safe custody were disturbed. For the rest of the conference, I was shadowed by two Russians, who were not on the list of delegates. I was reminded of the rough days with the underground.

"I can say she was really imposing in her uniform. I am surprised she did not wear a dress, but presumably, she wanted the Russian delegates to know that Big Brother was watching them."

"Stasys, you may be assured that Alisa knows you are not a Spaniard. She will not rest until you have been unearthed. Be careful in future dealings with the Russians. She wrecked our marriage and upset our son, and she would think nothing of fixing my brother," said Alex.

"You are quite right. She unearthed my real personality and there was a rough result for me.

"I had an invitation to attend the famous Anapakian Zonal Experimental Station of Viticulture and Wine Making in Anapa, Georgia. The station produces varieties of grapes suitable for the conditions this wine region experiences. In Anapa I obtained good information and some prize specimens. I passed them to a Spanish colleague who accompanied me. At the airport on way home I was arrested and sent to Moscow where believe it or not I was cross examined by Alisa in her imposing uniform.

"At her signal her bully boys roughed me up. She explained how she had broken my cover and she sent me to Lithuania to face punishment for my underground activities. Before I left, her bully boys roughed me up again and she added to their blows by kicking me painfully. You will understand when I called her a sadistic bitch whose Communist pals had wrecked our family's lives and how she had deceived you.

"I was flown to Vilnius. Lithuanian jails are not pleasant but I was not incarcerated for long. An influential Spanish Minister whose department sent me to Anapa threatened to stop a Spanish soccer team Real Madrid, from going to Moscow to compete with a Russian team for a major soccer trophy unless I was released. That would have created a storm in international football circles and I was freed. Jonas collected me and we had a happy family gathering before I returned to Spain. That is a short story of a Spanish agent exposed and in trouble because he spoke Russian. It was reminiscent of your being sent to the Arctic for the same reason.

"I am glad you got back to Spain. Yes, our knowledge of Russian has been a mixed blessing." said Alex who wondered *if Alisa would ever stop influencing his life.*

The next day, Stasys asked them if they would like a tour of the farm. They agreed, and he found them some riding clothes.

"The ponies are well trained and will take jumps if you want them to."

He spoke knowingly about grapes and his plans to introduce new varieties and showed them an irrigation system he had installed.

He said he had trouble with the regional water board authorities, who tried to block the scheme. He called on the organisation that had persuaded him to go to Russia, and they sorted things out.

"That must be a powerful body to be able to override local organisations," said Alex.

"Yes. It was the State Secret Police and their help was a sort of *quid pro quo*."

"You intrigue me. Aren't you treading in deep water?"

"I am afraid so, but my connexion has not harmed anyone."

That night, Alex said to Giselle, "It has been quite a visit. I am not surprised Stasys is reluctant to come to Canada. He is knowledgeable about grapes and wine and is well in with the top authorities. He was lucky t get out of jail in Lithuania. No doubt it is run by Russians whose wardens are a sadistic bunch."

"I was fascinated with Stasys's story. Your family certainly has an interesting history to tell."

They met Senor Cervantes, a bronzed, stocky man, who spoke to them in French and told them how pleased he was with Stasys. "He has a wonderful way with horses; he can shoe them; he can fix things; and he is beginning to understand grapes."

Alex and Giselle bade farewell to Stasys and headed for France where Alex showed her some of the battlefields he covered. He was proud to see that most of the bridges his team erected in a hurry and often under fire were still being used. They ended their trip with a few days in Paris, where they went from one museum to another and dined in the Eiffel Tower restaurant.

When they arrived home, Giselle thanked Alex and said it was a fascinating experience. She had enjoyed seeing Spain and France and meeting Stasys.

"He looks like you; he talks like you; he probably thinks like you; and now you share a common enemy: Alisa."

"Yes, that was an unusual tale. I am glad he told us, not that I can do anything about it. Fancy his working for Spain's top spy agency. He did not say so, but they must have exerted some serious pressure on him. Alisa was true to form as a fanatical Communist in hounding him and sending him to Lithuania to be punished as she thought he would be. Fancy a soccer match affecting international negotiations."

A year later, Arthur gave Alex a clipping from a Russian newspaper:

War Hero Killed by Rebels

Colonel Alisa Volgymko a veteran of the Great Patriotic War was killed yesterday. She was leading a raid on Ukrainian dissidents. Her party was ambushed, and she was burnt by a petrol bomb. Ivan Golymko and Afonika Petrov were also killed. Colonel Volgymko was decorated several times in her role as a wartime tank commander. Since 1946, she served her country in its security services.

General Nicholas Shermenko, the Moscow area police chief, said the perpetrators of the dastardly crime would be found and punished.

Alex was shocked, and when he broke the news to Ivor, they both wept. Ivor said the years in Canada when they were all together were the happiest of his life. There was something sinister about her departure, but they would never know what it was. He missed her terribly and would never forget her tales of Russian history.

Alex said she put her country ahead of anything else, which unfortunately brought pain to those close to her.

Alex and Ivor wrote to Irina Volgymko. She said she was proud of Alisa's record. She told them she displayed all her medals and hoped Ivor was practising his scales.

Always the professional, thought Ivor. He was grateful for her drills, which had helped him develop his skills.

The three Soviet agents who investigated Alisa's earlier disappearance met and over a few vodkas questioned whether the story of her death was true.

"We could not trace her, and then she was reported killed. Now she has been killed again. Is it true this time?"

"Yes it is. I checked her death certificate. She must have been hiding when we lost her. Where could she have been?" asked one of his companions

They found out the next day when their superior hauled them over the coals for not uncovering earlier who Alex Greenus's ferryboat companion was.

"How far back did you go in Greenus's history?" he asked.

"He was born in Lithuania, moved to Canada, fought in the Great Patriotic War, and was awarded our Medal of Valour."

"Did you read his citation?"

"No, we simply checked that the award was legitimate."

"What about Colonel Volgymko?"

"She was a highly decorated war hero with an excellent KGB record."

"What decorations did she earn?"

"Medal of Valour, Order of the Red Star, and Order of Glory."

"Both had the Medal of Valour. Here are the citations. Read them. Does anything strike you?"

"Oh hell. They were awarded medals for the same action. They knew each other. The Arctic connection fooled us. It was she who escaped with him."

"Indeed. Do you wonder why?"

"Presumably, she wanted to get out of Russia and used him as a means of doing so?"

"Did it not occur to you that they might have been lovers in the barren north?"

"That would have been impossible. Fraternisation with foreign soldiers was a punishable offence, and there was always a commissar to enforce it."

"Idiots. Love will always find a way. You should read Shakespeare's *Romeo and Juliet*. What did you find in her file?"

"There was a list of her war actions, the citations for her medals, and numerous favourable reports."

"What about her family?"

"Her mother was a widow and looked after her son."

"Son?"

"Yes, born in 1942."

"Did you look at his birth certificate?"

"No."

"Here is a photostat. Who is the boy's father?"

"Aleksandras Girnius. Oh shit, that is Alexander Greenus. I beg your pardon, sir. They must have been lovers. No wonder she escaped with him. We should have known that. She was lucky the hospital did not report that she had broken the fraternisation rules in a big way."

"It was war time. The hospital staff was overworked attending to wounded and injured people. They would not have worried about the name of a father and the registration people would have accepted it without query. The point is that you were slack and should have checked all her records. You had better be more thorough in future investigations. It does not condone your inefficiency but there is something you could not have known at the time of the escape. Her move to Canada was a KGB plot. She became a valuable spy in that country."

"Comrade, sir, we did not know we were competing with another KGB department. What would have happened had we discovered the truth?"

"Colonel Volgymko would have torn a mighty strip off you and told you to jump into the sea. The point is you failed in your subsequent investigation and let this department down. That will be noted in your files. If you breathe one word of the episode to anyone, you will end your careers monitoring dissidents in Siberia. You are to attend a refresher course in Kiev, and if you don't do well, it will be Siberia. You are dismissed."

At a restaurant afterwards, one of the agents said, "We were so close. I sensed that ferry clerk was lying. I should have followed my hunch and worked him over. It has been a valuable lesson. Old toughie Dimitrov's theory is proved once again: 'If it looks easy, try again,' he said that often as well as, 'Don't trust anybody.' Anyway, if it was another department's plan to let her go, we certainly would have been kicked in a sore place had we stopped her from leaving."

"You're right but fancy being spoofed by one's own organisation!"

"My friend, this is Russia. Nothing should surprise you. She must have returned. It's sad that she died such a violent death. I do not wish that on anyone."

10
Ivor

Ivor worked diligently at school and realised his wish to attend Queens University in Kingston, which was known as the "Limestone City." He met two other Quebec students there, and they agreed to share digs, consisting of a ground-floor apartment in Alfred Street. Ivor had learned cooking from his father and looked after the eating arrangements.

In addition to musical subjects, he studied mathematics. He played hockey, and that, along with swimming, kept him fit. His piano playing attracted attention, and he was invited to perform with the Kingston Symphony Orchestra. He agreed to play one of his favourite Beethoven compositions.

The following notice appeared in the Kingston *Whig Standard.*

> *The Kingston Philharmonic Orchestra is proud to host the local debut of Ivor Greenus, a Queens University student. Mr. Greenus began studying the piano at an early age in Moscow under the tuition of his grandmother, Irina Volgymko. He was sent to the famous Gnessin Music School at the age of five where Elena Gnessin supervised his training. He graduated to the Moscow Youth Orchestra with which he played in*

*many parts of the world. He left the orchestra during
a visit to Montreal to join his parents who were living
in Quebec. In his first public performance since coming
to Canada, he will play Beethoven's Piano Concerto
no. 5 "Emperor."*

He sent a copy of the program to his father and grandmother, whose early coaching had laid the foundation to his success. Alex was thrilled to receive it and congratulated Ivor on his debut. Ivor did not tell Alex and Giselle that he received a standing ovation for an outstanding performance or that he declined further invitations because he had been selected for the university's Golden Gaels hockey team. That entailed a great deal of travelling, leaving little time to practise for concert performances.

He received a letter of congratulations from his grandmother, who said it was time he returned to Russia.

He attended St. Mary's Cathedral and became friendly with the choirmaster and organist, under whose direction he began playing. When needed, he performed at weddings and requiem masses. He helped with other duties on Sundays.

In the summer, he worked at the logging camp, where he supervised children's activities. He enjoyed introducing them to environmental studies and the joys of an outdoor life. He did two recitals in Montreal, for which he was paid.

The next three years at Queens were a repetition of the first, with the exception that he served on the student council during his last two years and was captain of the Golden Gaels hockey team in his final year. In an exciting match against the McGill Redmen at the McConnell Arena in Montreal, he scored the winning goal of the intervarsity final at the last second. The *Montreal Gazette* featured the match in its sports pages. Their reporter said it was ironic that a Quebec university lost the final because of the brilliant play of a student who learned his hockey in Quebec.

Ivor laughed that one off.

In Kingston, he spent much of his spare time with a group of students who helped a local charity that catered to the needs of poor people.

After obtaining a bachelor of music degree, he was accepted for study at the Queens Centre for Teaching and Learning and looked forward to another year in the city. That did not happen, however, because he was persuaded to apply for a Rhodes scholarship and did so after consulting with Alex. His community work and student leadership stood him in good stead, and he was successful.

Ivor wondered if he would be spending too much time studying, but Alex told him he was lucky he had not chosen medicine with its long years of examinations. He advised him to make full use of his two years in Oxford and then spend another qualifying as a teacher.

At Oxford, he planned to study for a master of letters in music. He was admitted to Oriel College, the college at which the generous founder of the Rhodes scholarships, Cecil John Rhodes, studied. Ivor found the international university based on thirty-nine colleges and seven permanent private halls strange with its educational institutions within the university and its tutorial system. He soon realised their value.

His first year consisted of obligatory courses in historical musicology, analysis and aesthetics, and criticism of music. There were optional studies in early music, performance practice, and cultural studies of various periods, contemporary music, local history, and interdisciplinary subjects. Ivor chose cultural studies and early music. The second year would consist of writing a 30,000-word dissertation and the preparation of a final recital. There was a team of international experts to supervise students' research, and a college adviser was appointed for each graduate student.

He enjoyed the faculty of music, took part in its public performances, and listened to the various university choirs. He tried his hand at field hockey but soon gave that up. Rugby, cricket, and rowing were the major sports at the university. Rowing, he understood, but the field sports, particularly cricket, bewildered him. He turned to athletics and represented his college in long-distance races.

He joined the university's outdoor club and enjoyed its Saturday and Sunday outings and longer weekend trips. The club's members visited the Galloway Hills, the Peak District, the Lake District, and Snowdonia. He was pleased that safety standards were high. He bought the recommended first-aid equipment.

On a trip to the Forest of Bowland, one of the party, Angela Somers, an attractive, red-haired Australian studying architecture, twisted her ankle. Ivor bound it tightly, took her pack, and half carried her to a departure spot. When they arrived at her college, she kissed him and thanked him for helping her. He had enjoyed holding her on the return walk, and the kiss ended an eventful day for him.

He spent the following Wednesday evening with her at the meeting of the social club. The highlight of the club's social activities was its annual ceilidh. He learned that its original Celtic meaning was a party or gathering, but in England, it was dancing, polkas, schottisches, and waltzes with lots of songs and music.

Ivor was popular because he played current jazz and Scottish music on request. Angela encouraged him to dance, and he soon picked up the rhythm and steps. Their initial kiss had advanced to hugs and longer kisses. On weekend trips, when they were alone, she told him that if he wanted to explore further, she would not object. He did not understand her meaning. She grabbed him and said she would return to Australia at the end of the term, so he had better move faster if he wanted to love her. He said she was a beautiful *sheila*, a word he'd learnt from her, and they enjoyed the first of several love sessions.

When not busy with the Outdoor Club's outings, they explored the university's buildings, the features of which she explained to him. They were intrigued with the various chapels, many of which dated back for centuries. They attended Anglican Church services and were impressed with the organists and choirs. They both did well in their examinations and practical tests and parted sadly at the end of the Trinity term.

He thought about the final year's dissertation and considered music from Northern Europe that was unfamiliar to the public as a likely subject. In his reading at the Bodleian Library, he had come across a Lithuanian musician, Mikalojus Konstantinas Ciurlionis, who was regarded as the founder of Lithuanian national music. He was an artist in both music and painting. He was the son of a church organist and was born in Varena in Southern Lithuania.

His father had encouraged his children to play music, and Mikalojus, his youngest, could play the piano by ear at three years of age and could sight-read music by the age of seven. He was fortunate to be the protégé of Prince Organiski and trained at the Warsaw Conservatory of Music, after which he earned a living by teaching music. Later, he studied at the Warsaw School of Fine Arts.

He produced more than 270 musical compositions, 200 paintings, and 80 drawings. Unfortunately, like Van Gogh, his mind deteriorated, and he died an untimely death at the age of 36. It intrigued Ivor to read that somehow, his art and music were intertwined.

Ivor had learned Lithuanian from Alex and Arthur, with whom he also spoke Russian, and he had pondered the situation in Lithuania and its Russian presence. He knew the regime was harsh, that his uncle Stasys had fought against it, and that Alex and Arthur were glad to have escaped from the country.

He could find no evidence that the Russians had persecuted the country's artists though. He spoke to Alex, who said that one of the enigmas of the Russian occupation was that although they did their utmost to obliterate anything Lithuanian, they had left the country's musicians and artists to themselves unless they openly promoted Lithuanian independence. Ivor said he would like to learn more about Ciurlionis. Alex welcomed Ivor's interest in Lithuania.

"I hope if you intend to do research in the country, you do not have trouble in getting into it. They have the name Greenus in their records. I am sure I am recorded as an undesirable person. I think my regular articles criticising the Russian occupation would ensure that I have retained that classification. The abortive attack on me at the logging camp was an indication of the regime's anger. If you go to Lithuania, you may find the KGB pestering you."

Ivor spent as much time as he could speaking Lithuanian. He picked his father's and Arthur's brains on the history, geography, and social structure of the country. He read all the books he could find until he felt confident that he would be able to undertake research on Ciurlionis.

When he returned to Oxford in October, his proposed dissertation on a relatively unknown Lithuanian composer entitled, "Mikalojus Konstantinas Ciurlionis, a Forgotten Musician," was approved.

Ivor's supervisor said, "Mr. Greenus, I should like to explain the academic approach to a dissertation such as the one you contemplate completing. The technique is to state an hypothesis that you will prove or disprove. The dissertation must be based on original research, and it is recommended that you attend a course on research methods in the university's historical research department. Here is the director's card. You will find him a great help. I am here to guide you, and I am sure we will work well together. I recommend, too, that you study the copies of dissertations you will find in the Music Faculty Library."

Ivor followed the advice given by the historical research director. He spent hours in the Bodleian Library and the British Museum gathering preliminary information on the remarkable man who claimed he could hear colours and see sounds.

Before going to Lithuania to cover basic research, he maintained his interest in the Outdoor Club, but he missed Angela and wrote to tell her so. She said she retained pleasant memories of their days together and wished him success with his dissertation. She had obtained a position with a firm of prominent architects in

Melbourne. She had renewed her interest in Australia's aborigines, whom she believed had been badly treated.

The Russian occupiers of Lithuania did not encourage normal visitors, but as Alex had pointed out, they had left the arts alone and Ivor obtained permission to stay for six months provided he reported his activities to the Ministry of Culture each month. The Rhodes trustees kindly gave him extra funds for his research.

He flew to Vilnius and from there continued on to Druskininkai, a town situated in a picturesque landscape with rivers, lakes, hills, and forests. It was also famous as a spa. Ciurlionis had lived there for many years after his father obtained work as an organist in the town's little church.

Ivor found accommodation with Mrs. Daina Kipras, a widow who catered to visitors to the town's healing waters. There was a lull in the tourist traffic, and she provided Ivor with one of her largest rooms, which overlooked the Ratnycia River. She was interested in his work and told him that in addition to the artist's home, which was now the M. K. Ciurlionis Memorial Museum, there was another house next to it restored to its original state by M.K.'s sisters.

She told Ivor he could use her son's bicycle. He accepted her offer gratefully; it enabled him to explore the beautiful city, its wooded surroundings, and its river banks.

The officials at the museum were intrigued with his work and helped him with his research and the listing of Ciurlionis's paintings and music. He was encouraged to play the composer's sonatas against a background of his paintings to selected audiences.

He moved to Kaunas and worked in Vytautus, the Great Museum of Culture, which in 1997 would be renamed the M.K. Ciurlionis National Museum of Art. It was built in 1936 with an M. K. Ciurlionis gallery to house the composer/artist's collection. None of his canvasses was sold in his lifetime.

Alex was correct in assuming that he would be watched, and one afternoon, he was approached by three men who said they were from the country's security force. They wished to ask him some questions. Ivor asked for identification. The spokesman of the group said they did not need to identify themselves to a pipsqueak foreign student. They wanted to know where he had learnt Lithuanian. To irk them, Ivor replied in fluent Russian and again asked for some identification. One of the men pulled out a card and waved it at him. Ivor demanded to examine it. Its text was in Russian.

He read the words aloud and said, "You are KGB not Lithuanian security policemen."

"Yes. We keep this country safe. Once again, where did you learn Lithuanian?"

"I learnt it from my father and his friend who live in Canada, my home country."

"You gained entry as a student of an English university, but you have not enrolled in any place of learning. What are you doing?"

"I am researching the history of a famous musician, not studying in classes."

"Show us your entry permit."

Ivor handed his papers to one of the men who looked at them.

"Why are you a Canadian at an English university studying some unknown Lithuanian musician?"

"Because I am a musician and plan to publicise the work of the musician Ciurlionis, who was once famous but has been forgotten."

"There is no need to dig up old Lithuanian rubbish. You speak Russian, why don't you research our excellent composers?"

"I studied them during my days in the Moscow Youth Orchestra. They have been well researched. There is no real research on Ciurlionis. I am equipped to do it."

"You are really a Russian. Do not be taken in by anti-Russian nonsense you may hear. You are a mysterious person, and we will keep our eyes on you. Don't forget to report monthly to the authorities as you undertook to do."

"I am surprised you think me mysterious. You now know all about me. I shall have my head down in research here unless I am out of town collecting information for my work."

"Just be careful; that is all."

Ivor was amused by the visit. He assumed the agents had not connected him with his father but had given him the standard treatment for visiting students.

He worked at the existing museum and library where he found valuable material and many of the artist's paintings awaiting display in the new museum. After a few days, one of the library assistants, Audra Skruibis, handed him a note requesting that he meet her for lunch at a nearby restaurant.

He found her sitting at a secluded table. She said he no doubt wondered why she had asked him to meet her. Ivor nodded in agreement. She told him that the Russians had systematically destroyed many Lithuanian historical records, but her museum had secreted valuable documents in their basement. They included items important for his research. The museum was not strictly monitored, and she could show him the basement and how to find the material hidden under some junk.

Ivor said it was brave of her to trust him. He warned her that they would need to be careful, because he understood many Lithuanians collaborated with the Russians. She sadly agreed that was the case, but the museum staff was safe to deal with. Her plan was for him to move into the basement when the coast was clear and to tap once on the ceiling when he planned to leave. If there was a one-tap response, he could emerge; if two, he would have to stay until it was safe.

He thanked her for her help and made use of it. He was delighted with the access to information on Ciurlionis and told Audra so. She said he could help further by removing some valuable material and having it stored in England.

He was now a familiar figure in the museum, and people were used to seeing him carrying a briefcase bulging with papers. Daily, he removed important papers, and finally, some of the artist's early journals. By the time he finished his research, he had a substantial amount of material. He camouflaged it with his notes and a lot of pro-Russian books, which he used to cover the material in his suitcase.

Before leaving Lithuania, he visited his relations, none of whom was happy with the Soviet regime. They were surprised that the authorities were so accommodating to him. He said art and music were expressed in international languages that all could understand and posed no dangers to the authorities. They were intrigued with his description of Ciurlionis's activities and said it took someone from abroad to enlighten them on their own famous people.

On arrival in England, he dumped the Russian books and presented the smuggled material to the British Museum, whose staff had been so helpful to him. He asked that his part in the donation be kept secret, as he would probably return to Lithuania from time to time. He hoped that Lithuania would be free one day and the papers could be returned to its authorities.

Ivor's adviser was delighted with his dissertation and with his final piano recital, which consisted of some of Ciurlionis's work. At the *viva voce* examination, Alex delighted the examiners by illustrating the interplay of music on one of Ciurlionis's paintings. He was awarded the master of philosophy with distinction and was congratulated by his adviser, friends, and the Rhodes trustees, all of whom said he should continue his research.

He now had a substantial music background. He wondered what he should do with it. It was too advanced for schools. He thought he was unlikely to train as a teacher. The idea of becoming a priest remained. In Lithuania, he had been impressed with the stubborn spirit of the people who longed for the end of Russian repression and had clung to their religious beliefs in the face of atheistic outpourings from their rulers.

For his master's dissertation, Ivor had had to limit his research to the production of 30,000 words, but he had data on many aspects of the intriguing composer/artist left to explore. Among all the things that interested him, two stood out. The first was that although Ciurlionis's father had been a Catholic, the artist himself rarely mentioned religion and had expatiated on other beliefs and mysticisms. His mother was a Calvinist, who had to bring him and his eight siblings up on the smell of an oil rag and with little help from his wayward father. Perhaps she influenced him away from Rome. The second point was that little was written about the composer's nationalism. He was an early pioneer in the promotion of the Lithuanian language, despite his father's insistence on the speaking of Polish. He also arranged festivals of Lithuanian art.

Ivor felt he could obtain funds for a year's work from the Rhodes trustees if he decided to study for a doctor of philosophy. The thought of two Doctor Greenuses appealed to his sense of humour. He discussed this with Alex, who told him to go ahead.

"It is fatal to live on regrets and to entertain nagging thoughts about not having finished something important. You can rely on me if you run short of funds. We also have a vibrant Lithuanian community. They would be tickled pink that one of their members is resuscitating the work of a gifted Lithuanian. They would dip into their pockets to help you. All we would have to do is to arrange for you to play a recital of some of Ciurlionis's work."

"Dad, I have entertained the idea of becoming a priest and following the example of the priests and bishops who have helped our family. I can't fathom how more musical knowledge would fit in with that."

"It may not do so immediately, but it would be a great achievement to obtain a doctor of philosophy and another year before you enter a seminary would not set any hearts aflutter at the Vatican," said Alex who was impressed that his son, born a Communist and a well-travelled and talented musician, should contemplate becoming a priest. He pointed out that once a priest, he would be subjected to the rigid discipline of a bishop or order and that might mean the end or a limitation of the music he loved and to which he had devoted years of study.

"Dad, you're right but the music will always be with me. I will always be able to play if only with my flute, with which I am now proficient."

Ivor wrote to the Oxford School of Music and said that he would like to enrol for a doctor of philosophy degree. His proposed research would be on the life of Ciurlionis, the subject of his master's dissertation with special reference to the composer's years of painting and the composer's unique connection of his art with his music. He received a friendly reply and was requested to call at the university before the opening of the Michaelmas term, when he would be required to expand on his project with the faculty in order for his proposed work to be approved.

On his arrival at the School of Music, he was greeted warmly and congratulated on planning to devote another year to the study of music.

"Your dissertation has aroused a great deal of interest, and a further study of the same subject should answer some of the questions that have been raised," his adviser said.

He was asked to appear before an examining committee who questioned him on his plans.

"I understand there are some studies I must complete, and then I would be free to go to Lithuania. There is a problem that I encountered in my earlier research. I am fluent in Lithuanian, Ciurlionis's language, and when I was in Lithuania, it was natural to do my thinking and writing in the local language; in fact, I drafted my dissertation in Lithuanian and translated it into English. In so doing, there were several nuances of the language that were untranslatable.

"What I propose, and for which I trust I have your approval, is to present my thesis in Lithuanian and provide a translation for those not familiar with one of Europe's rare languages. My translation could be challenged, but that would not alter the accuracy of the thesis."

"Mr. Greenus," said one of the examiners, "that would not be a problem. As you know, our libraries hold works in a variety of languages, and it is up to scholars to decipher them. As you progress with your work, your adviser will accept your translations, because unfortunately, we do not have access to a Lithuanian translator. The fact that Lithuanian is a rare and difficult language would make your intended work of value to the university and others."

The meeting continued with questions on Ciurlionis and his dropping of an established reputation in music for a dubious one in art and how Ivor would assemble material to prove his hypothesis. Shortly afterwards, he was told that he had been accepted as a doctor of philosophy student and the year's syllabus was explained to him.

Ivor returned to Lithuania armed with a six months' residential permit. He went back to the museum in Kaunus. Once again, the KGB interrogated him, and he answered their questions politely. They were curious that he had returned and queried that he continued to research the life of a mixed-up Lithuanian musician who could not make up his mind whether to compose or paint. Ivor explained that the "mix-up," as they described it, was the reason for his interest in Ciurlionis.

Ivor concentrated on the pictures the artist had described in terms of his music. He readily understood the connection, and the pictures made sense to him. He compared them with those of artists of the same period and was startled at the contrast between Ciurlionis's expressive but often ill-defined pictures and the graphic exactness of the others.

But he got his message across and conveyed the mysticism with which he was engrossed. I shall concentrate on some of his major works, he decided, for which purpose he chose *Winter* and *Sonatas*.

He also wrote chapters on the composer's nationalism, his contribution to the development of the Lithuanian language, and the influence of religion on his work.

He returned to Oxford from time to time for discussions and guidance from his adviser. At his suggestion, Ivor obtained permission from Ciurlionis's trustees to reproduce some of the artist's paintings as an addendum to his thesis. He also included musical scores that supported his hypothesis.

The Oxford viva voce, the prelude to the granting of a degree was long, not because of doubts about Ivor's work, but because of the examiners' fascination with it. They congratulated him, said he would be awarded a degree, and suggested he remain at Oxford as a junior tutor. Ivor said he was flattered, but he needed to return to Canada to consider other options.

Alex and Giselle also congratulated him on his success and asked what he intended doing.

Ivor said he was still thinking about becoming a priest. He told them that he had met Father Staugaitis, of whom Alex had spoken with such reverence. He was impressed by the priest, who though emaciated by his sufferings, still helped people spiritually. He eked out a humble living and despite his tribulations retained his sense of humour. He quietly held services in his humble dwelling. Ivor was amazed and asked the priest how he got away with it. He was told that traces of religion remained with many Russians, and on that account, the local authorities left him alone.

"Ivor," he had said, "I am a decrepit old man and serve some purpose. I am unlikely to plant bombs or start a revolution, so they do not pester me. I quietly plant what they would regard as subversive ideas in the minds of people without the authorities knowing. Please remember me to your father. I know he kept the faith and was kind to your family." Ivor left him with all the money he could spare and wished him well.

He often thought of Father Masse, a cultured man who was content to serve a small parish and by whom no social problem went unanswered, and of St. Casimir Church, which had helped his father and other family members. Finally, he thought of his great friend Bishop Levesque, a no-nonsense servant of God whose example inspired many of the children at the logging camp to be serious about religion. If those remarkable men could devote their lives to the welfare of others, should he not consider doing the same? His volunteer work with poor people in Kingston had underlined for him the need for serious help to be given to the underprivileged. Would not service as a priest enable him to contribute?

"Ivor, I admire your thinking, but I sense you have some doubts. What are they?" asked Alex.

"You're right. Often, when I am playing or listening to music, my mind wanders to people's troubles, and, as an academic exercise, I once analysed the background of famous composers. Invariably, I found sorrow and problems in their lives. Subconsciously, my interest in music may have led me to my current thoughts. Ciurlionis, for example, who came from a religious family, rarely mentioned the Christian religion and was inspired by other forces. I admired his sad genius.

"My mother paid lip service to the Church but in private decried its practices. She poured scorn on the celibacy of the clergy. She knew it was not a doctrinal issue but was what she called the personal opinion of some Pope or other. She said it was an abnormal imposition and led to trouble. She said the Russian Orthodox Church, a sort of branch of Rome, that had defied suppression by the Soviets, was up-to-date. Its priests could marry, and the Church permitted contraception and divorce and had an open mind on abortions. She also decried, and this is understandable with her high army rank, that the Catholic Church humbled its women who could not rise above being nuns and servants to the male priesthood hierarchy."

"Ivor, I can understand your dilemma. Many aspirant priests entertained doubts about the Church but training at a seminary resolved them. I suggest you talk to Bishop Levesque."

Ivor followed his father's advice and met with the Bishop. He was warmly greeted and was told that during his absence, the bishop's impromptu hockey team had not lost a match, but with Ivor back in circulation, he expected some stern battles. Ivor said he might not oppose him for long, because he was leaning towards a life in the Church.

"Excellent, we need a good musician, and you would be a great asset as an organist and choirmaster."

"That's not what I had in mind, Your Grace. I want to serve people directly."

The bishop listened to Ivor's reasoning and suggested they pray for guidance, after which he outlined the training his young friend would need and the vows he would have to honour. He said the Church would welcome him but warned that a priest's life required discipline and brought few rewards other than those associated with helping others. Ivor outlined his doubts about the celibacy of the clergy, the minor role of women, and the Church's opposition to family planning. The Bishop said he was wise to entertain doubts and suggested that Ivor spend two years in a seminary where his doubts would likely be resolved and then make his decision. He recommended a seminary that would suit him and said the Church would bear the cost of the training. Ivor thanked him for his advice. He said he would enrol at the recommended seminary but that he would pay his own way.

Ivor thought of his lover, Angela Somers, with whom he had maintained a warm correspondence and whom he had thoughts of marrying. Dear Angela, that extrovertish and lovely person who had taught him to dance, would probably be concerned with her lover pledged to a celibate life—Angela, the architect who had entranced him for hours with her descriptions of Oxford's famous buildings and who had persuaded him to lighten up and play popular tunes. He had missed her badly, and the Outdoor Club ventures were not the same without her. How would she greet a decision to put his old life behind him and start afresh without her?

He wrote to her and outlined his thoughts. He said that no matter what he did, he would always love her and remember their association with affection. He said that despite some shining examples of priests who devoted their lives to their parishioners often in difficult circumstances, he had some doubts about the life of a priest.

She surprised him by recommending he attend the seminary and then make up his mind. She regretted that if he became a priest they could not resume their friendship on its old basis, but they could be companions. She said that she had always been impressed with his concern for others and remembered he was the first to help her when she injured her ankle. She thought that in the eyes of his Church, she, an Anglican, was a heretic, but she would understand if he pursued his inclinations.

He enrolled at the recommended seminary and enjoyed its programs and the companionship of the students, many of whom had abandoned good, permanent jobs in response to a call to serve God. They were a cheerful lot, and there was plenty of fun after the study periods. Ivor was in demand as a pianist and against his better judgment responded to requests for jazzy tunes.

When he expressed his doubts about certain restrictions in the Catholic faith, such as the minor role of women, a friend laughed and said he should read the First Epistle of Paul, "Let women keep silence in the churches for it is not permitted until then to speak." Ivor smiled and asked where in the Bible it said priests and nuns should be celibate.

11

The Anglican Priest

Several missionaries addressed the students, one of whom impressed Ivor. He had served in the far north of Canada and outlined the difficulties of working there despite which the missionaries succeeded in spreading the Gospel and helped the indigenous people in many ways.

Ivor decided to follow the speaker's example. He read all he could find on the early missionaries among the Inuit. He wondered at the incredible difficulties they faced and the work they did that went far beyond preaching the Gospel. They established the first schools and were backed by the federal government in that work. The more he read, the more interested he became in wanting to help the Inuits in the far north.

He spoke to Bishop Levesque about it. He applauded his thinking, because he knew how difficult it was to recruit priests for the vigorous and tiring work in the peculiar conditions in the north where winter meant almost complete darkness. He quipped that Ivor should take his hockey gear, because he would have natural ice on which to play all year round.

Later, Ivor said that he had decided to defer his ordination as a priest. His doubts had not been resolved, and he knew he would be a hypocrite not to admit that. He would still like to help the people in the Arctic and would explore ways of doing so.

"My son," said the Bishop, "I understand. There are examples of priests who have smothered their doubts and were obliged later to go through the sad procedure of resigning. God will guide you, and I am certain it will be towards helping others. Bless you and good luck."

Ivor told Alex of his decision. He said it did not mean he had abandoned his idea of helping people in Canada's north, people whose lives were being turned upside down by the intrusion of Western civilisation. Before he reached a final decision, he would visit Angela, his Australian companion at Oxford. She shared his humanitarian views and likely would help him decide on his future.

"Ivor, you are wise to think ahead. My generation was propelled into a long war, and our futures were predetermined for us. If one survived, one was advised to study and make up for lost time and then bring up a family. Today, you have more choices, and that is a mixed blessing, because one hesitates to select one. I sound like one of our pontificating politicians, but I am sure you get my meaning. Good luck in Australia. From what you have told me about Angela, I feel sure she will help you."

Angela was delighted to hear of his visit and met him at the Tullamarine airport in Melbourne. They hugged and kissed, and she teased that it was probably the anticipated repetition of such enjoyable practices that deterred him from becoming a priest.

He said, "Angela, you beautiful sheila, you have hit the nail on the head. I am unhappy about the celibacy of the clergy, particularly when I think of you. I would like to marry you, but I have a yen to serve in Canada's far north where I think the population is being exploited. I cannot expect you to give up Australia's sunshine for Arctic conditions."

He looked out of the car window and said, "Oh, what a traffic jam! At least you would not face one in the Arctic. I knew

Melbourne was a big city, but I have never seen traffic like this even on our 401 in Toronto at peak hour. What's going on?"

"You must have noticed that the Aussies at Oxford were sports mad. There are over 200 days of sunshine in most parts of Australia, and we simply have to get outside our buildings and enjoy life. Tomorrow, the Melbourne Cricket Ground will be jam-packed with spectators for the final of the Australian Football Rules, or 'footie' competition, hence this traffic. Tickets are as scarce as hen's teeth, and accommodation is at a premium, so you will have to share my apartment. My home team from Geelong is in the final."

"I see. Sports-mad Aussies. Footie final. Geelong. What have I come to? I was looking forward to the comfort of a hotel suite, but I'll grin and bear the thought of sharing space with you."

"Ivor, that is condescending of you, but you have not asked me what I thought about living in Canada's far north."

"Would you come with me?"

"Is that a marriage proposal? If it is, it is somewhat frigid. I am a little involved with our aborigines. It would interest me to help with yours, but I don't understand what position you would hold."

"I am still interested in religion, and as a long shot, I thought of working with the more enlightened churches that are doing good work in the north, in particular the Anglicans. They do not differ much from Catholics and old Henry VIII, the founder of the Church of England, shifted only slightly from Roman Catholicism to accommodate a divorce. He had the title of Defender of the Faith, a classic oxymoron. I am familiar with Anglican services, thanks to your guided tour of all the chapels in Oxford."

"How interesting. One hears of Anglicans becoming Catholics but rarely the reverse. Shall we check if it would be possible for you to be an Anglican priest?"

"Angela, I told my father that I thought you might have the answer to my problems, and you may have proved me correct."

The next day, Angela introduced him to her bishop, the Rt. Rev. John Mayne, to whom she had explained the purpose of her visit. He was intrigued with Ivor.

"You are a multilingual, highly qualified musician who has graduated from a prestigious Catholic seminary and you ask if you could become an Anglican priest. Why, may I ask?"

"Your Grace, it is simple. I want to marry Angela and then serve in Canada's Arctic regions."

"Well, I am sure you would be welcome in our Church. There would be no question of further studies, but you would have to serve a year in one of our churches under the guidance of its minister. I am afraid you would not earn enough to support two of you."

"That would not be a problem, because an uncle of mine has left me a small fortune, and should we marry, I would be able to support us," said Angela.

"In that case, all that remains is for you, Ivor, to contact the Anglican authorities in Canada and persuade them to accept you as a student priest. At the end of your probation, you would be tested on your knowledge of our procedures and protocols, and if successful, ordination would follow. What university did you go to in Canada?"

"Queens University in Kingston, Ontario."

"Does it have a divinity faculty?"

"Yes, a strong one; the university was founded on religious lines."

"One moment, let me look at a list of dioceses in Canada. I have it somewhere. Here it is. Yes, you should contact the Rt. Rev. Frederick Bartholomew of the Diocese of Kingston at 90 Johnson Street, Kingston."

"Your Grace, thank you."

"Not at all, my son, a pleasure and may you succeed in your endeavours. Bless you both."

Ivor and Angela left the cathedral and wandered down the street on their way to lunch at a restaurant fortunately free of footie enthusiasts.

"Well," asked Angela, "what do we do now?"

"I ask formally for your hand in marriage, and to save time, I suggest we have a civil wedding here and then head for Kingston. As my wife, you will have no trouble entering Canada. I can find accommodation from my business pals."

"We must see my parents first. They are easygoing, but there is no reason to shock them with a sudden *fait accompli*."

They headed for Geelong, which was about an hour from Melbourne, and met Angela's parents.

"So you are the man who helped Angela when she sprained her ankle on a hike," her father said.

"Yes, and I enjoyed her descriptions of the ancient buildings in Oxford."

"You are a long way from home. What brings you here?"

"I had a problem and thought Angela might help me solve it."

"She has always been free with advice. Did she help you?"

"Yes, but we needed to see you before we implemented her solution."

"Where do we come into it?"

"We plan to marry and felt you should be the first to know. After that, we shall head for Canada where I hope to become an Anglican priest."

"That sounds odd. We thought you were a musician."

"Yes, I am, but I also have a desire to help the less-privileged members of our society, in my case, the Inuits in the far north of Canada."

"Would our outdoor girl Angela be happy with a frigid existence?"

"Dad, it is not always uncomfortably frigid, and it sounds exciting to me. Imagine being able to ski almost the whole year round."

"Well, good luck to you two. In our day, one told one's parents before an engagement, but times have changed. When do you expect to marry?"

"We have obtained a special licence, so it will be next Wednesday. There will not be a ceremony. I'll tell friends and relatives about it later from Canada."

"I will not have to fork out for a reception, so I'll stand good for your airfares."

"Thank you, you have always been generous to me."

Ivor and Angela had lunch with her parents and returned to her apartment. She said, "I know a friend who wants this apartment furnished, so I'll do a deal with her. There is someone in our office who is a wizard with cars, and I'll hand mine to him for selling. I have a lot of holiday time; I'll use that in lieu of notice. Fortunately, I have just completed work on a big project and have not got my teeth into anything, so my employers will not have to handle awkward unfinished work."

Ivor phoned one of his varsity hockey friends in Kingston with whom he had remained in contact. Through him, he obtained the use of a house in Alfred Street shortly to be vacated by some students.

Six days later, they collected their air tickets at the airport, and Angela shrieked, "Ye Gods, Dad has booked us in business class! I knew he always travelled that way, but this will be a first for me. Mind you, Dad is well-heeled. He was a shrewd stockbroker and made a lot of money for his clients and our family. How super, the long trip will be a comfortable one."

They flew Qantas to Vancouver and then flew to Toronto by Air Canada. They hired a car, and Ivor said she would witness some interesting traffic on one of Canada's main highways, the 401, driven on the wrong side of the road according to Australian and British rules of the road.

She was impressed with the traffic in double and treble lines, but the countryside was boring, flat, and dry after a hot summer. She liked what she saw of Kingston, the Limestone City, and thought the house, although showing evidence of student neglect, would meet their needs. They unpacked, and after a meal at a downtown restaurant, they bought groceries. Then they relaxed after their exciting fortnight together.

The next day, Ivor said, "Now is the big test. I will phone the diocese office and fix an appointment with the bishop." He did so and was surprised to learn that the Bishop's secretary knew all about him. "Doctor Greenus, the Bishop of Melbourne phoned us and told us to expect a visit from you and explained its purpose. You may call on His Grace at two this afternoon."

They arrived in good time and were ushered into the Bishop's office. He was a tall, grey-haired man, dressed informally. He said he was pleased to meet an aspirant priest and his wife.

"It has become difficult to recruit trainee priests and to meet one who is an accomplished musician and well versed in the scriptures is indeed a pleasure."

Ivor quickly explained his position, and the Bishop smiled and said there would be no problem in Ivor becoming an Anglican priest.

"Our High Church members are for all intents and purposes Catholics, and you would be at home with us. I understand you spent two years at a Catholic seminary, so you have all the required academic knowledge. As Bishop Mayne no doubt mentioned, you will need to serve a year's probation with an Anglican priest. We would then check on your knowledge of our policies and procedures. Would that be acceptable to you?"

"Yes, Your Grace, that would be ideal."

"There are three parishes where you could spend a year. Here is a list of them."

Ivor read the list and said he would be pleased with the St. Mary Magdalene Church in Napanee, a relatively short distance from Kingston where he had spent four years at Queens University.

"Fine. I'll tell Reverend Hallowes to expect you. You must satisfy yourselves that you are compatible, and if you have any doubts, you could move to another church. Reverend Hallowes came from

Wiltshire to Canada as a skilled laboratory technician and gave up a good job, attended religious courses at the University of Toronto, and chose to come to this diocese. I suspect my obvious English accent had something to do with it. He is a serious person but has an underlying sense of humour that is quite refreshing. Here is his phone number. He'll be there any day except Monday when he will be in the woods somewhere. He is a great outdoorsman and hikes for miles."

Ivor knew his way around Kingston. He found the car he wanted and bought it with help from Angela. He phoned Reverend Hallowes and arranged to meet him after he had been to Quebec to see his father. Ivor had phoned Alex from Australia and told him of his marriage and plan to convert to the Anglican faith. Alex congratulated him and said he looked forward to meeting Angela. Ivor told him they would probably live in Kingston for a while, and as soon as they were settled, they would come to Drummondville.

Angela and Ivor set off on the 401 and headed east until they reached Quebec Highway 20 and then the 116 to Drummondville. Angela remarked on the absence of English signs. Ivor laughed and said a visit to Quebec would expand her knowledge of Canada.

"There is a nationalist movement with some strange ideas, including one that thinks Quebec is an entity separate from Canada. I think it is a romantic ideal. The Quebec separatists ignore the feelings of the province's 800,000 English-speaking citizens and the province's diverse First Nations population. Federal governments have to win seats in Quebec to stay in power and conveniently overlook Quebec's minority groups; one federal government after another throws industries, buildings, government offices, and money to Quebec to collect its citizens' votes. We have an expression that the squeaky door gets the oil and that describes Quebec. The ban on signs in languages other than French is nonsensical in today's global economy and travel business."

Alex and Giselle greeted the couple warmly and asked questions about Australia and Angela's views on Canada. She said she had only been there a short while but everybody had been pleasant, "eh?" They laughed, and she continued, "I think I have summed up Canada as one of the world's population melting spots with two big unanswered questions, namely, what are we going to do about our aborigines, and how do we make Quebecers into Canadians?"

"You are ahead of most Canadians in your thinking. I think that outside of Quebec, only one Canadian in a hundred will raise questions on those topics; the other ninety-nine will be too absorbed in hockey to worry about them. In any event, welcome and may you enjoy our huge country. It differs from Australia particularly in winter. Will you have time to go to the old camp?" asked Alex.

Ivor said as much as he would like to show Angela the old logging camp, he would have to defer that pleasure. He explained to her that Alex had once cut and carted timber in a logging camp and that accounted for his muscular build. Some years ago, he had acquired an old camp and he and his friends had restored it for the benefit of selected members of the public. Hundreds of kids had obtained training in environmental activities thanks to Alex.

When asked about their plans, Ivor said he would work on probation in a church in Napanee, after which he hoped to realise his dream of working among the Inuit.

"Dad, I will have a year in Napanee to use my musical knowledge in a small way. Who knows, I may find scope for research somewhere. There is music throughout the world, even among primitive people."

"Giselle and I wondered what to give you as a wedding present and decided on a five-year subscription to *Canada Geographic*; tickets to the Three Tenors' concert in Toronto; and a thousand dollars to buy something when you settle into a home."

"That is wonderful, thank you," said Ivor, who was echoed by Angela.

They left with their car full of fruit, preserves, and frozen food in an insulated box. They promised to return as soon as they had settled down in Napanee. Ivor said it was customary to give new ministers food, and Alex and Giselle were ahead of the pack in doing so.

They arranged to meet Reverend Hallowes and drove through farmland on Highway 2 to Napanee where they found the St. Mary Magdalene Church on Bridge Street. Angela noted that it was constructed in the Gothic Revival style using rock-faced coursed ashlar limestone masonry.

They went to the entrance, and Jasper Hallowes responded to their knocking. He was a blue-eyed blonde with a rugged complexion, the body of an athlete, and a handshake like a vice.

"Welcome, Doctor and Mrs. Greenus. I gather this is a shakedown session to decide if we are compatible. I have no doubt we shall be, and I would be delighted to have your assistance for a year. I will show you over the church and answer your questions, and then you are invited to lunch with me and my wife, Phyllis."

Angela said, "We would like to do that, but I should tell you that although married to Ivor, I am Angela Somers. Relax, Reverend Hallowes, I am not a women's libber; I just want to preserve my identity as an individual."

"Fair enough, Ms. Somers. Just follow me, and I'll show you around."

Angela was impressed with the church and noticed that some maintenance work was needed. Jasper noticed her looking at the roof and ceilings and commented on her interest. Angela said it was a conditioned reflex or professional curiosity; she was an architect.

"You are an architect? Splendid. If you come here, you could be a great help, if you are willing, of course. We are in the middle of a fundraising campaign to replace the roof and fix some interior damage. We have been given plans by a contractor with experience with church buildings, but it has been suggested that we obtain professional advice."

"Whether you accept Ivor or not, I would help you. You must realise that I qualified at Oxford University, a strict institution and then cut my practical teeth in the tough Australian construction industry. The workers had no respect for women as such, and some were rude to me until I put them in their places by swapping fruity language with them. My company was a no-nonsense one, fair but firm with clients and contractors. It is possible that I may be too plain-speaking for your potential contractor."

"Thank you for your consideration. Your approach could be a welcome change, because one hears one story after another of people being let down by builders."

They had a pleasant lunch with the Hallowes, after which Ivor and Angela had a short chat and then told Jasper that if he were happy, they would welcome working in his parish for a year. He and Ivor shook hands and agreed to meet the next day to discuss future activities.

Ivor and Jasper got on well together, and Ivor undertook to handle the church's small choir. He examined the organ and found some faults that he was able to correct. He soon had the choir in good shape, and its improvement attracted members who had dropped out for one reason or another.

As promised, Angela had a look at the proposed building project. She was soon pouring over blueprints and climbing all over the building, much to the amusement of passersby who were unused to a woman in overalls and hard hat moving huge ladders, mounting them, and then pulling out a tape measure and checking distances. She uncovered some shoddy work that had remained hidden. When she felt she had a firm idea of the building, she turned to the proposal given to the church by the potential contractor.

It was loosely worded, leaving loopholes the contractor could exploit: it did not have penalty clauses for delays; there was no proof of liability insurance, the absence of which would expose the church to all manner of claims; and there was no provision for the calculation of extras or savings in the work. She spoke to the church member in charge of its buildings and pointed out the changes that needed to be made to the proposed contract. He said that the contractor, William Armitage, had an excellent reputation and could be relied on to do a good job. Angela responded that if that were true, he should accept her recommendations with good grace.

He thanked her for her work and passed her recommendations to Armitage, who blew a fuse. He said his proposed contract was one he had used to the satisfaction of several church clients. He would have to increase his price if architectural interference was approved. Angela smiled. It was a familiar story. She said, "Mr. Armitage, be careful with your words. I am not an interferer; I am a professional committed to fair trading. My recommendations cover standard conditions, and their cost should be included in your price. I have carefully measured all the work to be done, and there are no complications to it. According to a schedule of local building costs I have compiled, you would receive a fair price for work done. However, if you persist in your attitude and attempt to denigrate me, I shall recommend that the work be put out to tender to contactors with liability insurance who would provide a bill of quantities to enable me to supervise their work."

The contractor left in a huff with a comment that he did not need a woman to tell him about construction.

He spoke to his foreman and said a bloody upstart female architect from Australia was about to throw a spanner in the works of the lucrative church contract they had drafted.

"Women are getting into everything. It was bad enough dealing with that female engineer on our last job; now we face one in total control of a job. Normally, I would tell the stupid bag to get back in the kitchen where she belongs, but we are short of work. We cannot risk losing the job and with that some of our skilled workers. That will happen if we remain idle. I'll have to eat humble pie and accept her conditions."

The amended contract, approved by the church's lawyers, was accepted and work started on time. The contractor was startled to arrive on site to find Angela in overalls and hard hat taking samples of concrete and measuring the layout of the groundwork that had to be done. The next day, she was on the roof examining the materials used and the crew's workmanship. Her close attention to detail kept the contractor's staff on their toes with the result that the work was completed efficiently, on time, and within the contracted price.

The church attributed this to the contractor, and Angela did nothing to disturb the praise given to him. Armitage had the decency to compliment Angela and said she had taught him a thing or two.

"If you intend to practise, I'll recommend you."

"Thank you, Mr. Armitage. I enjoyed matching my experience with Canadian conditions, but I doubt that I shall bother obtaining provincial registration. My husband and I will probably end up in the Arctic, where I will have to study igloo construction. What I suggest is that you use the contract upon which we agreed in your future work. It contained the essence of my long university studies and hard-earned experiences and was approved by the church's lawyers. I estimate it would cost you $20,000 to prepare a similar document, so in the end, you got a useful bonus for being a good boy.

"Your comments about that bloody Australian woman architect came back to me, but it was water off a duck's back. Your words were mild compared with what some Aussie contractors used to call me."

Armitage smiled and said his father had served in World War II in the Middle East with the Australians, whom he called diggers. He said fruity language came easy to them. Some were loudmouthed, but they were superb in battle. It seemed that their daughters had inherited some of the diggers' traits.

Angela smiled. "Mr. Armitage, I'm sure we have. The diggers called their mates with red hair 'Bluey.' For your information, because of my red hair I was known in the building trade alliteratively as 'that Bloody Brazen Bluey Bitch.' Good-bye and good luck."

She giggled when she told Ivor of her experience with Armitage. He said as a minister's wife, she would need to be more prudent with her language.

"Ivor, when you wrote your dissertation and thesis, you used appropriate academic language that would be totally Greek were you to use it from the pulpit. It would be useless if I acted sweet and proper with construction crews. I only told you about Armitage to amuse you. I shall be the epitome of decorum when needs must."

"Of course. As a matter of fact, I am to deliver next week's sermon. Should I discuss aggressive women and use Jezebel as an example? Perhaps you can give me a draft of her activities."

"I think you are hitting below the belt. Jezebel was not a nice lady. She had her own God, Baal, and turned people away from the Hebrews. She died a horrible death."

"That was quite good. You must have had a good Bible teacher. My point would be that women should not be like Jezebel but be the epitome of decorum, as you put it."

"You would use the pulpit to put me in my place, would you? Your sermon would go down with a dull thump. You should choose something more uplifting."

"Yes, of course. Should I talk of the messages in music coming from the hymns? Or would that send more than the usual number to sleep? How did the poet put it? 'Music that gentlier on the spirit lies than tir'd eyelids upon tir'd eyes.'"

"No, give the congregation something positive and uplifting."

"Thank you. I have always enjoyed chaffing you and will ban Jezebel from my thoughts."

At the regular reception after the service, several parishioners said how much they enjoyed Ivor's sermon, which was about the need to love one's neighbour. Others congratulated him on the stimulus he had given to the choir and applauded his visiting of the sick and bereaved. He smiled and said it was all in the line of duty, and he had the good example of the Reverend Hallowes to follow.

Ivor and Angela accepted an invitation to join Jasper on his Monday walks. He showed them all the local trails and then moved into the countryside where there were numerous parks of interest. Angela was particularly interested in the old buildings in Napanee and Jasper said that at one time, Napanee was more active than Kingston. There were mills on the river; there was an active passenger boat service to Belleville and beyond; and ships came to Napanee to collect barley, the source of the wealth that enabled the huge homes to be constructed.

"In the early days, when there were gangs hacking down all the beautiful trees and creating a wasteland, logs were floated down the Napanee River to Deseronto."

They joined the local branch of Amnesty International and the historical society and soon had many friends. Angela presented a paper on Australian aborigines to Amnesty International and Ivor one on Lithuania to the historical society. Angela told Ivor she was glad they had chosen a quiet part of the country in which she could obtain some idea of what made Canada tick. She would be sorry when his year was up.

One day, Ivor was in the A&P store when he heard something drop followed by *"Perkunas!"* the old "Damn it" from the logging camp.

He turned and asked if that was a Lithuanian word he had heard.

"Yes," said a tall man with finely etched features, "and I could add a few more. I have broken a dozen eggs."

Ivor quoted a Lithuanian proverb equivalent to the English "Do not cry over spilt milk." The dropper of the eggs smiled and said the last language he expected to hear in Napanee was Lithuanian. Ivor said his father was from that country.

"So was mine," the man said.

Ivor helped clear up the mess and suggested that when they finished shopping, they should go to the nearby Tim Hortons for coffee. They had a great chat, and Ivor learnt that Albertas Vilius had been brought up in Quebec but after a life in the oil industry had bought and restored an old waterfront house in Adolphustown about 30 kilometres from Napanee. He invited Ivor and his wife to lunch. He said had he not cursed, Ivor would have missed contacting the only Lithuanians in the district.

Angela was intrigued when Ivor told him of the incident.

"You criticised me for my fruity language, but a curse has led to a new acquaintance whose wife incidentally has confirmed his invitation to lunch next Saturday."

On that day, they drove through pleasant farmland next to a lake.

Elena, their hostess, welcomed them to her attractive and well-appointed home, which was full of examples of Albertas's craftsmanship. She provided a superb meal of marinated herring on caraway rye bread, cold beet soup with sour cream, chilled seafood salad, and a fruit salad. She chatted to Ivor in French and Lithuanian and a language foreign to Angela. She was told it was Polish and that Poland once owned Lithuania. Ivor regaled them with an account of his research in Lithuania and the life of Ciurlionis, the forgotten composer who could hear music in his paintings and see paintings in his music. Angela was impressed with the animation with which Ivor spoke of the composer and his music and wondered if he would regret heading to a musical wasteland.

She visited the Tyendinaga Mohawk Territory and spoke to the band chief who said that apart from a few small matters, they had little about which to complain. She would, however, be interested in the dispute over the Culbertson Tract, he said. He provided her with the official background to a dispute that had simmered for years.

The Mohawks of the Bay of Quinte submitted their Culbertson Tract Specific Claim to the Government of Canada, which completed a thorough historical and legal review of the submission and accepted the First Nation's claim for negotiations under its Specific Claims policy.

"What this means is that the government admits the legitimacy of the Mohawks' claim and the band now awaits a settlement of the dispute that has the township of Deseronto and its inhabitants in a tizzy," said the chief.

Well, she thought, this sounds familiar. *Ivor said there were property disputes in the far north, and they must be part of the Canadian heritage. One does not read about them in publicity handouts.*

Ivor was asked to preach in Christ Church, Her Majesty's Royal Chapel of Mohawks, which, he was intrigued to learn, was one of the six royal chapels outside of Great Britain. It possessed a double silver Communion set presented by Queen Anne as a token of her appreciation of the Mohawks support of British forces and a Communion chalice presented by Queen Elizabeth. He chose as his text the parable of the Good Samaritan.

Jasper Hallowes told Ivor that a member of the congregation, who had been posted overseas for a year was looking for someone to look after his condominium at 7 Centre Street South, Napanee, while he was away. If Ivor were interested, he would introduce him to him.

Ivor said he would like to meet him. When he did, the owner explained that he did not want any rent, but Ivor would be responsible for hydro, TV, and telephone expenses. Ivor asked if he and his wife could see the condominium and fixed a date to do so. They were pleased with it and its site on the Napanee River flanked by two parks and accepted the opportunity to occupy it. Ivor spoke to the owner of the Alfred Street property, who earlier had thanked them for their attention to the house and garden, and he said notice was not necessary; he had a list of prospective tenants. Ivor and Angela were pleased to be relieved of the drives from Kingston to Napanee and back and the saving of rent money.

Ivor attended meetings of the Ministers Fraternal of Napanee. Towards the end of the year, there were discussions of Christmas activities. Ivor was interested in what music was involved and spoke to the ministers of two churches with choirs. He asked if they had ever produced Handel's *Messiah*. They laughed and said that was beyond their ability. Their parishioners usually went to a performance in Kingston. Ivor said that he could handle the production if he could obtain enough singers. Would they consider an amalgamation of three choirs to achieve that?

"Doctor Greenus," said one of the ministers, "I well remember an outstanding performance of yours with the Kingston Philharmonic Orchestra, and I have no doubt you could create a wonderful *Messiah*, but this is little Napanee."

"If you would give me a chance, I will listen to your choirs and judge whether my idea has any merit. I have the time to work on the production."

He listened to the small choir of the Grace United Church and the bigger one at the Trinity United Church and decided that with them and his own choir, he would succeed with his proposed production. He was given the go-ahead and persuaded the choirs to join forces.

Ivor then thought of Father Sean Murphy, the newly appointed priest at Napanee's St. Patrick Church, who had been a tutor at the seminary where Ivor studied. He fixed an appointment and met the priest at his church.

"Doctor Greenus—or Ivan the Terrible, as we called you for your escapades—what brings you to the opposition?"

"Father, you were always a leading light on ecumenical work, and I have an opportunity for you to put it into practice."

"Wait a minute. You were always the students' spokesman and had a glib way of getting what you wanted. Are you trying to con me?"

"You misjudge me. You know that my passion is music, and I have three choirs lined up to produce Handel's *Messiah*. I could use more voices. Would you agree to your choir joining the others? The event will be cast as an interdenominational one. Gowns will not be worn. Ladies will wear long white dresses without jewellery. The men will wear dark suits, white shirts, and navy-blue ties. There will be an entrance fee with profits going to the Napanee District Charitable Foundation."

"I like the idea. It will be a success. You could play anything from boogie-woogie to a Bach fugue. I will have to get the consent of the church council and will let you know. 'Handel's *Messiah* in Napanee,' what a headline that will make!"

He phoned later to say his choir would join forces with the others. Trinity Church was chosen for practices and the final performance. The singers were enthusiastic and responded to Ivor's patient conducting.

The proposed performance attracted a lot of attention. Several musical students from Queens University and other singers asked to join the amalgamated choirs. Booking for the event was brisk, and they decided to perform twice.

Ivor was in his element, and the singers responded to his enthusiasm and beautiful organ playing. He persuaded a lecturer in the Queens University's Faculty of Music to conduct the choir during the final rehearsals and during the public performances while he concentrated on the music.

The performances were a great success and $2,500 was raised. Ivor sent accounts of the performance and pictures of himself at the donation of the cheque ceremony to his father with the comment, "I am making use of my musical and religious training."

The year passed quickly. Ivor was interviewed by a committee appointed by the Bishop, whose members questioned him on all aspects of the Anglican faith. He satisfied them and was ordained by Bishop Bartholomew in St. George's Cathedral in Kingston.

Ivor was delighted to see Bishop Levesque at the ordination along with his parents. At a reception arranged by Alex, he introduced him to Angela.

"I am delighted to meet you. I have heard of your good work in helping your church with its building renovations. I even heard of the alliterative soubriquet Australian building contractors used to describe you."

"Your Grace, that got me into hot water with Ivor. I have been a paragon of decorum ever since telling him about it."

"I will use 'Bluey Beauty' to describe you."

"Thank you, Your Grace. Ivor said you were imbued with ecumenical work as exemplified by your presence here today. I will remember you as His Ecumenical Ecclesiastical Eminence. I am sure you will be a cardinal one day and fit my description."

"You flatter me."

Ivor said, "Your Grace, excuse me for interrupting your semantics display. I want to thank you sincerely for coming today. You have always been an example of religion at work. Despite our opposition on the ice, you have guided me spiritually. Your presence here today comforts me."

"Reverend Doctor Greenus, I have always cherished our relationship. You had doubts about serving God, but they are now resolved. God has found a way. As William Cowper said many years ago, 'God moves in mysterious ways his wonders to perform.' The doctrines of your Church and mine are similar, and we worship the same God. I wish you success in your ministry. I will not belittle the sacrifice I made in coming to Kingston today. By doing so, I forfeited the pleasure of playing in the final of our hockey league. Ivor, good luck, and God bless you both."

"Your Grace, I realise what a sacrifice that was. It has been a joy to meet and introduce my redheaded sheila, Angela, the Bluey Beauty as you aptly described her."

Alex had enjoyed listening to the repartee. He regretted Alisa was not present to witness Ivor's commitment to serving others.

11
The Far North

Ivor had explained earlier to his bishop that he wanted to serve in the far north and had made enquiries to the Diocese of the Arctic. He was told that until he left he could remain with the St. Mary Magdalene Church.

Ivor found information on the Anglican Diocese of the Arctic in the cathedral library and Kingston Public Library. The diocese, by far the largest of the thirty dioceses in Canada, covered an area of four million square kilometres or one third the area of Canada and included the North West Territories, Nunavet, and the Nunavik area of Quebec. It contains only 55,000 people with the Inuit living above the tree line and Indians living south of it. The first contacts of the Inuits with the outside world were with whalers and traders who sought the resources of the area. Ivor was interested to read that the majority of the Inuits were members of the Anglican Church.

Over the years, the small nomadic groups of people who used to follow the caribou, seals, and fish for food gathered into permanent settlements, many of which had populations of 1,000 or more. The Anglican Church had congregations in 51 of these settlements grouped into 31 parishes. In all but six of these congregations, the native language of the area was used for the main Sunday worship.

The territory was harsh and was frozen and snow-covered for half the year. It was not possible to have paved roads on the tundra.

Ivor had some idea of Arctic conditions but thinking of them in light of the work of a priest alarmed him. He read that the winter in the Arctic was cold with temperatures from -20 °C to -35 °C and these would be exacerbated by wind chill factors. One had to dress appropriately with thermal underwear, thermal socks, thick long-sleeved shirts, a heavy jersey, a thick vest, a sort of balaclava, a thick coat, insulated boots, warm headgear, and goggles. The conditions would be rougher than he had visualized, and when he read the clothing requirements to Angela, she said, "It will take all day to dress, and how does one move around with all that heavy clothing?"

"We will have to learn, but I believe people skate, snowboard, play hockey, curl, and ski, so one can manage."

"What happens when one comes inside? Does one pull off the clothing? Are buildings heated?"

"I don't know about heat, but they must be insulated. Can you imagine -25 °C with a wind chill added?"

"What is a wind chill?"

"It is additional coldness created by a cold wind."

"Tell me, Ivor, what do you think a priest can do in Arctic conditions?"

"From what I have read, one can preach the Gospel and help people with their problems. There must be many as they change from nomadic to almost sedentary lives. There have been pioneer priests, so presumably, I will receive training in order to benefit from their experience. We will learn all about it if I am accepted, when no doubt full information will be sent to me."

Ivor and Angela immersed themselves in learning all they could about the Diocese of the Arctic. Angela soon learnt that the Inuits, whose homelands for centuries were annexed by the Crown without reference to them, were beginning to demand some independence and protection from oil companies and others intent on exploiting the territory's natural resources. She made notes for the occasion when she could add her voice to those of others.

She remembered the Mabo case, in which an Australian Court rejected the application of *Terra nulius*, meaning the land is empty and therefore was available to the conquerors in the guise of explorers. She told Ivor that she would be glad to be in the Arctic and free to help the Inuits. She said that at school and later, she had learnt that the people in Canada's north were Eskimos, who hunted seals for food and oil, spent their winters in igloos living on frozen seal meat and fish, and kept warm with seal-oil lamps. She knew now that Eskimo meant "flesh eater" and was no longer used to describe the Inuits. In her opinion, the Inuits were correct to define themselves as a separate race and to demand control of their own destiny.

"Angela, you are right and one wonders how they survived in the raw conditions over a huge area. There are Inuit in Greenland, and there is a connection with people in Northern Russia. It's rather like the Kurds, who stretch across several countries. There is a cultural shift of people from a nomadic hunting life to a settled one with dubious incomes. The oil and mining companies that you criticise may yet be the saviours of the Inuit with jobs and income from local resources."

"I hope so. The mining companies in Australia, bloated with incomes from gold, iron, and diamonds, paid scant heed to the Aborigines' way of life and sacred grounds. In South Africa, the only benefit the natives got for the plunder of their traditional lands was the opportunity to sweat thousands of metres down in gold mines where accidents and miners' phthisis wrecked their families' lives."

Ivor received his appointment and was told to report to the diocese office in Yellowknife, where he would spend six months under the tuition of an experienced priest. When he had acquired sufficient knowledge of the language to communicate with the Inuit, he would be sent to a parish for further training.

He was given a folder with detailed documents explaining living conditions in the diocese and the goods and clothing he should bring with him. He wrote to his father and outlined his future. Ultimately, his work would be in the outlying areas where there were scattered villages. There was still work to be done on a dictionary of some of the Inuit dialects, and with his euphonic ear, he expected to solve problems with mysterious words that had defied earlier lexicographers. He told his father that he was convinced he was doing the right thing and looked forward to helping the Inuit, who were battling to fit their way of life into that of the modern world.

Ivor received a letter from the University of Lithuania advising him of the award of its DPhil degree in recognition of his research on Ciurlionis. He was invited to attend the graduation ceremony. He was delighted with the honour but could not afford the long trip. He had not earned any holiday time and reluctantly declined the invitation.

He decided to accept another distinction when the curator of Vytautus, the Great Museum of Culture in Kaunus, advised him that the Lithuanian government had struck a medal in his honour. He was invited to attend the museum to receive the award with expenses paid. He discussed this with Angela, and she said he should go. His parishioners would survive a week of his absence. His bishop approved, and he phoned Kaunus with his acceptance. He knew his father, relying on his past credentials, had organised a family reunion in Lithuania and hoped they would meet in Kaunas.

Ivor phoned to tell Alex that the Lithuanian government had honoured him with a commemorative medal for his work on Mikalojus Konstantinas Ciurlionis and had invited him to Kaunus to receive it. He had accepted and hoped he and Giselle would be at the ceremony. They congratulated him and, to his delight, said they would be there. They were keen to see how Lithuania was faring.

Ivor booked his flights. He would travel light and hoped the jet lag would not incapacitate him in Kaunus. He kissed Angela farewell and drove to Kugaaruk on his dilapidated ATV. At the airport, he arranged for the vehicle to be parked.

"Father," said an attendant, "we'll put it in the back of a hangar. Scoundrels have been robbing vehicles around here."

"I doubt if my wreck would interest them, but thank you. I'll be back in a week's time."

The man at the check-in desk whistled when he saw Ivor's tickets.

"Are you going 'round the world, Father?"

"Almost. I did a lot of work in Lithuania and am returning for a short visit."

"Have you any luggage to check?"

"No, I only have a carry-on bag. I doubt if I would see it again if I handed it to be transferred at all the airports I am due to visit."

"Too true. Your plane leaves in half an hour. Have a good trip."

The flight to Yellowknife was uneventful. He caught a flight to Toronto. There were no direct flights to Lithuania, and he was routed via Frankfurt. He slept well on the planes and arrived at Vilnius midmorning, where he cleared customs easily. He was met by a museum official, who welcomed him and directed him to a bus that took them to Kaunas.

He asked his host to take him to a tailor where he could hire a dress suit, shoes, shirt, and socks for that evening. His companion obliged and paid the tailor. He said the clothing would be returned the next day. The tailor laughed and said he had bought everything except the suit. That was all that should be returned.

Ivor was taken to his hotel. It was lavish compared with the student accommodation of his previous visits. His host pointed out that it was within walking distance of the museum. He looked forward to the presentation and the speech Ivor was scheduled to deliver.

Ivor smiled. "I am used to composing sermons in an intricate Inuit language called Inuktitut. I hope I don't muddle that with my Lithuanian," he said.

"I am sure you will manage. There will be a large attendance. Your book has created a stir."

Ivor checked in and asked to be called at seven, an hour before the start of the ceremony. He enjoyed a small lunch. Experience taught him to avoid milk products; they restricted the throat and hampered the good delivery of a speech. He bathed, slept, and awoke on time. He put on his unfamiliar clothes and walked to the museum, where he was greeted by the curator and introduced to a number of dignitaries.

13
Recognition

At the time of Ivor's visit, references were made to *perestroika* and *glasnost* that heralded the collapse of the Soviet Union. They brought fresh hope to the Lithuanian nationalists and *Sajudis*, an anti-Communist movement.

Alex told Giselle that an independent Lithuania would be like the end of a long dream; it would be a happy conclusion, and he wished his homeland well in its endeavours. The family reunion he planned was a great success. It included Stasys and his wife, Juanita, a show jumper who had represented Spain in the Olympics; Terese; and the rest of the family. It was a great occasion and all were optimistic about Lithuania's future.

Alex had been delighted to learn that Ivor was to be awarded a commemorative medal by the Lithuanian government, and they had arranged to meet him at the Great Museum of Culture in Kaunus. He saw Ivor arrive. He was surrounded by some important-looking people.

Earlier, he and Giselle had been fascinated by the offerings in the museum. As they stood examining the exhibits, Alex felt a tap on his shoulder. He turned to see a grey-haired man with a stoop and a lined face who asked, "Doctor Greenus, how are the dogs these days?"

Alex was puzzled until the other introduced himself as Doctor Makauskas, formerly of the Klapeida Hospital. Alex was delighted to see him and said both the dogs had recovered. The shoulder-tapper said he had survived some rough years in a Siberian concentration camp. Alex introduced him to Giselle.

"This brave man, at great personal risk, helped me save the lives of two underground workers and was punished by the Russian overlords for his charity. Doctor, I am thrilled to see you and hope you have many years in which to enjoy the free Lithuania that is on the horizon."

"That is my hope, too, but my frail body will not last long, I fear. You must be proud of your son and the excellent study he made of our now most noted musician."

"Yes, I am, but how did you learn about him?"

"I read his book, which has been publicised. It is on sale near the entrance."

"That is the first I heard of it. You must excuse us. I see he has arrived. We must meet him and buy some copies. Is there anything I can do for you, for example, by the way of medicines?"

"That is kind of you, but I think I will manage."

"Well, good luck, but in case you need to contact me, here is my card. It is in English, but it is clear enough."

They shook hands all around, and Alex and Giselle went to a book stall to view copies of an edited version of Ivor's thesis on the life of Mikalojus Konstantinas Ciurlionis. Its frontispiece read:

> *This book is published with the permission of Oxford University and Dr. Ivor Greenus who has waived his royalties in favour of the museum. It is not generally known that Doctor Greenus recovered valuable historical material destined for destruction. In due course it will be stored safely in this museum.*

Alex decided Ivor was a dark horse for not telling him about the book. He bought several copies of it, and when he gave his credit card to a lady at the checkout desk, the curator of the museum, who happened to be standing by, noticed his name and asked if he was related to Doctor Greenus. Alex laughed and said he was Doctor Greenus, but if he was referring to Dr. Ivor Greenus, Ivor was his son.

"Doctor Greenus, we are delighted that you and your son were able to attend our ceremony. You may not know that our university honoured him with the honorary degree of doctor of philosophy. It was awarded *in abstentia* because your son said he was too busy to attend the graduation ceremony. He must have worked a point to get here tonight."

"Yes, he works a long way from here in the Arctic Circle. He is a modest man and is flattered that your government has cast a medal in his honour. He is over there chatting to that attractive lady in the red dress.

"Yes, Audra Skruibis, who is a remarkable woman. It is almost time for the speeches. There are seats on the podium for you, your wife, and your son."

Alex and Giselle greeted Ivor, and the three of them joined the curator on the podium. He asked for silence and said they were gathered to honour Dr. Ivor Greenus, a man who had researched and publicised an extraordinary person, Mikalojus Konstantinas Ciurlionis. As a result, that artist/painter's life was now well known and formed a major portion of their country's culture.

"Not only has Doctor Greenus written a detailed biography of the artist and created a list of all his works, but he was instrumental in discovering and preserving some of them. Dr. Greenus is a talented musician and has graciously consented to playing two of the artist's compositions. I request you to withhold your applause until the end of the second piece.

"Before he plays, I will present him with this well-deserved medal struck by our government in honour of his research."

He handed a container and citation to Ivor and shook his hands.

There was sustained applause at the end of which Ivor rose and said, "I could be described as a mixed-up kid. I am a Canadian born in Russia where my beloved grandmother taught me music. She was strict and did not hesitate to rap my knuckles if I was careless."

The crowd laughed.

"I am an example of Canada's multicultural population, a Russian who has come from the Arctic where I speak the native language Inuktitut, to talk in Lithuanian."

The crowd laughed again.

"As you may know, there is a sizeable Lithuanian population in Canada and its members have been wonderful in helping my family and in supporting my research in Lithuania." He paused for applause. "That research has helped to resuscitate a wonderful man's work." Again, the audience applauded. "It is outlined in my book, which covers his musical and painting activities. He was also an activist for Lithuanian independence and would be pleased with the country as it moves towards freedom. His father was a strict person, who insisted that his family speak Polish. The blighter made my research difficult when Ciurlionis wrote notes in that language. I, in turn, made it difficult for English scholars interested in my work by submitting my thesis in Lithuanian." The audience laughed. "Fortunately, Oxford University approved.

"Many of you have unhappy memories of the Russian occupation, but you should remember that the Russians did not interfere with our cultural activities. That made it possible for me to carry out my research. In doing so, some long lost heritage was preserved. It should be important for the people of the new Lithuania.

"I was interrogated several times by KBG agents. You remember, they always worked in threes, so I knew who they were when they accosted me. They claimed to be working in Lithuania's interests. I challenged them in Russian, and they said they made the country secure.

"I puzzled them. Time after time, they asked variations of, 'You are a Canadian at an English university. You claim you are researching art and music in Lithuania. You speak perfect Russian with a Moscow accent. You speak Lithuanian with a coastal accent. You must be up to something. You have good French and obviously English. We think you are a spy. Why choose an obscure Lithuanian to research? Why do you not research real composers like Tchaikovsky and Rimsky-Korsakov? You say you were born in Russia. Why don't you honour your own kin? Behave yourself. We will be watching you.'

"I answered them softly, and they let me go.

"They certainly watched me. Even when the sun was not shining, I had a shadow." The crowd again laughed. "Fortunately, they disregarded my fat briefcase crammed with notes beneath which lay valuable documents soon to be in this museum.

"I welcome the opportunity to thank Audra Skruibis for her wonderful support and guidance. She was of inestimable help in my research. We were joint preservers of records, were we not, Audra?" This was met with laughter and applause.

"I would like to record, too, the guidance and help of Oxford University. I am delighted that my father, a Lithuanian patriot, and his wife, Giselle, are here. I thank them for their support and encouragement. I regret that my beloved grandmother and my beloved mother have passed away and are not here to witness the honour you have bestowed upon me.

"Mr. Curator, I thank the government sincerely for this award. As promised, I will now move to the piano. I shall play two pieces. The first will be from 'The Sonata of Spring' and the second from 'The Sonata of the Sea.' They will be related to the artist's pictures with those titles I have arranged to appear on the screen. I suggest you watch the paintings as I play, and you should experience the extraordinary power of M.K.'s unique artistic work in two forms."

After sustained applause, Ivor played two pieces that received a standing ovation and requests for an encore. He obliged and returned to his seat.

The curator thanked Ivor and wished him luck in his pastoral work.

14
Sister Maria Celeste

Sister Maria Celeste asked her Mother Superior's permission to attend a ceremony at which a Dr. Ivor Greenus would be presented with a commemorative medal for his work on the Lithuanian artist/composer Mikalojus Konstantinas Ciurlionis.

"Sister, I did not know that you were interested in art and music."

"My mother and son were both concert pianists, and it is my son who is being honoured at the ceremony. By the grace of God, he will be near me for a short while."

"Before we admitted you to the order, you gave us a complete story of your life, including your marriage, your son, and the forced parting from him and your husband. Do I understand you want to re-establish relationships with them?"

"No, Mother. In their eyes, I am dead. I am devoted to the order and remain thankful for your mercy in accepting me. If you allow me to go, I shall be discreet and not reveal my identity, but I would like to hear my son praised and to hear his response."

"Go, and may God grace your son with success."

"He is a priest and works in the lonely wastes of the Arctic. I shall never again have the opportunity of seeing him and hearing his voice. Thank you, Mother, for your permission."

Sister Maria pondered her conversion to Christianity.

It was reminiscent of St. Paul's conversion on the road to Damascus, except he was young and active. I was older and at death's door on a bloody and burning Moscow Street when I saw the Light. The seeds of my conversion were sewn in the Arctic by my beloved Alex during the war against the Nazis. They germinated in Canada. They only grew to maturity after I was left for dead in that fight with a criminal gang. I chose a strict order of poverty and penance in expiation of my sins. Now I work for the poor in contradiction to my former life.

She attended the ceremony and sat at the back of the well-attended hall. She wore dark glasses. They, her nun's wimple, and a cowl hid most of her scarred face. Her clothing was in sharp contrast to the fashionable dresses of the ladies in the audience. She wept quietly when she saw Alex on the podium and when Ivor was introduced. She was proud of his address and piano playing.

"He is making good use of God's gift of music."

Ivor noticed the nun sitting in isolation at the back of the hall.

After his speech and recitals, he excused himself and approached her. He was startled by the nun's scarred face and wondered why a plastic surgeon had not improved it. He welcomed her to the gathering. She congratulated him in a soft voice in Moscow Russian. It contrasted with the evening's proceedings in Lithuanian and was vaguely familiar to his musical ear.

She then gave him an envelope, stood up, pressed her hand on his head, sobbed, and said, "God bless you, my son," and left the hall.

He was puzzled.

The solitary nun's attendance at the reception remained a mystery.

"God bless you" was a common expression, but only priests added "my son." He thought of pursuing her. He hesitated, put the envelope in his pocket, and joined Alex and Giselle.

"Who was that, Ivor?" Alex asked.

"A strange nun with a scarred face. She admired my work."

"You are famous and have obviously touched many people with your excellent efforts."

"A writer is always flattered to hear that. I did not write for a specific audience and little dreamed that my efforts would attract attention outside of academia."

"She looked strange and huddled up. She wasn't the spectre at the feast, was she?"

Ivor hesitated and said, "She was hardly that. Her face was disfigured. She wore dark glasses that I thought unusual. I assumed she was an admirer of my artist/musician, Ciurlionis. Apart from thanking me, she said little."

While Ivor circulated in the crowd, the curator said to Alex, "Your son is modest. He would have been a superb detective. He was persistent with his research and uncovered lots of fresh information on our famous musician. He was secretive in saving some valuable material. You must be proud of him."

"Yes, I am very proud of him."

Ivor signed a number of books. After thanking the curator for the ceremony and bidding good night to Alex and Giselle, he returned to his hotel.

There he opened the letter.

He cursed and shuddered. He recalled the Moscow accent and a sob. He regretted he had not followed his instincts and pursued the nun after she said, "God bless you, my son."

It was a standard Catholic blessing by an ordained person but not by a nun. She literally meant "son" but could not reveal why. How sad for her.

The letter read:

My dear Ivor,

Despite my intention to remain anonymous, I could not resist obtaining permission to attend your ceremony. You have no doubt heard of my death. The report of it, like that of the American Mark Twain, was an exaggeration.

I was indeed involved in a fracas with a criminal gang. I was shot, and one of the gang threw petrol on me as I lay on the ground and lit it. I learnt later that one of my team threw his coat across me and doused the flames My face and arms were badly burnt. I was unconscious and was reported dead. An attendant at the morgue to which my body was sent realised I was breathing. When my commander, General Sikorsky, was advised, he arranged for me to be sent to a leading hospital, and I was revived. My only recollection was the sudden burst of flame. What I have told you here, I learnt later. I suffered hours of pain and the discomfort of plastic surgery.

Although he was busy, General Sikorsky visited me several times. He expressed his sorrow at what had happened to me. He said that unfortunately my KGB days were over. He said he knew my mother had died, that I had no relations, and no one would bemoan my fate. He suggested that I allow the notice of my death to remain.

He said, "Colonel, your devotion to our country has been outstanding. You would find it difficult living as a disfigured retired soldier. We will give you a new identity and a generous pension so that you can live a life independent of others."

I realised my past life was over and agreed.

I was critically ill, but miraculously, with God's grace, I survived. You must be surprised to hear me refer to a miracle, to God, and to my being a nun.

I want to discuss my conversion and explain some facts of my life that might enable you to see me in a more favourable light than that you no doubt harbour. Alex, your father, whom I loved and will always love, argued in favour of Christianity against Communism when we were together in the Arctic in the 1940s. We exchanged viewpoints without rancour.

It was a difficult time. He was a tank specialist working for the British, and I was a Russian tank commander. We were involved in training Russian tank crews and handling tanks shipped from Britain through rough seas to Murmansk, a harbour free of ice all year round.

We fought alongside each other in two tank skirmishes. Despite Russian rules against fraternisation, we enjoyed a close relationship. One consequence was your birth. Another was my first experience of a reasoned argument in favour of a religion compared with Communism.

At the time, our efforts were directed to beating the Fascists of Italy and the Nazis of Germany. When that was achieved, the Soviets controlled most of Europe, including Lithuania, to which I was posted as a member of the KGB. That country's population was 80 percent Catholic. They supported and aided the underground forces opposed to us Communists. I could not help admiring them. Yes, I was part of the forces that enforced Communism on an unwilling population. Alex and Stasys, his brother, opposed it—Alex indirectly and Stasys actively. Alex operated from Canada where he published regular articles against Communist activities in Lithuania. He made two trips to the country to persuade his family to emigrate and to help the dissidents' cause.

I was aware through the KGB of both of their activities but did not order their arrests, as I could have done. On Alex's second trip, he was apprehended and I interrogated him and allowed him to be released. We met, made love, and escaped from Lithuania. We were married in Copenhagen, and I entered Canada without difficulty.

Then followed many happy years augmented by your arrival. In Quebec, I met several religious people and was impressed with their openness, their devotion, and their community work. It was performed voluntarily not dictated by a government. I was particularly impressed with Father Masse and Bishop Levesque and enjoyed discussing religion with them.

I began to entertain doubts about Communism that had started in Murmansk. Had I stayed in Canada, I would no doubt have converted to the Catholic faith. Unfortunately, I was forced to leave, much to my sorrow.

I apologise for any grief I caused. I had no alternative. You know that the KGB sent two agents to kill Alex. They were thwarted by him and his friend Arthur. It was the KGB who set up the plot for me to *escape from Lithuania and to marry Alex. Later, it was made clear to me that if I did not leave Canada, as ordered, they would liquidate me and you. I knew too much to be left loose. You were a thorn in their flesh for abandoning the Youth Orchestra. Our deaths would be a ghastly reminder to Alex of the KGB's powers.*

I decided that life as a live coward was better than one as a dead heroine responsible for the death of my son, so I returned to Russia. My new role there was one of the surveillance of Russian citizens and visitors to Russia. It was innocuous work. At a viticulture conference in Tbilisi, I was startled to see Alex sitting opposite me at dinner, and I exclaimed in Russian, "How is Ivor?" The man, a Spaniard named Jiminez, was puzzled. He asked the delegate next to him what I had said. He shrugged his shoulders when he heard what it was.

I apologised for my outburst. It was unusual for a Spaniard to have blue eyes and fair hair and to be a dead spit of Alex. My detective instincts took over. A KGB investigation determined that Jiminez was not born in Spain but was Stasys under an assumed name.

My curiosity was satisfied, and as far as I was concerned, the matter ended there. Unfortunately, his particulars remained in the KGB records, and when he visited Georgia, he was arrested. I knew he might do that, and I had left an instruction in his file that I should be contacted if he was taken. My idea was to take him out of KGB hands when he would have received rough treatment and transfer him to Lithuania. There he would be able to refute trumped-up charges against him, and the Spanish authorities might be able to rescue him. When he arrived in Moscow, I interrogated him. In the presence of the KBG guards, I had to act severely. Understandably, Stasys was not impressed with me and was bitter and abusive. I was compelled to exhibit violence that would match my reputation as the Iron Maiden. I faked some kicks to safe parts of his body and used the excuse of another appointment to avoid administering further punishment. As you know, Stasys went to Lithuania and was released, thanks to efforts by the Spanish administration. It was something to do with soccer that I did not understand.

My work switched to combating urban violence with which the regular police were confronted. In my last assignment, I was shot and burnt. As I explained, I was reported killed. Plastic surgeons did their best to repair the fire damage to my body with indifferent results.

My usefulness to the KGB was over. As I mentioned, I was given a new name and identity papers and a pension. As you will appreciate, I had plenty of time in hospital to ponder my future and my misgivings with Communism.

As a new person, I had no contacts. People could not avoid shuddering when they saw my face. I decided to escape from society, if possible in the sanctuary of a nunnery. I remembered Father Masse saying it was never too late to repent and seek the Lord. That is what I did. I remembered the sterling Catholics I met in Canada and their counterparts in Lithuania. I decided to seek a Lithuanian Catholic Order in which I could help society.

I found a willing helper in Father Stanilus in Vilnius. He patiently guided and tested me. I was baptised and took my first Communion. The order of which I am a member accepted me, an elderly and unusual novitiate. I told the Mother Superior that in the words of Matthew XXV.35 "I was a stranger and you took me in."

I arranged for my pension to be paid into the order's banking account. I have named the order as the beneficiary of my death policy. It will benefit substantially when I die. You might say I paid an entry fee for my salvation. You will understand that I did not leave anything to you as I originally intended. It was essential to retain my anonymity even in death. It was providential that I chose an order close to the venue of your wonderful award. It is thanks to God that I will see and hear and hopefully meet you.

I now have a small cell. I am poverty-stricken. I work with poor people. The order cares for sick people, and I have added to my knowledge of first aid. I was able to assist when the Communists continued to harass Christians.

I have come to terms with my disfigurement. A sister, a former professor of literature comforted me by telling me the story, The Picture of Dorian Gray *by an English author, Oscar Wilde.*

"Like Dorian Gray, you have a beautiful face behind the scars," she said. *"We all love you; admire your tenacity, your acceptance of discomfort, and for working hard with us."*

Ivor, I am not entirely the ogre indicated by my negative actions. The title of "Iron Maiden" was given to me because I stood no nonsense from criminals. But I was not rough with dissidents.

As far as your family is concerned, I regret that Stasys was arrested. I have explained my role in that affair. In the early days, we knew he was a dissident and that Alex connived with him. I prevented their arrests on the grounds that they would lead us to other agitators.

I saved your family's priest from being sent to Siberia and asked the KGB to close their eyes on his illicit religious practices when he became a teacher. I obtained scarce accommodation for your grandmother. She was not aware of it, nor were your uncles aware of the fact that I helped them obtain their jobs. I secretly helped your grandmother and aunt to emigrate to Canada. I would like to think that I was a good mother to you in Canada.

When I sit or lie in my small cell, I ponder on what might have been. Could I have refused the plot to get into Canada?

No .The KGB would have pursued their vengeance against Alex. They knew that if we were married, he would unconsciously provide me with first-class credentials and unknowingly would help my spying.

Should I have called the KGB's bluff when ordered to leave Canada?

No. Had I stayed, I would have been jailed for spying and our lives would have been at risk.

Could I have made a new life in public as a disfigured woman with a new identity?

No. I agreed with General Sikorsky on that.

These questions are hypothetical.

What is factual is that I have found the Lord. I am content with my lot. I am at peace with the world.

I have one wish.

You abandoned music in favour of religious service. You were gifted by God, and it is wrong not to use your talents in His cause. My advice is for you to seek a position as organist of a large cathedral and to serve God through music and through service as an assistant priest. You could augment a cathedral's funds with public piano recitals. If you follow my suggestion, I am sure you will be fulfilled in a glorious way, unlike me in my humble way. I know you are an Anglican priest and married. I hope you have children. Should they ask about their maternal grandmother, tell them that I am devoted to the poor. If you have a daughter and can now see some merit in my life, you might call her Alisa.

Ivor, I am content.

Please do not try to locate me.

God bless you, my son.

Farewell.

Your Loving Mother

Ivor was shattered by the letter and wept.

I should find her and tell her I love her and will follow her advice. Father Stanilus will know where she is. But I have to leave tomorrow, and soon, I will be thousands of kilometres away from here. What would my father think if I showed him this letter? Do I not have a duty to tell him that she left Canada to save my life? Would he believe her? I cannot reveal her secret. He and Giselle love each other, and he has come to terms with Alisa's "deceit." I must not open old wounds.

Alisa leads a secret life. I must honour her secrecy. Curse, my hands are tied. I shall pray for her daily.

The next day, Alex remarked on his drawn looks.

"Ivor," he said, "is something worrying you? You should be preening yourself after last night's ceremony."

"I think it is a reaction to all the excitement. I'll be fine later."

He thought of his parents together in the Arctic and the start there of Alisa's conversion. He thought too of his work in the Arctic. His father had often reminisced about his Arctic connections. Little did he know that, in addition to giving him a son, the connections were responsible for an unlikely convert to Christianity: Alisa.

He bade farewell to Alex and Giselle and hoped they would enjoy the rest of their stay in Lithuania.

His guide met him and said he would return the suit to the tailor and hoped Ivor would find the rest of the clothing useful.

"Perhaps, one day. Usually, I am well buttoned up with warm clothing, and occasionally such as now, I wear a clerical collar. Nevertheless, thank you. The items will be mementoes of a memorable occasion."

"It certainly was. We were fortunate you were able to attend. Is there a possibility of your doing further research into our music?"

"That is a tempting thought, but I am committed to work in the far north of Canada."

They caught a bus to the Vilnius airport where the guide reiterated his thanks for Ivor's attendance, shook his hand, and wished him good luck.

On the long journey to Nunavut, Ivor thought about his meeting with Alisa. He again cursed himself for not pursuing her.

When he spoke to her at the ceremony, he had felt something was familiar and he should have been alert to that. Why was she wearing dark glasses in a well-lit hall? She used Russian when the evening's proceedings were in Lithuanian. It was the Moscow Russian the KGB said he spoke. When the nun smiled, her mouth, despite the damaged lips, seemed familiar. Why did she sob as she blessed him? Was it not customary for nuns to say simply, "God bless you" and for priests and their superiors to add "my son"? Also, what could have induced a nun to attend a ceremony relating to someone not connected with her religion, and why had she sat in the back of the hall?

As a researcher, he put disparate items together to see if there was a connection, but on this occasion, he had failed to do so. He speculated on what would have happened had he stumbled onto the fact that the nun was Alisa. He would have hugged her to the surprise of the audience he knew had watched his walk to the back of the hall.

Media representatives would have smelt a story. Alex would have rushed to the scene. Alisa's secret would have been blown. Was it Divine Providence that had blocked his mind in order to protect someone who had suffered enough? Despite his initial sadness at not identifying Alisa, he realised that it would have been fatal to do have done so.

His guide had touched a point of interest, and he wondered if he would ever see Lithuania again. He would like to research its dialects and music. It was a country wide open for musical researchers and philologists. It had been ruled by Poles, Germans, and Russians. There must be vestiges of each in dialects and music.

Instead of Lithuania, he would intensify his work among the Inuits. They had links with Russia and stretched across to the east to Greenland and possibly Denmark. They were like the Kurds with their horizontal country stretching across Turkey, Iraq, Iran, Syria, and the Caucasus. It would be fascinating to research all the Inuits, but he knew he would never test his hypothesis because of the impossibility of travelling across the icy wastes.

He left the flight at Yellowknife to report to his bishop, who congratulated him on his award. He said nothing of importance had occurred in Ivor's absence. He thanked him for the good work he was doing in his region and wished him Godspeed.

Ivor collected his ATV at Kugaaruk and drove home slowly still overwhelmed by the events of the past few days. Angela greeted him warmly and wanted to know all about his trip. He described everything except his meeting Alisa. He kept that for last and explained what had happened before handing her Alisa's letter. She read it and burst into tears. She said how sad it was that Alisa, by all accounts a beautiful and dynamic woman, had been harmed and reduced to the lowest order of nun's work.

"Ivor, should you not have rescued her?"

"That option has burned my soul. But where would she go? She could not be admitted to Canada. Would she wander the Russian streets as a disfigured nonentity? What would the effect have been on my father, who has come to terms with her deceit and death? As you can read, she wants secrecy. She says she is content. Though reduced to a humble position, she has accommodation with understanding sisters for company. I am convinced that although there were obvious signs that I should have followed and I would have identified her, Divine Providence prevented me from doing so."

"Of course. She is at peace. It would be wrong to disturb it."

"Angela, you read her last wish about my music. To pun, she has struck a musical chord. I have enjoyed my work here, but I am not fulfilling myself and you are denied the normal blessings of life. I feel I should look south. I suggest that in the coming winter you go to Australia's sun and improve your vitamin D content. I am sure your father would welcome you and hopefully finance your trip. On your return, we could discuss our future."

"That is a wonderful idea. Dad has been pressing me to visit. He quotes business class travel as an inducement. But what about you? How will you cope without your architect companion?"

"Our maid can cook reasonably well. We have a freezer stacked with goodies. I am certain to receive gifts of seal steaks, caribou haunches, frozen and smoked fish, possibly fresh fish caught through the ice, and possibly whale meat. You have taught me to make whole wheat bread. I have a backlog of journal entries to make. In short, I would cope."

"Fine. I'll think of you as I struggle with choice lamb, Angus beef steak, roasted chicken, pawpaws, pineapples, avocado pears, and assorted mousses. Whilst you are in the dark, I'll be sunbathing at a beach. I might even see the footie final, the traffic of which impressed you."

Ivor threw a cushion at her and said, "Go thou taunting wench. Go to your antipodean repasts and strange activities that masquerade as sport. One must not be surprised with a population that sprang from the jails of England."

"Ha, you have stumbled there. Our forefathers were selected by the best judges in England."

They tussled and retired to the bedroom where the argument was settled satisfactorily.

14
Farewell to the Arctic

Ivor wrote to Alex and told him that he and Angela had decided to move to Toronto and enclosed a copy of an article in the Queen's University Alumni Newsletter:

> *Ivor Greenus, a former captain of the Golden Gaels hockey team, known for scoring a spectacular goal in the last minute of a match against the McGill Redmen to clinch the intervarsity hockey title, is now an Anglican priest in the Arctic.*
>
> *He is an accomplished pianist, and his debut with the Kingston Symphony Orchestra, Beethoven's Piano Concerto no. 5 "Emperor," when a student at Queens, a drew a standing ovation.*
>
> *After four years at Queens, he obtained a bachelor of music degree and was awarded a Rhodes scholarship. He obtained a doctor of philosophy degree at Oxford for his study of an unusual Lithuanian artist/composer, Mikalojus Konstantinas Ciurlionis. He was awarded an honorary doctorate of philosophy by the University of Lithuania and, for his book on Ciurlionis, a best*

seller in Lithuania, a commemorative medal by that country's government.

He spent two years at a Roman Catholic seminary and a year at the Church of St. Mary Magdalene in Napanee, Ontario, before his ordination as an Anglican priest. He chose to serve in the Diocese of the Arctic. He is fluent in English and French and, thanks to his Russian mother and Lithuanian father, in Russian and Lithuanian. They also taught him the rudiments of German and Polish. In the Arctic, he solved the meaning of many Inuit words that had defied earlier missionary lexicographers.

He will be leaving the Arctic to assume the post of organist and choirmaster with pastoral duties at the St. James Anglican Cathedral in Toronto. Doctor Greenus and his wife, Angela, an Australian architect whom he met at Oxford, and their small daughter, Alisa, will arrive in Toronto in September.

Alex was delighted that Ivor would be living in Toronto. He would enjoy being closer to him. They had drifted apart since Ivor began work in Lithuania. He thought of the conference curator's comments on Ivor's detective abilities.

"Was Ivor a good detective like his mother? He certainly produced a quality dissertation that required detective work. Was he secretive like her? Yes, he did not mention his smuggling, the publication of his book, or an honorary degree. I wonder if Ivor, my last Arctic connection, hid anything else from me?"

He thought sadly of his first connection, the beautiful and secretive Alisa, who died such a horrible death.

Acknowledgments

I acknowledge with thanks the help and encouragement given to me by two children of Lithuanian immigrants, Albert and Nellie Skruibis, of Adolphustown, Ontario. They showed me the immigration papers of her father and described the hardships his family suffered, which stirred my imagination and inspired me to write this book. They are multilingual Canadians, whose knowledge of Montreal and Lithuania stood me in good stead. We had many an enjoyable discussion while savouring Nellie's delectable Lithuanian and Russian dishes.

Angela Miller and Linda Murray kindly read my draft and corrected errors and omissions.

I hope readers unfamiliar with cricket were able to decipher my references to that wonderful competitive game, which is played throughout the British Commonwealth. Its terms, such as "hit for a six," as Field Marshall Montgomery planned to do to Hitler, have a meaningful place in the English language, as bizarre as they sound to the uninitiated.